'*Devotion* is a romance and a horror story, a tale of obsession and betrayal, revolving around two women divided by the chasm of class. In breathtaking prose, Stevens illuminates the ugly, stunning danger of love. This novel gripped me gorgeously and still won't let me go.' Hannah Lillith Assadi, author of *Sonora*

'*Devotion* is a dangerous novel – sharp, glittering, and sexy – and Madeline Stevens is a significant new talent. I read this story of obsession, friendship, and betrayal with my heart in my throat.' Julie Buntin, author of *Marlena*

'Madeline Stevens' tale of jealousy and obsession is the next big psychological thriller debut, featuring two women who become dangerously entangled. One has everything, and the other wants everything – and will do anything to get what the other has.' CrimeReads

'A clever, sharply satirical and unsettling novel that perfectly captures the contradiction of wanting everything, but ultimately having to lose yourself in the process.' Years of Reading Selfishly

'A sharp and sensuous read . . . a quiet exploration of the obsession, malevolence, and jealousy that can lie at the heart of misguided devotion.' The Shelf of Unread Books

DEVOTION

Madeline Stevens

faber

First published in the UK in 2019
by Faber & Faber Limited
Bloomsbury House,
74–77 Great Russell Street
London WC1B 3DA

First published in the United States in 2019
by Ecco, an imprint of HarperCollins Publishers,
195 Broadway,
New York NY 10007

This paperback edition published in 2021

Typeset by Typo•glyphix, Burton-on-Trent DE14 3HE
Printed and bound by CPI Group (UK) Ltd, Croydon CR0 4YY

This is a work of fiction. Names, characters, places and incidents are products of the author's imagination or are used fictitiously and are not to be construed as real. Any resemblance to actual events, locales, organisations or persons, living or dead, is entirely coincidental

A CIP record for this book
is available from the British Library

ISBN 978–0–571–34908–1

2 4 6 8 10 9 7 5 3 1

DEVOTION

PROLOGUE

The footsteps outside my door were not the usual clicking of my neighbor's heels, but scuffling, like a rodent. I stepped quietly, heel-to-toe, from my bedroom to the hallway, wearing only a thin T-shirt and ratty underwear. The peephole on the door was old; you had to swing aside a silver-dollar-sized medallion in order to look through a little circle of semitransparent glass. The change in light was obvious from the outside so I never used it. Instead, I placed my ear against the door.

I heard my roommate Sam's thin voice from her room hiss, "What's happening?" but I didn't answer. It was past midnight and someone was pacing back and forth in our hallway. The door shifted against my face a little as someone leaned against it.

The knock made me jump. I saw Sam's little pink face peek around her doorframe at the end of the hall. The knocks started coming rapidly then.

James's eyes were bloodshot when I opened the door, his cheeks hollow, the hair on the back of his head had grown out unevenly. I stood in the doorway, in my underwear, holding on to the brass knob, jiggling it back and forth in my palm. "What are you doing here?" I said. At first I couldn't think how he found me in the first place, then I remembered all the times I'd given him my address so he could order cars home for me at night.

"Can I come in?" he said. I could smell alcohol on him.

I glanced at Sam, who ducked back into her bedroom. The apartment had no common space, just a galley kitchen, little bathroom, and hallway. I wavered, not yet stepping out of the way.

He opened his wallet. "We owe you money," he said. "We never paid you for that last week. I told you not to let us get away with that."

I didn't say anything but moved aside to let him pass.

I watched him look into my bedroom—the first unfurnished room I'd lived in since moving to New York—the futon mattress on the floor in the corner, the ripped-up sheets, the books piled against the wall. I wondered if he'd realize how many came from his house, how many I'd taken from the walls of shelves in his wife's office. He wiped sweat from his chin. There was nowhere to sit down.

"May I have a glass of water?" he said. The politeness of the question bothered me.

I moved to the kitchen and he walked past me and into Sam's room without asking. "Oh," I heard him mumble, "Sorry."

"My roommate," I said, handing him the water.

He took a sip and set it on the counter. "Just you two?" he said, looking around. "It's a one-bedroom then or is there a living room?"

I just stared at him in the harsh kitchen light.

"You don't know what happened?" he said.

"I don't know anything."

"Lonnie left. Disappeared." He took a step toward me. "She didn't drain the money, but she left me with William."

I could smell his cedar-scented aftershave under the sweat and alcohol. I realized I hadn't shaved my legs in days. "You're doing well, right?" he said.

I didn't respond. It wasn't hard to imagine why she would leave him. I tried to remember exactly how long it had been since I saw her, since everything had gotten so messed up in the Hamptons—six months at this point. Maybe it took her that long to get up the courage.

"What do you mean disappeared?"

He didn't answer the question. "I'm sure you found a new job?" he said instead, slurring his words, staring at my mouth. "Must be easy to find a new job."

I don't know if it was the news about Lonnie or this vague come-on, but something switched then. I wanted him gone.

"You're drunk," I said. "It's late. You should go."

He looked around again, his eyes turning big and glassy like those of an insulted child—surprised at any slight. I walked to the door and opened it, waiting for him to follow. He shoved a wad of money into my hand at the threshold. "I didn't want you to come after us," he said. "For not getting your last payment."

I took the cash without saying anything, though we both knew I could never go after him for anything. There was no record of me. Legally, I never had anything to do with the whole lot of them. I took it because I was used to needing money or maybe because I thought he needed to give it to me. I locked the door quickly behind him, then looked down to find all I was holding were some crumpled ones, two fives, and a wad of receipts.

1

I never signed a contract. The wife handed me house keys with a flippancy I found unnerving, despite my desperation. I held them the whole way back to Brooklyn, to reassure myself I had indeed been given the job, that there had been an agreement, fingering the ridges until my sweaty palms smelled of metal. The ring had a leather strap attached featuring a monogrammed "L" that made me wonder if she'd given me her own set by accident.

I was still clutching them, the strap wrapped around my index finger, when I sat down at a bar and ordered a drink that evening. I gave the bartender my credit card, and said, "Keep it open," thinking I might just leave when I'd finished. The card was maxed out by then; he could have it.

I'd had such a long list of jobs. All the girls I knew got the same start in the world. We were hired part-time, as hostesses or maybe retail associates. The jobs were all essentially the same: stand around, smile, look pretty, look thin, look stylish. I was told, "You are the face of this establishment," which was given to mean I was the first person customers would see, but really meant I was nothing more than a face to them.

Those positions made the mind shrivel. Reading was not allowed, even on the slowest of days. Sitting was not allowed. I would envy the servers just for being able to walk around. Standing still was what made the ache in my feet noticeable. The clock ticked. The same songs repeated. People came; they complained or they didn't. They left. And then, when I quit, I was left with nothing—no savings, no unemployment, no severance.

My reflection in the mirror behind the shelves of alcohol had dark circles under the eyes, thinned-out cheeks. Walking around Crown Heights had started to give me a terrifying awareness of my body. It was brittle, milky, weak. I could feel the hip bones showing through the skin. It wasn't that I felt like a child, it was worse—I felt like a patient. My summer sundresses transformed into hospital gowns. Everyone around me looked very strong by comparison.

I'd been surviving for weeks on bodega coffee and prepackaged pastries—those little glazed things, more chemical than food, more air than bread. That afternoon, right before the interview, I'd used my pocketknife to slice open a ripe avocado because I'd read somewhere that a person could survive, however deficiently, on avocados alone. The knife had been a gift from my dad on my twelfth birthday, and it had been blunted on twigs and sharpened again and again in the woods around his house. One summer evening I made a small trap out of sticks and twine, placing food carefully inside. After dinner I found a rabbit stuck in it, its blank eyes blinking at me. I picked the animal up by its scruff and quickly snapped the neck, then slit the throat.

I was testing myself. My mom had decided to become a vegetarian, and had explained it to me this way: "I could never kill an animal, so why should it be all right to have other people do it for me?"

I hadn't expected the blood to spurt out the way it did. I returned home covered in it and had to explain to my dad what I'd done. Though I'd felt all right walking back from the rabbit's tiny grave, a lump formed mysteriously in my throat when I had to justify my actions to someone else. I wiped away tears, unsure if I was embarrassed by my actions or my emotions. My dad laughed at me and tossed me a kitchen rag.

When I remembered the rabbit now, I was filled with a useless regret that I hadn't cut off the muscle and eaten it. But a beer on an empty stomach had a wonderful effect—a combination of much-needed calories and alcohol working together to numb everything. I tried to keep myself from gulping.

The bar was new. Thin wood paneling ran up the wall from the tall backs of black-cushioned booths and curved around the ceiling, like the inside of a sailing ship. The man sitting next to me was a cop, his sturdy frame filling out the navy uniform.

"This place," he said, raising a hand to gesture at the room.

"I know, right?" I replied, excited to have someone talking to me. It had been a long time since I'd been out with anyone. It'd been a long time since I'd been out at all.

"You live around here?"

"Yeah, pretty close."

He nodded, ran a hand over his shaved head. "I used to work in this neighborhood in the nineties," he said. "That's where they put the new guys. We were on Franklin on my first week, on Franklin and St. Marks. We turned the corner and some guys had these girls tied to a lamppost on the street. These guys were chucking bowling balls at them. Fucking crack cocaine. They were playing ninepins with a group of screaming girls. Stopping traffic and no one even called us. We just walked in on that scene."

"That wasn't very long ago," I said.

"And now you live here," he replied. I felt he was stopping himself short of saying "little white girl." It was what a strange man on my block had called me that morning, accompanied by a sucking sound against his teeth. Though I felt self-righteous about this sort of treatment—I was poor, what did he know?—I tried to understand that my face alone was a threatening sign of rising rent. He didn't want me there, but I couldn't afford to live anywhere else.

I didn't think anything about the story of the girls tied up on Franklin. What I did think about was getting this man to buy me dinner. I studied his body—the bulk of his shoulder muscles under his uniform, the sharp, clean-shaven line of his jaw. I guessed he was in his forties, though it was hard to tell. His dark skin was unwrinkled. I didn't often end up with men who looked like him. I usually went home with skinny white boys no older than me. They rarely knew what to do.

"My name is Ella," I said. "Tell me more about Crown Heights." I cradled my chin in my palm, looking at him wistfully. "I'm from very far away."

He gave me a side-eye in which I could see him sizing up my body as well. He took a swig of beer, and then said, "You know about the riots, Ella? Everybody knows about the riots."

I didn't know what he was referencing, but I nodded.

"No, let me tell you about something else." He squinted at me. "You know about the LeRoi family?"

A bead of condensation dripped from my glass onto my leg. I felt it trickle all the way down to my ankle. I shook my head.

"They ran a church out of a brownstone around here, but it wasn't a real church, it was more like a harem of women. The pastor was this guy Rev. LeRoi. He liked 'em young. The girls would dress up like nuns and go beg for money in the subway. They had all kinds of this guy's kids. Nobody understood how so many kids fit in that house. There were rumors LeRoi made them keep 'em upstairs in cages. When one of the girls wanted out, she disappeared. This went on for years. They finally busted LeRoi, and found where he'd been dumping the bodies."

"Where?"

"This land he owned up north somewhere. In a lake. He killed some nineteen girls. Thing is, his son still runs the church. Supposedly it's squeaky clean now, but I'd stay the hell away from it."

I looked down and found my barstool was rocking back and forth and my beer was gone, though it didn't seem like enough time had passed for me to drink it all. It was quite a twisted story by way of introduction, but I didn't care. I still wanted to have dinner with him. The cop turned to the bartender. "Another round?" he asked. I couldn't stand the thought of more beer so I ordered a gin and tonic—tonic was supposed to be good for nausea, wasn't it? I laughed, repeated the word "tonic." It was going to restore me.

The cop looked at me out of the corner of his eye again. I put my hands on the bar, fingers splayed, my new set of keys hard and sharp against my palm.

"Do *you* live around here?" I asked.

"Nah, Brooklyn Heights."

I struggled to find my straw. "You still work around here?"

"In Manhattan."

"What are you doing out here?"

We were playing twenty questions; he was losing interest.

"Nostalgia, I guess. Or more like curiosity."

"You just came out here to have a drink alone?"

I drew out the word "alone," trying to make it sound sad. It's not hard with that word.

"Could ask you the same question."

We stared at each other. My little legs had somehow become entwined in his big ones. It just happens that way, when you're at a bar and turn toward each other. The barstool was still rocking underneath me, but at least it was good for something.

I said, "Do you want to get out of here, get some food?"

He didn't answer but opened his fat wallet, paid both our tabs, and drank the rest of his beer in one gulp. The bartender handed me back my card, uncharged.

Outside, twilight was gathering, but the air was still warm, the warmth swimming around me. My legs felt watery. I was so weak, I was evaporating. I wasn't sure I could make it to the restaurant. I grabbed his arm, a gesture disguised as flirtation but really meant to steady myself.

He laughed. "You okay?"

I smiled at him, my face indolent, droopy. "I'm great. Hungry."

"Let's get you some food."

As we walked I felt him reach over and pull down my skirt in the back. He did it quickly, not saying anything. I didn't feel embarrassed; I was still holding the keys to my new job. That was the important thing.

On Nostrand Avenue we ordered roti at a counter. There were stacks of cake in clamshell containers next to the register. I asked for one and then took out my wallet, even though it was empty. He put a hand on my hand, pulled out his own again. I smiled and couldn't stop smiling, though it made my sad, weak face hurt. I was going to eat on someone else's dime. I commended myself. He was such a good find; cops want to take care of people. I thanked him, patted his arm, a little over-eager, but what did it matter?

I realized as we sat waiting for our food, I had no reason to continue speaking to him. He'd already paid for the meal. Counter service was a good idea, rather than waiting through a whole meal to see whether he would ask to split the bill. I made a mental note as I snapped open the plastic cake container, not caring what he thought about me eating it before the other food. The frosting was the kind of sweet that made my teeth feel loose in my skull. I ate it anyway, all of it, gobbled it down. It was a good thing the roti took so long to come or I probably would've devoured that as well and thrown it all up in the street.

I'd never had roti before and had to watch the cop to figure out how to eat it. I followed his lead as he unwrapped the tinfoil and ripped off a bit of thin, unleavened bread, using the piece to scoop up the chicken and potatoes inside. I was delighted, when I bit into it, to find the bread was flaky and soft and the chicken tasted of butter and curry. Then my teeth bit into something hard.

"There's bones in there," the cop said, watching me.

I didn't look at him; I just spit the bone into my hand, set it down on the table, and went back to eating. It was enjoyable, using my hands, fishing out the chicken bones. I didn't give a shit what I looked like to this cop, since he'd already paid for all this good food.

"Girl's starving," he said, as I scooped up bite after bite.

"I've hardly had a minute to eat today," I said, my mouth full.

I realized then that he hadn't asked me a single question about myself. Didn't he wonder why I hadn't eaten all day? Didn't he wonder what I did for work? Wasn't that the question everyone always asked?

When the food was gone I was very full. I was grateful to him for providing me with this lovely full feeling. I didn't feel I owed him for it, but I felt like repaying him anyway. He had a good face—friendly wide-set eyes and perfect white teeth. It was dark outside. I slapped a mosquito away from my leg as we stood together on the curb. The seventeen-year cicadas were supposed to hatch and outnumber the city's population six hundred to one that summer, but they never came. The eggs had died; the newspapers said we'd filled too many vacant lots with condos. Mosquitoes were already swarming in their place. "Subway's that way," he said.

I pulled on his thick arm and said, "Yeah, but I live over here."

We didn't say anything else. He was kissing me by the time we got to the front door of my building—his lips tasted of curry and beer. I held his head between my hands, the keys pressing into his cheek, thinking it was wonderful to have a man walk me home at night. I was so obliged to him. He didn't ask why my bedroom had no real furniture, and I was thankful for that too. He just pinned me on my futon mattress in the dark. It was good—friendly and nice, like his face. I knew I wouldn't see him again.

The LeRoi "house of evil," as the *New York Post* called it, was down the street from my building. For a while after that night I made a habit of walking past the house, though it required circling the block to head toward the train. I liked to pass it when the morning sun streaked gold across the cream-colored brick. There were blue patio chairs out front, and potted hedges flanking the front door. An American flag hung like a curtain in one of the bay windows on the lower level. It was these everyday details that struck me.

Once a man whistled at me from an upstairs bedroom. "Come here!" he said, and I noticed that he wasn't yelling, wasn't even calling, but was talking just loud enough for me to hear. I didn't stop.

It's easy to become interested in a story like this. It only requires the same kind of curiosity about evil as watching a horror movie, but why did I continue to visit the house? That month I traced my daily routes around the city in a thick notebook—a project I'd picked up in order to prove my growing intimacy with New York. According to this hand-drawn account I walked past the LeRoi residence almost fifty times that summer, each time on my way to work for Lonnie.

2

She was young, young enough that everyone in the city, where the rich aged slowly, called her too young. I liked to watch her when she wasn't looking. The smooth curve of her legs above thin little ankles, flat stomach, pert round breasts. Dark hair and too much of it. "The kind you can't do anything with!" she whined, because the effects of a flat iron or hot rollers quickly wore off in the city's humidity, leaving rumpled silken waves instead. Eyebrows thick, manicured, usually drawn in enough to crease the skin between them, that little crease, the very beginnings of her first—her only—faint wrinkle. The nose, upturned, not a ridiculous ski jump, only slightly. Do the rich breed those upturned noses? Her eyes, heavy lidded, green, but not so radiant in color. The kind of eyes you think are plain brown because of all that brown hair, but then find no, those are flecks of jade.

The mouth. How does one describe a mouth? A mouth is flesh—movement—characterized by those white tips of teeth, by expression, by the rose that deepens when bit, when idly played with by fingertips. The way the shape of a face changes with a smile, a frown, a story, a wedge of pineapple between the molars.

There is no way to describe a face. Not really. No way to explain how it moves. We put women like Lonnie on film—nations fall in love. Not with the women themselves, not with the characters, not with those beautiful features even, but with the movement of their muscles, the way the pliable flesh is stretched across bone, the way it changes. The way it makes us feel something—elation or sadness, it doesn't matter which. Emotion is a stirring—a movement. We fall in love with a moving body. And so it moves us.

She wore a man's robe, gold with black trim, and you could tell, the way it plunged down her chest, she was naked underneath. Getting dressed was the last thing she did before leaving the house. She sometimes asked me to zip her dresses, so I ran my fingertips from the base of her spine to the nape of her neck without actually touching her. She would let out a tiny sigh as I was doing it, as if the basic process of putting on clothes depressed her.

At the beach she mixed Pimm's and 7UP in a thermos, then passed it around and smiled. Something about her posture became unfastened in the sun and she melted into her towel, running her fingers through the sand around her, as if she were raking the whole beach, slowly, inch by inch. She didn't seem to be listening to anyone; she didn't say anything; she didn't read. She just smiled and touched the sand and sometimes put her cheek to her own bronzed shoulder, as if to feel its warmth.

I worried about her in the water. She ran to it like a

child who had not yet been hit by an unexpected wave. She always swam out farther than I did. She would turn horizontal to float and I would lose sight of her from my vantage point close to shore.

I worried about her everywhere. She was always late. She was the kind of person who would arrive at a restaurant an hour after expected, run into the room, throw her things across three chairs, plunk down on a fourth, and then sigh and smile as if she'd lived in that spot her whole life. She never apologized. Her purse was always dribbling out MetroCards or tubes of eyeliner or important receipts. She left a trail of bobby pins wherever she went. She was always losing something but never frantic about it. What did it matter when you could just ask anyone for a swipe into the subway or a slick of lip balm or a tampon? Could it be that everyone had treated her that way her whole life? We all wanted to give her whatever we had.

I knew some details about her past—her mother had died young, her father was in finance. She was an only child. Her paternal grandparents were French, her maternal grandparents, Italian. She had gone to Marymount School, the religious bent of which had given her what she described as "a hard-on for Catholicism," though apparently she didn't mean this in a sacrilegious way. She still considered herself a member of the Church.

There were two photo albums jammed between thick art books on a shelf in her hallway, each containing no more than fifteen photos, mostly of people I never met alongside a few shots of flowers or rooms. Lonnie was featured in only three of them. In the first, she was probably twelve years old and away at summer camp, wearing thin white cotton shorts and a silly old-fashioned handkerchief tied under the collar of a white polo. She was standing in front of a cabin, leaning against the wooden handrail leading to the screen door, her little ass sticking out from the angle of her posture, her face turned slightly away from the camera, like she didn't know the photo was being taken. She was slimmer, flat chested, a little gangly even, but with tanned, flawless skin and the same thick waves streaming down her shoulders.

The other album was obviously from high school. Lonnie was in two of these photos. In one, she was standing in front of a school bus, wearing a long coat with toggle buttons over the Alice-blue pleated skirt of her school uniform. She was standing next to two girls who were talking to each other, but she was evidently not a part of the conversation. She was holding an arm up, her hand touching the hair by her temple. Though the image captured her full face, she was not smiling or looking at the camera here either; she was looking down. It was impossible to tell whether she was again unaware of the photographer's presence or attempting a model's pose, trying to look natural.

I'm looking at the last photo as I write. One day I slipped it from its plastic casing into my purse. She is sitting on the wood floor next to an unmade bed. A white sheet is falling next to her. Her cheeks are a little fuller, her hair a little shorter, but otherwise she looks exactly like the adult incarnation I knew. She's not in her uniform, but a pair of white denim shorts and a navy halter top. She's barefoot, her toenails painted a deep red. Her knees are bent, so you can see the full flesh of her thighs and the small strip of denim covering her crotch. She is leaning back, resting her palms on the floor behind her. Her lips are pursed and her eyes a little narrowed at the camera. She is ready to devour the photographer.

The photo was easy to steal. I didn't think she would suspect me, I didn't think she would even notice its disappearance, but that wasn't why I took it. I wanted to be the photographer or Lonnie, maybe both, though I knew owning the photo would not get me any closer to either experience. Did I have an inkling that I would need to record her? That I would spend a long time trying to work out what she was to me? Did I have a suspicion that she might not be real? Was I grasping for evidence?

I am picturing us together at the beach, but I can't be sure if it is a real memory. We are the only ones in the water. The lifeguard's chair is empty. I look behind me and see the men, her men, asleep on the sand with the baby. I am waist deep in the water, numb to the cold but still goose pimpled. I keep turning around so the waves don't hit me in the face, then looking back out, searching for her. She is past where the waves are breaking, just floating on her back, bobbing in the water. I catch glimpses of her arms, stretched out and gleaming wet in the sun, then I lose her again. I can't go back to the shore because I am the only one watching.

3

They owned a four-story town house between Park and Lexington in Carnegie Hill. I didn't see their home until my first day of work. My interview had been conducted at the playground. They told me about William's routine as we followed him around the sandbox. He was sixteen months old, walked on the balls of his feet like a tiny ballet dancer, and could say a few words. "We may need you to stay late occasionally, but generally, you'll be off by four."

The husband gestured to his wife and said, "Lonnie doesn't work, but she needs the days for her writing."

Lonnie knelt down next to William and ran a little toy truck along the ledge of the sandbox, keeping her knees together. She was wearing a pencil skirt and heels as if she were the one being interviewed. I worried about my appearance, though I'd dressed carefully that morning and pulled my hair up so the humidity wouldn't affect it. I was wearing flats and carrying a backpack instead of a handbag. It felt too casual; I looked like a teenager compared to her.

She left her big caramel-colored purse on a bench rather far from where we ended up standing, and I felt like going over to grab it for her, but also sensed it was not my place to do so. She wasn't even keeping an eye on it; her attention was focused on her son. They didn't ask me very many questions. I gave them a few details about the invented families I'd listed on my résumé, not mentioning my latest month of unemployment or the way my stomach cramped with hunger all day long. I reassured them I had no interest in moving back home. "So much to do all the time," I said of New York, trying to sound eager about the cliché.

I never knew what to say when someone asked me why I'd come to the city. I felt I'd moved for the same reason my ancestors had packed up wagons and made their way across the wide expanse of the American prairie —I wanted to see the elephant. I'd loved that idiom from the first time I heard it. The pioneers had invented a way to sum up both the naïve optimism of someone setting out to make their fortune as well as the jaded cynicism to which it was inevitably coupled. The contradictory nature of the phrase was particularly relevant early that summer, as I struggled to sustain myself. Hungry, broke, yet stupidly self-righteous about my lack of privilege and the very fact of my continued survival in a strange new place, I kept asking myself, *Have you seen the elephant yet?*

Oregon, or my memory of it, exists mostly in nighttime or the gloaming hours of dusk. I learned to live in that funny dark space. Those houses I occupied were familiar by touch and sound—the popcorn texture of my father's spackled walls, the smooth wood of my mother's antique radio, the ticking clock in the kitchen, the quiet creaking of the floors. Life happened by climbing out windows after midnight curfew, wandering through all those big backyards, so big the owners would never find me and the boy I was with. Which boy? Any boy, it didn't matter; it was dark. Life happened in the dark back seats of cars. Everyone was pale.

I could see my father in his robe sipping a beer in the backyard at night while the rain petered out. His lawn chair—a rainbow-printed number from the seventies—squeaked as he turned toward the dark field past our backyard, the darker trees beyond the field, and said, "Why would anyone ever want to leave this place?" I knew I wasn't supposed to answer and I also knew that the question was meant for me.

I didn't know what to make of her—of either of them, really. I felt a certain amount of resentment—for their wealth, their beauty, their confidence. It wasn't envy exactly. I didn't want their life, but I resented them for being able to live the way they did at all.

I had never worked for a boss my own age. The husband, James, was also young, in his mid-thirties. He was fit and tan with only a little gray mixed into his thick, honey-blond hair. I assumed, despite our closeness in age, that because of their obvious wealth, they would end up treating me like a servant instead of someone helping raise their child.

At the end of the interview, Lonnie (purse back in hand) told William to say goodbye to me. He tiptoed over and wrapped his little arms around my legs.

"I think that settles it," she said. "When can you start?"

Of course, it strikes me now, how trusting she was. What did she see in me? A girl in a thin ten-dollar dress, raised in a truck-stop town in rural Oregon, who'd never finished college? Maybe it didn't matter who I was.

I spent a long time, that first day, deciding which door to come through. I had keys to both, but going up the stoop and through the arched double doors of the main entrance seemed presumptuous, and entering through the ground level, servile. I'd never been faced with a decision like this before. In my three years of living in the city I had not once entered a single-family house.

I ended up flicking the latch on the iron gate and going through the ground-floor entrance, under the stoop. The door opened into a small mudroom. Weak morning light seeped in from the next room, illuminating an antique mirrored hall tree directly opposite the door, where a cream trench coat hung crookedly by its sleeve. I peeled off my canvas backpack and jean jacket and placed them next to the trench coat on a filigreed hook. The presence of the coat comforted me. The ground-floor entrance was used by the family, not just the help.

The next room over was a breakfast nook, which led to the kitchen. There was a baby monitor on the counter showing a grainy little picture of William asleep in his crib, his arms up over his head. Everything was quiet. Lonnie had told me, "Just let yourself in, I'll show you around. And when Billy wakes up you can give him some breakfast and take him to the park. You can go home early after that. We'll just get him used to you."

I'd assumed she'd be waiting for me at the door. I felt intrusive touring her house alone. I thought maybe I'd come through the wrong door after all, so I climbed the wooden stairs to the right of the kitchen, which led to a large foyer bounded by a formal dining room at the front of the house and a living room toward the back. Though the walls were an airy white, all the furniture looked like it had been acquired at an estate sale or a bordello—heavy oak, leather, red velvet in a time and place where it was a sign of wealth and taste to buy everything new. Mirrors in baroque frames hung on the walls. Both rooms were empty, save my own reflection.

"Hello?" I said, my voice coming out smaller than I expected.

There was no response. For a moment I wondered if it were possible I'd let myself into the wrong home. But no, it had been William on the baby monitor. Lonnie was probably just in a bathroom somewhere. I stood still in the foyer. The house smelled of lavender and something earthy, like modeling clay.

It felt too intimate to climb any higher. I had no idea what to do with myself. I decided abandoning my backpack by the door had been a mistake, so I went down to retrieve it. As I passed through the kitchen, the baby monitor started to emit the coos and whines of William waking. I stood staring at his restless form on the little screen, waiting for something to happen. For Lonnie to rise from the depths of the house and do something. For a creak that would signify movement. I was so still and anxious I thought I'd be able to hear the latch of a door two flights up. I heard the footsteps of someone on the sidewalk outside, the barking of a dog in the distance, the hum of traffic on Lexington Avenue, and William's sleepy moaning. I heard my own heartbeat, but I didn't hear Lonnie.

Was she testing me? Was this her version of a trial period? Will you let my baby cry or do something? How empathetic of a nanny are you? The clock on the stove read 7:45, fifteen minutes after my scheduled arrival time and too long to pretend I wasn't there yet.

It wasn't until I started to climb the stairs that led from the main entrance to the bedrooms above that I realized I didn't know where William's nursery was. Crying was coming from the room at the top of the stairs and I found the door partly open. I gave it a gentle push and it swept back to reveal Lonnie, naked, tangled in the pin-striped sheets of a four-poster bed. She lay on her side, her back to me, her dark locks spread around the pillow, the thin line of her neck emerging through the hair. A square of sunlight illuminated the concavity of her waist, the little white hairs on her skin, and the dust swirling in the air above her. She drew one leg slowly up and the sheet came with it, sliding up her inner thigh. On her nightstand was the source of the crying—another baby monitor, through which she was apparently having no trouble sleeping.

I stepped backward—not breathing, leaving the door agape—and ran up another flight of stairs where I could now hear, in the room at the front of the house, William's fussing starting to turn to wails. He calmed when I lifted him out of his crib and stared at me for a moment before, having judged me kindly, he rested his head in the crook of my neck. I hummed to him and looked around his room.

It was not cluttered with toys or decor, though a wooden train set was spread out across the greater part of a wool shag rug. A mobile of downy sheep hung above the crib and next to it a painting of an endearing frowning lion. Above the changing table I recognized an Edward Gorey illustration, a tiny, serenely smiling bow-tied boy at a long white-clothed table with a tiny fruit plate and tiny dinner bell. Behind him, the back of an enormous Gothic chair and then crosshatched shadows.

As there was still no sign of Lonnie, I walked William over to the changing table and unbuttoned his onesie. He stuck two fingers in his mouth and stared at me as I worked. He was long, skinny, and light to lift, like he was made of hollow bird bones. Something about his expression, whether serious or smiling, was a little vacant and dreamy. After I buttoned him back up, he squirmed to be put down and toddled on tiptoe back to his crib, yanking a matted grayish-white blanket lined in satin through the slats. He gripped a corner to his nose, and then made his way back to me, holding the same corner up, offering me a turn. I bent down and gave the blanket a good sniff. The fabric smelled like baby powder and, more faintly, urine. Without taking his fingers out of his mouth, he laughed.

Lonnie threw the door open then, startling both of us. She was wearing her robe, her hair a tangled nest on one side of her head, pillow marks on her cheek.

"Oh God!" she said. "Elle!"

She was the only person I'd ever known to shorten my name—Ella usually being diminutive enough as it is. I liked the way "Elle" sounded in her mouth, though—a sort of sleek exclamation.

"I completely overslept!"

"It's okay," I said. "I hope it's all right I came up here. I heard William crying—"

"Oh God, of course! Thank you," she said, picking William up.

"Mamamamama," he droned, leaning into her chest.

Downstairs, she poured milk from a gallon jug into a bottle. "Our last nanny wanted to transition him off the bottle when he turned one," she said. "But he was still asking for it after she left, so I just gave it back to him."

She pointed to a fruit bowl on the counter. "You can cut some up, if you like. And make coffee too. Eat any of our food anytime."

Obediently, I boiled water in the red kettle on the stove and poured grounds into a French press. I also warmed some milk for William's oatmeal and cut a banana into chunks. As I worked Lonnie said, "We've had some problems with nannies in the past actually." She balanced William, still vacantly sucking his bottle, on her hip. "She was heartless, our last nanny."

I looked at her, but she didn't go on. Instead, she moved toward the fresh coffee like a moth toward light. "We can go out to the terrace," she said. "I hate eating down here in the dark."

Before following her up the stairs, our food loaded onto a bamboo tray, I turned and grabbed a peach for myself, just the right amount of yielding underneath the skin. I ran the fuzz back and forth under my fingertips while we sat in the sunlight on the terrace. It was my first peach of the season. Lonnie stripped off William's onesie, set him in his high chair, and handed him a spoon. He set to work trying to eat the cereal. Most of it landed on his naked belly, but he didn't mind.

The terrace extended past the living room over what I would later learn was the laundry room, guest bedroom, and bath behind the kitchen, taking up the remainder of the lot. Below us, on either side and to the rear, I could see the narrow, well-pruned backyards of neighboring houses.

Lonnie sat in front of a palm that rose up over her head. She twisted her hair into a bun, and, holding it in place with a raised arm, turned her face to the sun, as if photosynthesizing her breakfast. I never saw her eat more than coffee and fruit in the morning and that first day was no exception. She seemed content at the table, though, whether eating or not. She didn't say much, so I didn't either. She was still waking up and I liked the silence that fell between us as she did so. It was as if to say, we'll be spending a lot of time together, no need to rush things. I held the peach to my nose, savoring the anticipation.

At one point she said, "You know what you're doing. I'm not the kind of mother who hovers or tells you what to do. You can do what you feel like with him. There will always be cash inside the cigar box on the table in the foyer. You can buy him or yourself whatever you need—toys, coffee, food. I don't want you to spend your own money when you're with him. I never want you to want."

"Okay," I said. "Thank you."

She watched me bite into my peach and smiled. "They're delicious, aren't they?" she said. "They're not usually good yet."

I used my hand to wipe a dribble of juice from my chin and nodded, calculating how much cash I could reasonably take from the cigar box, how much food from the cupboards, in order to eat dinner that week. I could feel myself starting to believe her, to trust her, to earnestly like her, though it might have just been the promise of nourishment. Not being hungry felt the same as being happy.

That first week, after the peach, I devoured a square of bread, toasted brown, soft on the inside, slathered in a thick smear of salted butter with a French label. I followed it with raspberries, placed on each fingertip and popped off, one at a time, into my mouth. I ate thin slices of sharp cheddar and Gruyère, letting them melt on my tongue. I started simply, like a child, and with time moved on to forkfuls of sour kimchi, chili jam on nutty crackers, and garlicky green olives. I took to eating during William's naptimes in order to fully concentrate on the food, training my body to register hunger between normal meals.

Food was better than I remembered, not just because I was ravenous, making up for lost time, but because Lonnie purchased only the best of everything—all the produce ripe, sweet, juicy, fresh, mostly from local farms. The eggs gave up bright orange yolks, the likes of which I'd never seen. They tasted almost like a different food they were so rich. Once, craving the crackers I'd tried not to finish off that afternoon, I went to Dean & DeLuca after my shift and found the tiny box cost ten dollars, which came out to more than fifty cents a cracker.

One day, watching me struggle, Lonnie showed me how to cut open a mango, avoiding the hard middle, then running the blade along the flesh of the two sides in a crisscross pattern. I imagined the knife sinking into her hand as she cupped a half in her palm, pictured her blood like juice. When she bent the slice back so all the little cubes of fruit popped out, ready to be cut free, I exhaled a delighted laugh. "Not quite done," she said, picking up the middle, and carefully slicing the peel off all the way around. When the ribbon fell to the cutting board she brought the pit to her mouth and sucked at it, scraping what was left of the meat away with her teeth. She handed it, half-eaten, to me, and I put the slippery thing to my own mouth, juice running down my hand.

4

I've always watched a lot of horror movies. As a kid I'd liked them simply because they were forbidden. Though they gave me nightmares, I watched anyway, just to feel like I was getting away with something. I grew to appreciate them for other reasons, though. I like the way a good one feels like something lifted from your own nightmares. I like the way the body is treated with reverence by the camera during its destruction.

Though they rely on the element of surprise, most horror movies actually work in a very predictable way. It's not difficult to find a sense of comfort and reliability within the darkness; you only have to know the formula. The main character is given one real clue before they know they should be looking for it, followed by a series of red herrings. In this way, the plot is essentially a story of recovery. They are not really discovering things, as much as it may seem that way, but rather trying to work out what they already know, trying to remember whatever it was they were shown back when they thought things were random and unrelated.

I remember my dad driving me to the video store in his pickup truck the year my parents got divorced. The dark of the Oregon woods at night spun out around us, as I bounced up and down in the middle of the bench seat, fooling with the cassette player, with him to my left, one hand on the wheel and the other bringing a cigarette to his mouth.

I would follow him to the horror section and examine the plastic-encased covers—demented clowns, zombie dogs, the screaming faces of beautiful blondes. My mom would never let me see those kinds of movies. We would rent a few at a time, setting them in a pile on the counter. Once Dad said to the teenage girl working, "Shame you have to spend your Friday nights here."

She didn't look at him.

"When you're so young and pretty."

"Isn't she a little young for these kinds of movies?" she replied.

"She's older now," Dad said.

I'm not sure what to write about now that I'm married. I scratch in small letters, trying to remember, then:

> *Wasn't able to pick up a pen for all the sickness my whole first trimester to mention the fact that I'm pregnant. Now that I'm three months along I am nothing but alert and hungry. I could ravage everything. It's scary, this tapeworm baby. In the park I stuck my fingers into the dirt under the grass and licked them clean. I wanted a handful of*

earth. Pillie said, "What harm can it do?" but the doctor told me not to eat it.

The baby. The baby itself seems too strange a thing to comprehend. C keeps asking me why I did it, or at least why I did it now. Why why why. What is it with everyone and their questions? As if it were some kind of cruel and ruthless thing to do.

I've decided to rewrite her journal—the last one—from memory. I've decided to write down everything. I don't know how accurate it will be, but it seems like the final task, the only way I can hold on to her.

5

The first time I met Carlow was at Lonnie's birthday party. Lonnie had covered the house with Chinese lanterns and colorful flowers—arrangements of wild roses and cosmos, spider mums and wisteria. The floral scent mingled with the lamb chops and cheeses on the dining room table and Lonnie's own musky perfume. "Pilar told me not to put flowers in the dining room," Lonnie said, referencing the housekeeper who came twice a week. "But it's summer so I wanted the whole place lousy with flowers."

I'd been asked to put William to bed and then stay the night. It was the first but not the last time I'd sleep over, their house gradually becoming more familiar to me than my own austere apartment. At that point I'd been William's nanny for two weeks. He was an easy baby, though I was rarely off by four and Lonnie was rarely writing in the big office opposite the master bedroom. There were lunches with friends, shopping, manicures, waxes, and an endless stream of doctor's appointments. I'd been raised in a family without health insurance; I went to a doctor only if I was very sick. Lonnie had screenings for everything imaginable as well as acupuncture and massages for stress.

Though all the appointments seemed unnecessary, in fact I understood what it was like to fill a whole day up with nothing much. I was a single woman. On weekends, I slept late, I took long baths any time of day I felt like it, I read books, I watched meandering foreign films, I would sometimes spend an hour masturbating—not even watching porn, just lying there, trying to think of nothing but the sensation like some kind of meditative exercise. If I had something specific to do but no time frame in which to do it, like clean the house, I could make the activity take all day—doing a little, then turning on an episode of something on my laptop, sitting down to watch for a while, doing a little more, stopping to eat something, watching another episode, making tea, having a snack, and so on. As an adult one didn't get bored. Or rather, one got bored only at work.

I spent a long time carrying William around that party, trying to look like I was having a good time. When people surrounded us, he dug his little nails into my shoulders with fear but kept an uncomfortable smile on his face that everyone found very winning.

"Look at this skinny baby! Lonnie, you're so lucky he's so *skinny*!"

"He's tall too, look how tall he is!"

Lonnie mixed drinks at the gold bar cart in the corner of the living room. She'd dressed in front of me. I tried not to look at the glow of her skin, but it was impossible to stop my eyes from following her as she paced naked around her bedroom, digging through piles of clothing. She had a light stretch mark that ran from her navel to the dark patch of neatly trimmed pubic hair, the only evidence that William was indeed her own.

I'd been thinking about a time in my middle school locker room, when I had been scanning the lanky body of Jennifer Howell as she peeled off her sports bra and then expertly clipped a lacy pink one over her little round breasts. I remember standing in cotton panties printed with cartoon cats, a white undershirt on my flat skinny torso, and her turning toward me, her shoulders gleaming with glitter lotion, somehow tan despite the rain all school year long, saying, "Stop looking at me, lesbo."

All the girls spun around, their faces contorted with disgust. I looked down at my skinny legs, noticing all the hair on them, and mumbled, "I wasn't," the only thing I could think to say.

Lonnie didn't chide me; she didn't seem to notice my gaze. When she finally found what she was looking for—a long coral dress with a low back and square neckline—she ran her hands over her tits, directing my attention to her nipples, rigid against the silky fabric, saying, "Is this okay? I can't wear a bra."

Carlow was sitting in the green wingback chair next to a pyre of yellow beeswax candles in the fireplace. I noticed him around the time the carefully arranged dining room table became covered in stray drinks and cocktail napkins with rings of cherry-colored wine stains. The living room, reflected in the windows, vibrated with laughter. I watched Lonnie, barefoot, weave away from him, refilling glasses without permission. People were beginning to sway as they spoke, to lean in closer together.

There was something boyish about his face. I tried to pinpoint where the impression came from—he had full cheeks, large brown eyes, and thick unkempt eyebrows just asymmetrical enough to make his face look a little doubtful. His dark hair was cropped close on the sides but fell in a long perfect wave on top. These details were all inconsequential in an interesting way—his features floated around his smirking mouth as if they existed only to give it form. The smirk wasn't mean, but rather made him look like he was amused by something no one else had noticed. He wasn't talking to anyone; he was smiling dopily to himself.

I walked over to him, William, still nibbling a cookie, sitting astride my hip. He smiled up at us and said, "Hello."

Emboldened by the fact that no one was watching me at that moment, I said, "You look content for someone sitting all alone."

"I'm not alone," he said. "I'm at a party."

He was still smiling, wrinkling up the skin by his eyes. I wished I weren't carrying this baby. And I wished I owned a nicer dress than the cheap belted cotton thing I'd thought would be sufficient.

"Carlow," he said.

"I'm Elle," I said, choosing to use Lonnie's nickname for me.

He offered a firm handshake.

"What did you do for your twenty-sixth birthday?" I asked.

"You think I'm older than twenty-six?" he said.

I smiled.

"Oh God, I don't remember," he said. "It wasn't like this. Only a woman can throw a beautiful party like this."

As if he were reading my thoughts, he reached his hands out. "Let me hold the baby!" he said.

I passed William over and watched him snuggle into Carlow's chest; they obviously knew each other. I leaned on one arm of the chair, next to them, conscious of how close my hip was to his bicep.

"When did you meet Lonnie?" I said.

Carlow bent closer to me as he spoke, his face coming up to my shoulder. "I'm friends with James," he said. "We met her at the same time. It was her twenty-first birthday, which I guess makes this the five-year mark. She was having a picnic on Governors Island—a day party before the night party—she's always made a big deal out of her own birthday. It started raining, actually a terrible summer thunderstorm, and everyone on the island ran to the dock. We didn't know her, we were there with other friends, but we were all crammed together under the awning."

I pictured wet tendrils of hair plastered to her chest.

"What I really remember," Carlow said, "was telling James she was probably too young, but, the way things turned out, what the hell do I know? You know, that first day, I told James she looked like trouble to me."

I wanted to ask him why he'd said that, what he meant, but he smiled then, and held out William to pass back to me, which I took to signal the end of the conversation.

When it was finally late enough, I took William into the kitchen. Pilar had gone home and the lights were turned down low; small yellow circles illuminated the countertops. The dishwasher was gurgling and hot against my thighs as I reached up to get a bottle. William had his fingers in his mouth. His shirt was untucked and wrinkled, with chocolate stains on the collar. He nuzzled into my neck, his eyelids drooping as I filled the bottle with milk. I sat down at the kitchen table with him on my lap, deciding to give the bottle to him there. He slumped his little body into mine, sucking absently at the milk.

I heard footsteps on the stairs and soon after saw James saunter over to a kitchen cabinet, followed by Carlow and another man I didn't know. Carlow saw me right away, giving me a smile in greeting, but it took James a moment. He was focused on finding a bottle of scotch buried somewhere in the back of a cupboard. "Gentlemen," he said as he pulled it out and swung around. "Oh, Elle," he said. "Time for him to go to bed?"

"He's getting tired," I said.

"Lonnie wanted you to know how she appreciates your not taking your eye off him, even when other people were holding him."

I nodded. "Of course," I said. "He's my responsibility tonight."

"She always has an eye on him, and she noticed you do too."

I nodded again. He was drunk.

"I noticed too."

I nodded a third time and pursed my lips into a smile for him. William unlatched his mouth from the nipple and whispered, "Dada." James didn't hear or didn't care. He kept looking at me and I felt very sober. Carlow was leaning against the counter, taking in the conversation.

The third man, the one I didn't know, clasped James on the shoulder, jolting him to attention. "Are we going to try some of that?"

"Yes," James said, turning back to the cupboard to retrieve tumblers. "Alexander Murray, 1964." He poured three glasses. "It's meant to be drank, boys."

They clinked glasses and sipped the amber liquid. "Don't tell anyone where you got this," James said.

As they walked out of the room, Carlow lingered behind and set his glass down on the table in front of me, then headed back upstairs behind the others.

I smiled and sipped at the offering as William finished his milk, though I felt I didn't deserve it. I'd expected it to be indistinguishable from the cheap whiskey I drank, but there was a smoky undertaste of something I couldn't quite identify—raisins, licorice, figs. I ran my tongue along the roof of my mouth, trying to single it out—molasses maybe, or almond extract. When it was gone, I had to stop myself from licking the glass.

When I laid William in his crib he sprang back up, tears streaming down his face and onto his crocodile-print pajamas. All night he had tried so hard to please everyone, but alone with me he was comfortable enough to fall apart. His screams were accusatory: *Why didn't you send all those people away?*

I picked him back up and brought him over to the rocking chair. I hummed softly and rubbed his back while he cried, burying his face in my shoulder, making it slimy with snot. Finally, he dozed off in my arms, his small body going limp and leaden. The vent above the door was quietly streaming in cool air and I liked the feeling of his hot body against my chest. I wanted to lay William down with me in the guest bed across the hall and fall asleep curled around him. I didn't want to leave him and I didn't want to go back to the party, but I felt obligated.

I clipped the baby monitor to the thin plastic belt around my waist and made my way slowly back down the stairs. Many of the guests had left by now. Lonnie had finally stopped pushing drinks and was lounging on the leather sofa, slumped into it. She was trying to take a drink from a champagne coupe without sitting up, moving the glass very slowly toward her mouth, giggling a little, her hand shaking with the effort of not spilling. She was sitting alone, so I walked over and lowered myself down gently next to her.

"I put William to bed," I said. "He's asleep."

She didn't move the glass away from her mouth even after she'd stopped slurping at the bubbling liquid. She nodded, a vacant smile beneath the coupe. When the glass finally detached from her mouth she passed it over to me, and I grabbed it with both hands, narrowly avoiding the drink sloshing onto my dress.

"Try it," she said. "Have you tried it? You have to catch up now."

I put my mouth over the faint smudge of coconut oil from her lips and sipped, then gulped the rest of the drink down. Lonnie watched me, still smiling.

"It's good," I told her. "It's very good."

My lips glided against each other. She rested her head on my shoulder.

"There's something about you I really love, Elle," she said. "I don't know what it is about you, but I really love you."

I had a desperate urge to believe her, while at the same time a thought came unbidden and unexpected in its strength: *I might hate you*. Carlow approached before I could respond. He handed Lonnie a crown of flowers taped together with green florist tape. She gasped. "What is this?"

"A birthday crown," he said. "Put it on. But be careful, I used one of your wire hangers as a base and the hook is still sticking out under the flowers."

"You *made* this?" Lonnie exclaimed.

"I used your flowers," he said. "I took some from a vase."

"These are my flowers!" Lonnie said as she put the crown on. Carlow leaned over and adjusted the wire, molding it to the shape of her head.

The creamy blush of the petals offset her complexion in a way that made her look soft and dreamy in the candlelight.

"I want to see," she said, taking the crown off and passing it over to me. "Put it on so I can see what I look like."

I placed the crown on my head and turned to face her, a potent floral scent swimming around me. The wire fit snugly against my skull. We stared at each other.

"You used the moonflowers from the terrace too!" Lonnie said. "This is a dangerous crown! Wire hook and poisonous flowers!"

"I used to do things," Lonnie said, one hand touching her face in the bathroom mirror, the other trembling a little and pinching a joint between two fingers. "You know, I used to do a lot of things. I don't ever *do* anything now. And I can't remember what I think about so does that mean I don't think about anything? Ever?"

She had walked in on me in the bathroom, her bathroom, and didn't bother to leave when she saw it was occupied. The lock on the bathroom door was faulty, I'd discovered earlier that week, when William had burst in while Lonnie was showering. I apologized, grabbing him, embarrassed, but her voice from behind the semi-transparent shower curtain just said, "Oh, the lock is broken. Don't worry."

I wadded toilet paper tighter and tighter in my fist, unable to pee in front of her. The tiny windowless room was filling up with smoke. "It's better," she said, "when it feels a little secret—the smoking."

I wanted to let my dress go, to cover myself back up. Would she know I hadn't peed? Eventually, I dropped the wad of toilet paper into the clear water and, standing up, quickly shut the lid. She was completely oblivious. She handed me the joint.

The weed made the ache in my bladder worse. I could feel my whole body more acutely; I could feel my heart pounding. It was scary to fixate on, scary to think too long about being a body—just a mess of physical needs. If this pounding were to stop that would be it.

Carlow was lying on the floor when we came back downstairs, the selected Pablo Neruda hovering over him. The living room was clouded in smoke. "This book has a history," Carlow said.

"Look at his smug face," Lonnie said, pointing to the book. "What a bastard, you can tell."

"That smug face got laid. You can tell that too," Carlow replied.

"That smug face got *us* laid, you mean," James said. "We used to carry that around, remember? We had our little journals and our Neruda."

Carlow was laughing, his long flat belly moving up and down.

"You're still in love with that girl in France," James said.

His face fell a little. "She was an angel," he said. "That girl was an angel."

"That girl was fifteen."

"We were basically homeless by that point. We came to Europe with all this money and blew through it so fast. Our parents gave us so much money and we just spent it *all*. We'd been sleeping outside for five days, and I hadn't bathed except in the ocean."

"When was this?" Lonnie asked. "If she was fifteen, how old were you?"

"You're so hung up on the ages," Carlow said. "I was nineteen, okay? I asked her if she wanted to go for a walk in the woods."

"And what did she say?"

"She did. She wanted to go for a walk in the woods." Carlow's smirk was in full effect now. "That's all I'll say, you can't know everything." He reconsidered, though, and spat at us. "Do you know what she said? You want to know what she said? She said, 'You taste like the ocean.'"

Lonnie and James exploded with laughter, but Carlow just smiled, turning pages in the Neruda. "That girl was an angel," he said again. "And I have no way to find her."

"It's better that way," Lonnie said.

"I could've had a whole other life," Carlow said.

"Yeah," Lonnie said, "if she had taken you home to meet her parents. If she had told them, 'Hi, Mom, this is the nineteen-year-old bum I'm dating.'"

Something seethed inside of me and made Lonnie's teasing of him unbearable. I was chewing on my bottom lip. He wasn't looking at me. He wasn't looking at Lonnie either, he was looking up at the smoke crowding the ceiling, but that wasn't good enough. What was it about these dumb preppy men? These men who had no concept of poverty at all. I still had to pee, but I was suddenly very thirsty too. Thirst, thirst, thirst—the word ringing in my mind. What a dry word, like saying it out loud would suck all the saliva from my mouth. The heat of Lonnie next to me was making it worse. Her legs were draped over her husband like they were so in love.

Carlow held the book up to our eyeline. "This one," he said, tapping a page.

"The rain, the rain," Lonnie said, leaning forward to look. "That one's about the girl who can you-know-what."

*

In the middle of the night the baby got sick. I heard him crying through the monitor, struggled to pull on the T-shirt I'd brought as pajamas, and walked in to find the nursery filled with the sour smell of vomit. He was sitting up in the crib, his onesie wet with puke and tears. My first thought was that he'd somehow ingested alcohol at the party, but that was impossible, I hadn't taken my eyes off him.

My whole body had tilted off its axis—that turned-stomach feeling from the champagne combined with the rank smell filling William's room—but I walked over and picked up his little reeking body. He stopped crying, his screams turning to a gentle whimper.

I stripped his onesie off, then drew him a lukewarm bath. He was drowsy and I had to hold him up. I was beginning to feel less dizzy now that he didn't smell like vomit anymore and it was kind of nice, being the only one awake with him in the quiet house. I looked at his funny little body in the water and thought about how a little more than a year ago he had been a part of Lonnie. How strange, at least in the middle of the night, that people come from other people.

After I put William back to bed, I took his soiled bedding and clothes down to the laundry room past the kitchen. I tried to see into the dim living room, wondering if Carlow had fallen asleep on the floor, but it was too dark.

Downstairs, the guest room door was open, the lamp

on the nightstand switched on. When I got a few steps closer I also saw that it wasn't just Carlow in the bedroom.

Lonnie had him pressed up against the wall. Actually, no, he had her pressed up against the wall—why do I remember it the other way around? She was pressed up against the wall and pressed up against him. He was bare chested but still wearing pants. She was wearing her robe, so I gathered what had happened. She went to bed with James, got up, and sneaked downstairs. The robe was slipping off her shoulder and he had his hand underneath it. All that soft silk and all that soft skin.

I realized they could see me at any moment, so I ducked to the side of the open door. I was close enough to hear their breathing. Why did they leave the door open? As soon as I had the thought, one of them pushed it closed. This must have just started—if I'd been a few moments earlier I might've met Lonnie on the stairs.

I was still holding the sour sheets from William's crib. I'd tried to wad them up around the vomit, but I could feel a wet spot against my hand. I could still smell them.

I waited a long time outside the bedroom. Maybe I was waiting for sex noises as confirmation. There were never any squeaky bedsprings, but what I did hear, eventually, was a single muffled moan, like it was coming from behind his hand, or like she had sighed into his mouth.

Maybe I should've thought about what this knowledge meant for my job or what it meant for Lonnie's marriage or, at the very least, what it meant for my attraction to

Carlow, but instead, I stood there, with some kind of stomach-sick bursting inside of me, and considered what kind of sex they must be having. The quiet fucking. He couldn't bite her or slap her around. The restraint like a form of poetry. I stood there holding the sheets on which her baby had just vomited and compared their fucking to a sonnet. It must just drive him mad, I thought. The things he must want to do to her would be impossible to cover up. How could you fuck a woman like that without needing to leave a mark?

6

After I found out about the affair I started opening drawers I had no business opening, taking an inventory of her home in a notebook. I wrote it all down, partially to slow my progress. I was conscious that I could look through everything, every nook and cranny, in a matter of days—or hours, even, depending on how well behaved William was—but this gave me a sick feeling, like eating an entire cake by myself. I could digest this secret information only in thin slices. Listing everything I found was a way of considerably protracting the process.

Junk drawer, kitchen, I wrote one day, *light bulbs, batteries, rubber bands, thumbtacks, empty baby food jar, yellow-handled scissors, large white knit doily (folded in tissue paper).*

Another day I swung the door of her medicine cabinet open and I was immediately enraged by the lack of products, the empty shelf space. I found the cheap tube of liquid eyeliner Lonnie used to dress up. A single bottle of ballerina-pink nail polish. French men's cologne with a black and silver label. James's shaving set. A tube of coral lipstick. A slippery jar of coconut oil sat on top of the cabinet near the vanity lights, a few globs in the process of dripping down into the cabinet. That was all.

I slid the shower curtain back and examined the caddy hanging from the nozzle. Peppermint shampoo, a diluted jar of apple cider vinegar she probably used as conditioner. Simple castile soap and a goo-filled jar without a label. I opened it, ran the product between my fingers, tasted it with the tip of my tongue—coconut oil and salt.

What had I been hoping to find? A complicated skincare routine that would explain her utter porelessness? Expensive hair masks, a lot of unnoticeable makeup? Something that said I am this beautiful because of class? Something that said if I lacked funds I might be as flawed as you are?

I wrote it all down. The cologne was labeled 1899, a date instead of a name. This struck me as romantic. The coral pinks of the lipstick and nail polish also struck me as romantic. I had probably ten tubes of cheap lipstick, at least ten bottles of nail polish at home, accumulated since adolescence, half of them gone gloppy, packed in my suitcase each time I moved as if they were precious. It was much more beautiful to have only one—the perfect one.

I had the sensation of stepping blindly as I listed the contents of her house's hidden spaces. Of grasping at textures, trying to make out changes in light. I didn't know what it was yet that I was inside, only that whatever I was immersed in was larger than my current understanding.

I was going through the rooms of her mind. Secret arrangements, shadows and light. There's something feminine about boxes. Nothing I opened revealed anything about James. It's girls who hide objects inside other objects—jewelry boxes, hope chests, dollhouses, decorative compacts with mirrors inside, boxes of love notes, tampons.

In her nightstand there was a wooden box with a peony inlay on top and a mirror inside, which reflected the contents when opened. I found a small jar of tiny pink crystals on a string, a lock of blond hair tied with a gold ribbon, an old dead corsage, a folded note in someone else's handwriting:

On the balcony
I saw a girl,
Fucking asshole,
Who made a jerk of herself
And delighted in it.
Is it good? I asked her.
It is crappy-crappy, she said.
But I do it because it is crappy
And because it is vain

I copied the Stephen Crane satire into my notebook. I described the corsage—once-pink roses, yellowed baby's breath, rhinestones on hair-thin wires.

I couldn't find any of the writing she was supposedly working on, either in the desk or online, but I found old notebooks inside a small chest in her office. She wrote stray phrases and paragraphs without reference to one another:

> *So many men without women . . .*
>
> *Jean says something like When in love one survives on air and cold water. All I want are apricots and strawberries.*
>
> *Mallory, drunk and swaying, pointing for emphasis, imitates the Asian boy, David, in our class. She tells us that the nun wears that bandage around her ankle because it has little metal pieces in it that poke into her leg every time she walks. To remind her of Christ. Isn't that creepy? she says. I don't know.*
>
> *Amy gave me her Marilyn Monroe lighter. No, in real life we would not be friends. But this isn't real life.*

There was a whole page where she cut the name "Johnny" from magazines and books and pasted them together.

There were doodles—she was a good artist—always body parts that led off the page. Little hands and yo-yos, braids coming from nowhere, girls' legs descending from the top of the paper, in saddle shoes and lacy socks, with bleeding knees.

What revealed more than the journals were old notes from school friends—folded into tiny rectangles, with pull tabs that popped the corners out. There was a stack of these inside an unused Chinese food box in a desk drawer. I imagined them falling from her high school locker when she pulled it open, the pleasure she would've felt. The same pleasure I felt now, discovering them. The same pleasure I had once felt when notes fell from my own locker years ago.

So, you remember the guy? Of course you do. He had the balls to IM me last night and tell me he wanted me to know it wasn't planned. That he had been surprised. That I had started kissing him (!) and he had no intention of things going as far as they did. What a tool. He also didn't know what Planned Parenthood was if you can believe it. I wanted to call you so bad but my mom would see your number on the phone bill and figure it out like she always does. You're the only person who understands what I'm going through, and I love you so much. I have to cut this short because Mrs. K, the menopausal bitch, is staring at me like she knows I'm not doing the assignment.

I ran into Mr. Mullany at Mimi's on Friday. He told me he thought we were kindred spirits or something. He also told me he thought we had been together in a past life. The thing is! I don't not believe in past lives? I actually think the idea of them is pretty cool? But he's an old skeeze with shit always stuck in his teeth so I just told him he'd have to find me in his next life. What is wrong with us that these guys like us?

Patterns emerged within the notes—which I told myself were clues as to why she might cheat on James. Multiple girls had been banned from talking to Lonnie by their parents, though they clearly found ways around this, by simply saying they were meeting different friends and passing notes or chatting online instead of talking on the phone.

Older men were often mentioned as having "creepy" attractions to the girls—Lonnie, her friends, or the group as a whole. It was difficult to decipher how old these old men were or how the girls knew them—whether they were parents or teachers or men they met at parties or bars. This was never desirable. They may have admitted to teasing them a little, but it always ended in obvious rejection. At least that's what the girls always claimed. Why the men continued to pursue them was a constant source of poorly concealed delight and intrigue for them.

Lonnie's girlfriends were repeatedly taken advantage of. They never said "rape," they never seemed to think these instances were anything more than annoying, but phrases like "I was too drunk to stop him," "I wouldn't have let him sober" were all over the place. Was this a way to spin regrets into victimization? Or had Lonnie grown up entrenched in a culture of date rape? Had they just come to expect that it was something that happened, if they got drunk with boys?

These notes were probably not very different from the ones I had passed in school with girlfriends of my own, but Lonnie had kept them. I had not, so there was no way to remember, no way to compare.

I also found a childhood jewelry box, shaped like a piano, velvet lined, with a ballerina pirouetting to the tinkling tune of the "Nutcracker Suite" when open, but instead of jewelry, inside I found baby teeth in the little compartments—a whole set, incisors, canines, molars, their insides browned with decay. I arranged them on my palm, in order, ran my fingers over their jagged edges. Lonnie's childhood mouth, kept inside pink velvet. This was so perfect it filled me with an unexplainable rage. I slipped one—an eyetooth—into my pocket.

7

Sam's and my apartment faced away from the street. With her window open I could hear the call to prayer of a distant mosque, an occasional siren, the automated announcements of the Long Island Railroad, and, more loudly than anything else, the church down the street at odd hours, not just Sundays but nights during the week too. There were words thundering into a microphone, a choir, the hammering of an organ. The fact that I couldn't understand any of it made it haunting—that stentorian male voice following me around my home, accusing me of something, though I didn't know what it was.

Sam was hardly ever home. She worked long hours in administration somewhere in the city and had other friends, family, a whole other life. We'd never been close. I'd moved in only after responding to her Craigslist ad.

Lonely after work, I listened for the stray sounds of my neighbors—bumps, the sound of a tap turning on, the comforting muffled hum of a television, a blow dryer, a coffee grinder. The old plaster walls were thick and I rarely heard anything coming from inside the building except mice skittering in the walls and, in the hallway, footsteps—the clicking of heels. Lying in bed at night, I counted the steps, trying to figure out which apartment those heels led to, measuring my own steps later, but it never quite added up right. Whoever owned those heels had a gait much different from my own.

The footsteps reminded me of when I was a very small child and my mom worked nights at a diner. That was before she got the teaching job, long before the divorce. In our little house I'd hear the thuds of her shoes on the porch at two a.m. and creep out of my room, desperate for a glimpse of her. I understand now, from watching William, how she must have felt to see a child awake when she shouldn't be. She must have been exhausted. She'd shoo me back into my room without comfort, despite my tears.

One night, though, she waved me over when I opened my door and mumbled, "I can't sleep." My usual line. My dad was in their bedroom, likely passed out in front of the television on their dresser. I could hear the sound of commercials drifting down the hall.

"Want some?" my mom said. She was bent over the kitchen counter, wearing her baby-blue work blouse with a pair of my dad's boxer shorts, eating fries from a Styrofoam take-out container. She'd already washed her face and I loved the way it looked without all her usual makeup. She had a beautiful peachy-cream complexion.

I doused a fry in ketchup and placed it on my tongue, relishing the sour-saltiness. They were still hot. She lifted my little body onto the counter next to her and together we devoured the whole container of fries, one crispy morsel at a time. They were the best fries I'd ever eat—before or since.

"Middle of the night food," she said. "It's a secret. It always tastes best."

Unable to sleep, I curled up on the loveseat in Sam's room and searched the Internet for anything about "Rev." LeRoi. The cop had been right about the details: he'd had a host of "nuns" who spent their days on the streets begging for money for the church, and supposedly brought in a significant income—enough to purchase sixty acres upstate, which LeRoi claimed to use as a camp for orphans. It also happened to be where he chopped up the bodies of the "nuns" who wanted out—"nuns" who were murdered while the rest of the women sang hymns to cover up the sounds of the screams.

LeRoi was eventually charged with the murder of four people, but police speculated he had killed at least a dozen, and as many as twenty-three of his parishioners had gone missing over the years. He'd fathered forty-six (some articles say forty-two and some say they are not all his) children with these "nuns."

While LeRoi died in prison in 2006, as far as I could tell, his family still lived in the tall corner town house at the end of my block, and the church was in operation, headed by LeRoi's oldest son.

The story had come back into the news lately; maybe

that's why the cop had brought it up. I clicked play on a recent video from a local station's website—deep dramatic narration over slow zooms of black-and-white photos—a crying woman had been abandoned by one of LeRoi's nuns as a toddler. She was fully aware that LeRoi was her father, but her mother had gone missing shortly after leaving her with an aunt and she had never been able to locate her.

Tears stream down her cheeks as she says, "I went to my father in prison when he was still alive. I said, 'Did you kill my mom?' He told me, 'No.'"

She says, as if to reassure herself, "I believe him." The girl chokes back a sob, looks around anxiously, and then says, "He has never lied to me."

The newscaster asks anyone with information to come forward and the story ends.

I found myself continuously clicking this video, despite knowing that it all comes to nothing. I was waiting for the old photo of the mother standing among LeRoi's family in the eighties. It's a big group shot, with LeRoi front and center in a maroon velvet suit, looking directly at the camera, his face serious. He's handsome—smooth skin, pouty lips, curly hair slicked back with pomade. The camera pans across all the women of various ages and skin tones standing around him, zooms in on the mother. She is young, but not as young as many of the girls. She's looking at the camera expressionless with serious, dead eyes.

There was a middle-aged black man who sometimes said hello to me in the elevator. We spoke as the old contraption made its sluggish climb to the fifth floor and I tried not to stare at his glass eye, tried to look into the real one.

"You live in Roxanne's old place," he said. "Across from the trash chute."

I nodded.

"She used to have me over sometimes. To smoke pot with her—weird old lady, but nice."

"Do you hear the church?" I asked him.

"The church?" he said. "Which one?"

"You don't hear singing from the church down the block?"

He frowned and shook his head. I squinted at him, as if he were lying to me. This made him shift uncomfortably on his feet. We didn't say anything else to each other for the rest of the ride.

8

One day Lonnie suggested we take William to the Met. Lonnie didn't often suggest outings between the three of us, and I couldn't read her motivations. I worried she'd begun to feel panicked about leaving William alone with me for some reason, and had the urge to check up, but she gave nothing away. She babbled uncharacteristically in the heat. She was talking about a camp upstate.

"I went every summer for years," she said. "The whole month of July, and when I returned Dad would take me to the Hamptons until school started again. It still feels a little unnatural for me to be in the city in July. Seems full of tourists."

She was right. Fifth Avenue was crowded, and I struggled to stay by her side as she pushed William in the stroller, parting a sea of people in sneakers.

I didn't have to ask any questions; she kept talking. "No boys!" she said. "We had boys in preschool, when we refused to play with them, and then kindergarten started and they all disappeared. It's a problem, don't you think? School is supposed to teach you to socialize as much as it's supposed to teach you math or reading. How are you supposed to learn to socialize with boys? They're not just for special occasions, they're a sort of everyday incidence."

Incidence? Had she selected the wrong word?

"No boys at camp either, not lucky like my friends, but it was somehow more all right—it was just a big sleepover, the counselors hardly older than we were, and actually more interested in rebelling than the younger girls. They taught us how to drink and smoke, they thought it was funny, the little bit of knowledge they had on us, and they'd crack up if one of us coughed or threw up.

"It sounds funny—having to learn something like how to drink, but you do, not just because you have to learn how to recognize the perfect amount before the spins set in, but you have to get used to the taste, so you don't just spit a shot out. It's like cough medicine at first. You forget that once you like it. Better not to have boys around for all of that. Better to act like an old hand when one passes you a flask."

She switched subjects suddenly, randomly. "How's your love life?" she asked.

I laughed, startled by everything she did. "Not much to talk about there," I said.

"You don't have a boyfriend?"

"Not right now."

"You go on dates though?"

I could only think about the cop I'd fucked because he'd fed me. I nodded. "When the mood strikes."

"I know I'm sort of your boss," she said. "But we can be friends. We're probably not very different."

"Did you have a nanny?" I asked after a beat, something I'd wondered often, while trying to figure out why Lonnie was so nice to me all the time. "What was your nanny like?"

"My first nanny? I loved her," she said, shaking her head.

"How long did she work with you?" I asked.

"I was probably five or six when she left. After her there was a very strict woman. She taught me to behave properly, I guess. I have her to thank for teaching me manners, but I didn't love her. My last nanny was a young girl, younger than we are now, and she let me do whatever I wanted, in secret."

Lonnie explained how she hadn't been allowed to watch television, but the nanny would warn her when she heard the elevator door slam in the hallway signaling her father's return. I imagined a complicated walkie-talkie system, little Lonnie getting the radio signal and scrambling on skinny legs and oversized adolescent feet out of her father's bedroom. I pictured her flopping onto her bed, throwing open a book, and glaring at the man over the top of the cover, daring him to interrupt her from her reading.

She also told me there had been a boyfriend who would come over when her father was out late. They probably waited for Lonnie to go to bed so they could fool around. They gave her junk food for dinner—whatever she wanted—and handed her cassette tapes—of Nirvana and Bikini Kill. I tried to imagine little Lonnie struggling to make sense of grunge and punk from the Northwest—the same music that had seemed a natural extension of my teenage existence—but within the context of her privileged childhood it somehow made less sense.

"Hair like this," she said about the boyfriend, making a chopping motion on either side of her chin with her hands. "You know, and parted in the middle. Always greasy."

"*My So-Called Life,*" I said.

She laughed. "Yes, exactly."

"Are you in contact with any of them now?" I asked. "Do they know you had a baby?"

"No," she said. "I don't know how to contact anyone."

Lonnie stopped pushing the stroller. She turned to me and said, "I know you're young, and maybe you don't know what you want to do with your life, but I hope you'll be with Billy for a while, Elle. I hope you'll stay with us for a long time."

I couldn't stop picturing Lonnie at camp—easy to see the smooth-skinned gangly girl from the photo album nervously knocking back a swig of vodka, sputtering a little, laughing, tucking a lock of greasy hair behind her little tan ear.

Inside the museum she picked William up to show him the half-survived busts from ancient Greece. She imitated their faces and he looked back and forth from the statue to his mother, smiling. "Wow," he said in his small voice—he'd picked the word up earlier that week and had been using it constantly.

In the American wing every painting she paused in front of was a reflection of her: the nude with round breasts splayed on the floor, her hair spread out around her head, one arm held over her face as a perch for a parrot. The dark-haired woman in the coral dress scowling, her mouth open in disgust. Even the pale woman in the low-cut black gown, her face turned to the side, revealing the tender pink of one ear seemed somehow to reflect Lonnie, if not in actual appearance, at least in authority.

We paused for a long time in front of John White Alexander's *Repose*. I felt embarrassed to tell Lonnie "It's you," though the mouth, the bored expression, the nonchalance that somehow suggested intense eroticism, was exactly the same. I silently let her and the painting have their moment of recognition, wandering into the next room to study Frieseke's *Summer*—a nude lounging in the dappled sunlight of a tree, while another girl, fully clothed, sits upright, just watching.

Peeking back around the corner, I realized she was gone.

I walked into the next room, and the next. I weaved in and out of room after room but didn't see Lonnie and William anywhere. At first, I thought how silly it was; we must've been walking in opposite directions, circling each other, but then I started to feel the first twinges of panic set in. I remembered playing hide-and-seek as a kid, the way the game would go from a group of six or seven kids all giggling together and then the sudden devastating shock of no one. I became vaguely aware that my body had broken out in a cold sweat. Without knowing why, I suddenly felt very protective. I worried that something had happened to Lonnie—then, I worried that she was hiding from me, that she had some reason to escape, some reason I didn't know about, and was leaving me behind here on purpose. At the same time, I knew this couldn't possibly be the case, but it was as if the actual configuration of reality suddenly existed on a different plane from my body. The real museum, full of other normal people, existed, as did Lonnie—just around another corner—but I was somewhere else, wandering alone through illusory rooms. Or maybe Lonnie was somewhere else, and I was stuck in the real museum with all these loud, tennis-shoed families. I didn't know which delusion was more frightening.

I found myself back in the room with *Repose,* having apparently walked in a circle, though it felt more like the room was repeating itself. I swirled around and came face-to-face with another slack-mouthed girl in a painting—this one, a beautiful redheaded child, listening to her mother read from a book. Her face had the curious effect of calming me down as I tried to work out what exactly it was about her I found disquieting. She was sitting on a bed next to her older sister, whose expression was calm and poised.

The younger child's face was dead center, and unusual in its lack of expression. I'd never seen a face like that in a museum. She wasn't reacting to the book—it wasn't a look of interest or fear or contentment. It was just the face of a girl not being watched. How could a face like that exist inside something painted by a man? The model must have been young enough to sort of forget that she was posing. She was bored, distracted. It was the face of a girl who was somewhere else entirely.

What disturbed me, I realized, was the similarity of expression between the redheaded girl and the woman in Alexander's *Repose*. Was it really only a sideways glance of the eyes that could thrust a face into the realm of sexuality?

When Lonnie came up behind me and whispered, "Boo," I nearly hit my head against the painted face of the little redheaded girl. I was stunned by her sudden reappearance, and standing, I realized, far too close. An alarm sounded, a rapid bleep that made everyone in the room turn. A guard peeked around the corner. "Sorry," Lonnie said to him, already starting to laugh at me. "She tripped."

As we made our way out of the room, her arm in mine, my cheeks flushed and my back dripping with sweat, she whispered, joking, "I can't take you anywhere."

Alone, back at the brownstone that day, I found a ring. A strange item, not in her jewelry box, but in a small butter cookie tin from Saint-Malo shoved in the back of the closet in her office. The ring was the only thing in the tin, just rattling around in there. It was cheap metal, adjustable, like a trinket from one of those candy machines outside pizza shops and corner stores that sat dirty, full of stale hot tamales and gumballs and junk in little plastic eggs. On top, the metal was bent into a chunky heart frame inside of which was a glittered lime background with a tiny outline of the Virgin Mary, her hands open and welcoming, her smiling face looking down, a little askew, her usual pose—like she is above you, but magnanimous, accepting.

Knowing that shade of lime, I held the ring up to Lonnie's desk lamp, then cupped my hands together around it, peeking in with one eye. Sure enough, it glowed in the dark, a faint green shine inside my hands. I slipped it onto my index finger and it fit without my having to bend the metal at all. I liked the way it looked on my hand. I liked the weirdness of the object. Where had it come from? It was childish, but too big for a child's finger. It was religious, but also seemed like a joke, the way you could make the holy Virgin glow. It was clunky and gaudy and cheap, not something you would see Lonnie wear now, so what was it doing in her house?

I thought of her as a teenager, punctuating her style with weird accents like this. I already knew I was taking it home with me, but I pulled out her photo album again, looking for the picture of Lonnie in her coat, in front of the school bus, with her hand up by her temple. Her fingers were laced in her hair, but you could see, on her index finger, her right hand, the same one I'd slipped it on without thinking, a flash of metal, thick and clunky.

At first I slipped the ring off before I left my apartment. Then I started wearing it all the time, even in front of Lonnie. I did it because I was bored. Because watching a baby is so repetitive. Because it thrilled me. Because it made me feel sick with worry. Because feeling anything is better than feeling nothing. Because I didn't feel guilty. Because they had so much stuff and I had no stuff. Because it meant nothing to her and a lot to me. Because I wanted to prove to myself this job didn't mean anything to me. Because this job meant a lot to me. Because it was a test of trust. Because I wanted to know how far I could push her. Because I wanted to feel powerful. Because I wanted to feel powerful like Lonnie must have felt powerful, growing up, wearing this ring.

She grabbed my hand one day while I sliced honeydew melon for her breakfast. The green melon, the green ring, the metal knife, the metal band. I was still holding the knife, and the way she grabbed me was risky, the knife veering unexpectedly.

My whole body bloomed with sweat. She looked at the ring for what felt like a long time, her brow a little drawn.

"That's so strange," she muttered. "I used to have that same ring."

"Really?" I said, my voice coming out a little too deep as I tried to make it sound natural.

"I lost it a long time ago," she said. "It's just bizarre because I thought it was such a funny weird thing, I'd never seen anything like it. I guess it makes sense that it would be mass produced though, it's just a cheap charm."

"Where did you get yours?" I said.

"This seaside trinket store."

"I found this one," I told her. I'd planned this part of the conversation. I knew exactly what to say. "I thought it was weird too. Maybe there's not more than one, maybe this one is yours."

She smiled and let go of my wrist. "I like that," she said.

After she turned away I found she'd made me cut myself, a little slit in my left index finger, which I'd been using to hold down the melon. I didn't say anything. I watched the blood rush to the tear, then put my finger in my mouth and sucked on it, a sweet sticky metallic taste.

9

It wasn't long after Lonnie's birthday that Carlow started to come over during the day while James was at work. Before he arrived, Lonnie spent a long time bathing, emerging from the tub dewy, smelling of musky amber cologne and toothpaste. The bathroom was foggy when she opened the door, plumes of condensation rising into the hall. She usually threw on a dress for him, something simple—short, shapeless cotton with delicate patterns—but somehow the curves of her body, the slenderness of her waist, emerged through the thin fabric in glimpses as she moved.

She ran to let him in. She grasped the end of the banister, swinging her body off the stairs and toward the basement door (he never came in through the foyer), childlike in her movements, just as I'd pictured her switching off the forbidden TV and running out of her father's room. I thought, if William and I hadn't been there (and at one time, we weren't), they would've collapsed in front of the hall tree, falling on each other, the door still half-open, making love instantly, loudly, on the floor there.

As it was, she always said, "You remember Carlow," as if he were so forgettable.

"Of course, hi."

"Elle"—everyone had started to call me that—"always a pleasure."

We didn't hug or shake hands or exchange Lonnie's usual European cheek kisses when we met in hallways like that. He just smiled at me and then, as we passed each other, he gave me a quick pinch on the elbow. What did that pinch mean? It was like a wink. It was a sort of extension of his innocent, amused smirk.

She would say, "I have a book to give him" or "I need to show him a book" or "he's helping me edit my book." And I would say, "Okay," and accept that little pinch on the elbow as they went upstairs.

I tiptoed around the house when they were in the office. I was trying to impress on them some sort of distortion of sound—even though she knew her own house, she knew the squeaky wood floors, the thin walls. I wanted them to think, if they couldn't hear me, I wouldn't be able to hear them. I wanted to let them know they could be a little louder if they wanted. When William was awake I took him to the far reaches of the house—the breakfast nook or the terrace, so he wouldn't be heard. When he was asleep I tried to get as close to that office door as I could.

On the other side of the door: footsteps, laughter, silence, furniture moving sometimes, but nothing very obvious, just the scraping of a chair's legs across the floor, the thud of a body sitting on the couch. Sometimes the smell of weed.

On the other side of the door: the music swells. I imagine everything in the room swells. There's darkness all around, but the room is flickering like a movie screen. I picture it lit up, translucent as the sky at twilight.

Carlow must be able to take in everything. It's a temporary magical power—his sudden ability to observe and remember. She has a lot of male writers on her bookshelves. She's been studying the unhappy American man—Carver, Singer, Malamud, Cheever, Harrison, Salter. The room is already encased within a haunting nostalgia. The affair has ended at the same time it is happening. At the same time he can touch the perfect white of her smooth throat he can also feel the silence of his life without her. He can imagine her death, his own. We love only within restrictions.

She has a rabbit pelt on her desk, an old clock that plugs into the wall and makes an obnoxious sound like it's about to overheat. He doesn't know what's in the drawers or the closet like I do, but he can see into the top one—she never closes it all the way. It's full of pencil shavings, the wood chips and those zigzags of kelly green and school-bus yellow. She sharpens her pencils right into the drawer. He doesn't know about the baby teeth, the old journals, the notes folded into triangles. Instead he knows the secret smells of her, the taste.

The first time he expected the act to be secondary—for the encounter to really be about possession—but it isn't like that at all. She controls the room like a cat. Her submission is intentional, calculated. She's selfish, withholding for long stretches, and it makes it unbearable. He's at her mercy. He doesn't know why she's chosen him.

I don't know why she's chosen him. I think about it constantly.

I guessed it was because every day is like the day before until it isn't. Because nothing ever happens. And when something happens it feels like the only thing that has ever happened. Because sometimes we have to tear ourselves away from the people who know us best in order to remind ourselves that we all die alone. That we really live alone.

Of course, there was a possibility that they weren't fucking at all. I could only imagine weirder things, though, when I imagined their not-fucking. Lonnie using Carlow to write her book, making him pose for her, touch himself, not touch her, smoke her out, making her fall into some kind of desire-trance until she put pen to paper out of something like desperation.

Eventually they came out of the room. We sat on the terrace in the orange evening sunlight while I fed William. Once Lonnie gave him a slice of lemon and he kept the sour thing in his mouth, moving his tongue around it. She'd beamed, putting his cheeks between her palms, "Yes, I knew I got a good one."

I thought, *He'll spend the rest of his life trying to find another woman who looks at him the way she did that day.*

Carlow told me about his artwork and how he grew up in one of the buildings I walk past every day. He had apparently taken a very famous photograph when he was in his twenties titled *Woman in a Double Frame*.

He seemed thrilled when I admitted I hadn't seen it, but I wondered if his satisfaction was posturing—feigned humility. "I can't get past that photo," he said. "Every time I do an interview they want to talk about it. I'm not even working with photography anymore. I would much rather talk about my paintings."

His paintings, I gathered, hadn't yet garnered much interest, though he'd been doggedly churning them out for about five years. He didn't actually tell me what the subject matter was, or what style they were in, he just said he was dealing with "light, and the history of the body."

I pictured nudes, I pictured Lonnie naked in his studio, fooling around with random objects—telephones, chairs, those fake birds they sell in art supply stores made from Styrofoam with real feathers pasted on. A studio would be a fantastic place to make love—just a large blank space for messes, for inventiveness.

I asked Lonnie what James did for work, realizing no one had ever mentioned it before.

"He's in finance of one kind or another," Lonnie said, laughing a little.

I hesitated, then decided to venture, "Of one kind or another?"

"My father got him the job. They work together."

Her face fell a little at this last bit of information, as if she were disappointed in how things had turned out for James's career, so I quickly changed the subject. "Do you ever see anything interesting in those apartments?" I asked, gesturing toward the tall building at the end of the block.

"They're either watching TV or doing sad old people exercises," Lonnie said. "Nothing ever happens."

While everyone else was in the water C lay down next to me and said, "I'm going to kiss you someday." His hair all slick from the water. He said, "I don't care how long I have to wait." Anyway, I got mine. Poison ivy all over my left hip. Agony.

I look more like those old photos of my mom every day. Some things have happened. I made some things happen. Everything always happens all at once. "We become the people we need to be in order to finish the book." One of those things I wrote down, thinking I'd remember the reference and promptly forgot. But what book am I finishing?

I started fucking C. Well, I fucked him once, but it will probably happen again. He says I remind him of someone else. He says a lot of things when I'm sleepy afterward. He's sort of sad, this boy, at least right now, when I happen to know him, sort of drifting with a lot of passions that burn out too quickly. He talks too much but he's funny and weird. He said, "Remember me among your lovers." I didn't tell him he was the first new one, in fact I told him he wasn't.

It's not that anything is better with C. It's just that everything is new.

I mean, there was something like five hours' worth of sex. Not just sex, but everything that goes with it. It wasn't that, though, not exactly, though lips chapped from kissing was nice, chin red from his stubble. It was smoking in the hallway—him in pajamas, me in my dress. It was neighbors arriving home from the movies, from somewhere, dinner, dressed nice and climbing up six flights of stairs, out of breath, telling C, "Don't worry about it, we're about to do the same thing."

And then C saying, "We're adults, you know?" in the middle of one of his weed-induced monologues. Adults. Adults. Adults.

"I feel more like I'm sixteen than I have in a while." I shouldn't have said it, but I wanted to feel like that one time I sneaked out of the house in Southampton when M tapped on my window. The window tap, the last resort when there were only landlines and a phone call at one a.m. would wake up Dad. That one time when I sat a little cold on the beach and told M, "I don't want to

date anyone anymore, I'll just make out with all of my friends."

C's reaction: a little smile, a little side-eyed bitterness. Everyone knows the situation. It's not like I said I love you. It wouldn't be true, not really, maybe in one sense. A temporary sense. Then again, everything is temporary. What does time have to do with love?

All I do is compare times to other times. Though they're not the same, not at all. You could look at it either way. Everything is fundamentally the same and fundamentally different. These men are both exactly the same and completely different. It means the same thing. It means the exact opposite thing. There's probably some kind of explanation for that in physics.

He said, "Do you want my critique of your pussy?"

"Your critique?"

"Yes."

"Okay?"

"I love the taste. The smell. I love the lips, the clit, the hair. I love the way it feels inside. I love your asshole. I love all of it. The whole thing."

I'd like to remember it all somehow, though I know how dangerous that is.

Trying not to think about what came next in high school, right after I told J I would just make out with all my friends, or rather, right after I went about kissing a few of the girls. The way those soft-lipped things each decided I'd talked them into something sickening afterward. The way everyone started turning their backs on me as I walked by. It was the first time I realized whole years can be awful. Not *sure I learned a single thing that year. I wish they had just sent me away, instead of letting me slowly unravel in front of everyone, all alone. It wasn't until I tried to slit my wrists in the lunchroom that anyone said they might have overreacted, that anyone noticed anything was really wrong. And by then none of their moms would let them talk to me.*

Something awful is going to happen.

10

It was early June and the sprinklers were off and on in playgrounds across the city, depending on the temperature that day. I watched the girls from Marymount, nearing the start of their summer break. The time of year when the sun makes children agitated and jovial. They spent their recesses at the playground. Sometimes I saw them at the one kitty-corner to their school, next door to the Metropolitan Museum. Sometimes they ventured north, as William and I did, to the playground at Ninety-Sixth. They were easy to pick out, those Alice-blue skirts giving them away. They came with nannies and organic chocolate milk after school. The game I played—which little girls were most like Lonnie? Where did Lonnie fit into this configuration?

Two girls were perched atop a pyramid, not letting the other children climb up the internal ladder that led to the top, laughing and kicking at anyone who tried. Was she withholding as a child? Was she mean like this? Was she territorial? Did she assert her dominance with force?

Other girls—in a larger group—came up with another game, a different method of governance and control. They kept stealing the scuffed black loafer of a classmate, throwing it back and forth to one another while she lunged after it—always too late—over and over again. Would Lonnie have been a joiner in this group? Would she have started the game? She wouldn't have been the poor girl with the dirty white sock, hopping on one foot, her braids coming out in thin wisps—would she?

I saw her sometimes as the solitary soul on the monkey bars, yelling to the other girls occasionally, but not playing with them. She was more concerned with her own body's dexterity than anything else. She was hanging upside down, her hair standing on end below her red face, a headband on the ground below her, her pleated skirt flipped up over her shirt, her white cotton panties fully exposed. This girl was at least eight years old—too old to be showing off her underwear so brazenly. Too old for her obvious lack of shame.

The older Marymount girls, the middle school girls, still came here after school sometimes, not to play, but to sit and gossip as they waited for the time they must return home. They no longer used the playground for recess, but once I spent a half hour watching them use the fire poles and pull-up bars for gym class. They were not wearing the skirts of course, but little cap-sleeved tees and navy cotton shorts emblazoned with the school name. Many wore blue hair bows above their ponytails, pearl earrings. I watched them climb up the pole—most doing so quickly, a few struggling and being cheered on by their classmates. I watched them jump and hang from the pull-up bar. I watched the way their muscles moved as they learned to use their own bodies as weights. I watched them line up and drop to the pavement for push-ups.

I suppose my school had been militant like this in gym class as well, but there had certainly been a wider range of ability—and a wider range of body type. Their little cap-sleeved T-shirts all fit snugly across taut bellies, the thin legs of their blue shorts showed clearly a dozen sets of skinny thighs and perky asses. Where was the overweight girl struggling to keep up? Where was the too-skinny one—as I had been—looking two years younger than the rest of her classmates, swimming in her gym clothes?

I saw these same girls, back in their blue skirts and stark white tops, eating crepes out of little paper triangles at three o'clock when William woke from his afternoon nap and we ventured again onto the streets. They laughed as they licked melted Nutella from their fingers. They owned the city already, yet they were nothing, had done nothing to earn it.

In the Ancient Playground across the street from Marymount, half-naked children disappeared in the tunnels beneath brick pyramids. I followed William, crouching in the darkness and then emerging again into the dappled brilliance of sun streaking through the trees. I slipped my shoes off to feel the coolness of the sprinkler water on my feet, to feel the littered sand from the sandbox, dribbled out of heaping plastic buckets, strewn along the cement.

The mineral smell of the tap water, the taste of it on a sunscreen-smeared finger.

William knelt at a crack in the ground, poked a finger into the dirt and weeds peeking through. He ran his hand over the cement, testing the roughness, and scraped himself, a bright streak of blood on his knuckle, a visceral cry. To watch a baby is to think about the feel, the taste, the texture of things.

To watch a baby is also to learn what to do with monotony. The playground—the playground over and over again. The same routes, the same tests of balance and skill, always trying to climb the same diagonal wall of bricks. The back and forth of the baby swing. The back and forth. What do you do with your mind during the back and forth?

One afternoon there were two teenagers at the playground, probably thirteen years old—not far off from Carlow's girl in France—and at first I thought one was on a mission to get a babysitting gig. She was trying to make friends with a two-year-old in the sandbox—talking to her in a silly high-pitched voice, dragging her toy cars through the sand next to her—but then I noticed the real reason. The two-year-old was with her father, her young father. The girl was talking to the baby but I could tell she was conscious of the father's eyes on her. She didn't say anything to him but looked sideways every once in a while to make sure he was still there, still watching. She was wearing neon pink leggings and you could see the workings of her sinewy thighs through the thin stretched fabric.

He wasn't reacting to her, but she was clever, she was really too clever, because he couldn't look away if he wanted. He couldn't leave his daughter unsupervised. The girl's friend, the gawky type of teenager that reminded me more of myself at that age—frizzy haired, hiding her stick-thin body beneath baggy jeans and a hoodie though it was far too warm for the sweatshirt—stood a little behind, watching the man watch her friend, watching her friend pretend not to notice the man.

When the little girl tired of the sandbox she climbed out and ran down to the swing set, where two baby swings were open. The girl followed, the father followed, and the friend, slowly, wandered behind. The father lifted his daughter into a swing, ignoring the girl lolling on the angled pole of the swing set. The girl held the pole with one hand, swinging her body around it a few times, but the man just looked straight ahead at his daughter. The girl was staring at him now, not just looking slyly sideways anymore. She knew she was being ignored.

Her next move was a bold one. She grabbed the chains of the baby swing next to this man's daughter and hoisted herself up. "Leila!" I heard her screech. "Let's see if I can still fit in here!"

Her friend, standing a few feet back, on the edge of the sectioned-off swing area, shook her head a little, her face unsmiling. The girl's thin legs slid into the hard plastic holes of the baby swing with little room to spare. The swing was set too high for her feet to reach the ground, so she thrust her torso back and forth until the swing moved a little with the motion. It didn't take long for her to realize that her skinny arms were far too weak to lift the rest of her body back out of the swing. "Leila!" she screeched and laughed at the same time. "Leila, oh no!"

The friend walked over to the swing, but kept her hands in the pockets of her hoodie. "I don't know how to help," she said.

The man was still pushing his daughter back and forth, though he was now watching the drama next to him as he did so—she succeeded in that. The girl tried unsuccessfully a few more times to lift herself before he finally turned to her fully and said, "Okay, this wasn't a good idea."

The girl, shrieking with laughter, did not respond. The man walked behind her and just looked for a moment. He had to touch her. There was no way around touching her, it was expected now. He put his hands beneath her arms as if she were a small child but her legs were wedged into the swing and she only screamed, still laughing, her body not cooperating. It took a good five minutes to get her out and required the assistance of not just the man and her friend but someone else's mother to tilt the swing parallel to the ground so the man could slide her out. She ended up in a laughing heap by the man's feet. "Thank you, thank you," she uttered between fits of breathy laughter.

"These are too small for my four-year-old," the mother said. "Get it? Don't do that again."

The girl nodded, and turned her face up to the man hovering over her—her eyebrows drawn toward each other in an absurd laughing apology. The concentrated unsmiling way he looked down at her made me feel terrified.

"Eva!" A tall woman with dreadlocks and a Caribbean accent came marching over to the swing set, dragging a little blue-eyed boy behind her, Eva's little brother. "You were supposed to be home an hour ago, your mother is about to kill both of us, you get over here right now."

The girl still couldn't stop her breathy laughter, but she climbed up off the ground and ran to the woman, who seized her by the arm. The girl looked back—I expected her to shout goodbye to her friend—but she didn't shout anything and she didn't look at her friend, she just flashed a big white-toothed grin at the man, her adult teeth still a little too big in her head. At first I thought this Eva was the closest I had gotten to Lonnie's incarnation but then, watching the friend amble off with her shoulders down, I questioned it. Was Lonnie's sexual prowess as inborn as I imagined, or could she have been more like the friend at some point—watching, studying, waiting? Self-conscious and then later, feeling like she needed to make up for something?

The floor of Lonnie's office: a little puddle, I wrote in my notebook, marveling at the innocence of the noun, but there was no other way to describe it—not a dripping or gush anymore, just the sad little result. Too thin and clear to have come from him, and too much of it anyway—this was hers, pooled next to her writing desk like spilled ink.

I dabbed a finger at the edge—marveled at the way liquid molecules attract, despite a lack of container. The smooth slick between my thumb and forefinger. I tasted it. Finger to my lip like I was trying to get a feverish baby to drink. The saline sweetness reached the tip of my tongue. Why had she left that there? Had she simply forgotten about it? Had she wanted to save it for herself? Had she been trying to leave something for her husband to find? Was it completely crazy to wonder, just for a fleeting moment, if she had left it there for me?

11

The picture was the next thing I stole. Sultry teenage Lonnie next to an unmade bed. I wanted it. I took it. I kept it. I never thought about putting it back. I plucked a piece of used chewing gum from her bathroom's wastebasket, placed it in my own mouth to make it soft again, and stuck the picture to a page in my route-mapping notebook.

That piece of gum. I watched her throw it away that morning, as she teased William with the blow dryer while getting ready. I stood in the bathroom doorway, feeling intrusive, though she was giggling with William like she was glad he was there, so I didn't pick him up and take him elsewhere to play. She stood upright for just a moment, looked at herself in the mirror. Her hair was puffed out in disarray from the blow dryer, stray wisps arching upward. She brought the gum between her front teeth with her tongue and then pinched it out of her mouth, flicking it into the little metal garbage pail under the pedestal sink.

"I can't buy gum," she said. "I chew all of it at once, all day long. My jaw hurts."

I smiled.

There was nothing else in the trash can. There was just the gum, the little sticky lump that had been in her mouth that morning. I knew where the tape was, but that gum was the closest gluey substance, just a few steps away from the bookshelf. Putting it in my own mouth will make it soft and sticky again, I said to myself. It was the only logic I was willing to consider. These things are only strange when viewed objectively. And there was no one else home then.

I never considered taking anything of any value from her house, maybe because none of her actual objects seem to matter to her at all. Once she said, "You can borrow any of my books anytime," so I started sneaking them away as quickly as I could read them. She had so many, she never noticed, even as they began to pile up on the floor of my bedroom, as my mind began to pile up with the same stories, the characters, the beautiful sentences she already knew. I felt if I could just read all her books I could absorb a large portion of her mind. I could catch up with her, best her even. I didn't want her things, I wanted her life.

Even so, books and trinkets were not the only things I decided to steal.

When I imagined myself with Carlow, I pictured us at his parents' apartment, the one I walked past when I took William to the playground.

In this fantasy, there's fancy champagne in the fridge

and we pop it open even though we shouldn't. Even though it's for some party that hasn't happened yet. I sit on the counter, swigging comically from the big bottle and handing it off to him, laughing, and then I look at him and say, "Come here."

A body between my legs. His slim hips between my thighs. The way a dress creeps up.

"So this is where Carlow grew up." "So this is the bed Carlow slept on." His bedroom is not a shrine to his former self, of course; he's a grown man. It's been remodeled and repainted. There is only an imaginary idea of him becoming someone in the space. He tells me where his stuff used to be.

That's when his parents arrive home unexpectedly. It's a big dumb secret that I'm in the house too, as if this thirty-some-year-old man is still scared of his father, still scared of his opinion. I make fun of him for this, and respond a little too loudly to his caresses, out of spite. I say, "What, are you embarrassed of me?"

He says, "No."

He says, "Yes."

He says, "You better shut up."

He says, "You don't understand anything."

He puts one big hand up my skirt.

I recognized my best opportunity when Lonnie and James spent one night away early that summer to attend a wedding, leaving me alone at the brownstone with William.

Lonnie didn't exhibit any of the usual signs of stress of a parent leaving her child. She held him on her hip, snuggled her nose to his face, but didn't frantically go over phone numbers or emergency instructions. She didn't give me that pleading look. The one that said, "Just. Please. Take care of him."

Was it because she trusted me or because William was not the centerpiece of her world? I didn't think of that possibility with judgment. Actually, I thought, it's better. It's easier for everyone. What a magnificent liberty for William, to be a cherished amusement, free to have his own experiences, instead of being her whole personality.

"Is Carlow going with you?" I asked.

"No," Lonnie said. "Why?"

"Oh, I don't know. Just wondering if he knew the couple."

"Actually, that's what I wanted to tell you. If you have any questions you can contact him. He knows the house pretty well. And William of course. You know, for anything small. I'll let him know he's on call."

"Okay," I said. All I had to do was come up with a question that would get him over here after William was in bed. "Stay and have a drink, now that I dragged you out. Lonnie said I should drink their wine before it goes bad, but I hate drinking alone."

This wasn't true—of course I had never minded drinking alone, but it would probably work.

After William and I waved goodbye from the stoop, I

took him up to the guest room across from the nursery to look around and think how I could lure Carlow inside, but the room was fairly devoid of interest. It was white and airy—white walls, a white textured rug and bedspread. A rolltop desk stood in one corner. I pulled up the wooden slats on the desk but it was like one at a hotel—a blank notepad sat on an otherwise empty desktop with tiny cursive letters at the top spelling out *Laurel Nicole Bernard*. I hadn't put together until just then that Lonnie was a nickname. The realization made me feel foolish and slow.

I took a bath in Lonnie's tub after William fell asleep that night. The master bathroom had the biggest tub in the house—a beautiful deep claw-foot that dipped in the middle like a banana split dish. I filled it up to the very top. There were no windows, but above the tub there was a strip of fogged glass running the length of the room, which during the day let in sun from the skylight covering the ceiling of the upstairs bathroom. The house was full of skylights and deftly placed mirrors allowing for natural light in every room. A purple passion plant trailed from a hanging planter over the tub, its fuzzy leaves nearly within arm's reach as I soaked in the water. The night was cool, the bathroom steamy.

I stayed there for a long time and when I emerged I wandered into Lonnie's bedroom. Her closet was already open, some of the clothes falling off hangers and onto the shoe rack below. I ran my hand over the fancier dresses, settled on a cotton shift dress, the kind she wore when Carlow came over. It was white with eyelet lace at the hem. I slipped it over my head, then found a skinny leather belt to wrap around my waist. In front of her oak-framed mirror I turned from side to side, pulling my hair up in one hand and letting it down again, examining myself. It wasn't unflattering, though white looked better against her skin; I was still too pale. I'd started wearing skimpy shirts and shorts to work, avoiding the shade at the playground, trying to soak up as much color as possible. I knew I couldn't match Lonnie's golden hue, but I'd never been able to tan before—I'd alternated between white and pink in Oregon—then suddenly, that year, it started working, at least a little, my skin toasting like a marshmallow held carefully to a flame. I was fascinated by the slight variation.

My phone rang as I was standing there.

"I'm sorry to bother you," Carlow said when I answered. "Lonnie gave me your number. I'm downstairs. I didn't want to ring the doorbell in case the baby was asleep. I just left something over here last week and wanted to pick it up. You're here, right? If you're busy don't worry about it, I can come back."

"No," I said. "I'm here, it's okay. Can you give me one minute?"

I thought about changing, but decided against it. Instead, I ran back into the bathroom and used my fingers to clear condensation from a little circle on the mirror, peering at my face. It was flushed and shiny from the warm water. I opened Lonnie's medicine cabinet, but of course the only makeup inside was the tube of coral lipstick. She'd taken the eyeliner with her. I popped it open—the tip was still pointed and factory cut. I closed the cabinet and smeared it across my lips. Anything was better than nothing.

Carlow was sitting on the stoop's railing. The sun had only recently set and the sky was still a luminous blue. He gave me a smile. "You're the best," he said. "I just got off work and I wanted to go home and read, then I realized I left my book here."

"What book is it?"

"I'll show you."

We went inside and he rummaged around through some magazines on the coffee table. "Damn," he said. "Where did she put it?"

"All you wanted to do on a Friday night is go home and read?" I asked him, my mind telling me, *You imagined this into being* and also, *You must start the conversation that will make him stay*.

"I've been working late all week, you know, I just didn't have the energy for a night out. You probably know. You've been working late today too."

"Not that I could go out if I wanted to anyway. I mean, tonight."

"No," he said. He was leafing through the stacks of mail on the bureau in the foyer. He paused over each letter as if it were his own mail. Was he going through her stuff? Was he jealous? Or maybe drawing this out on purpose? I became self-conscious about the way Lonnie's dress gaped at the chest. I remembered I wasn't wearing a bra and touched the neckline to make sure everything was still in place.

"Do you want to have a drink with me here?" he said, looking up from the mail. "That's maybe the only thing I have energy for tonight. I can go buy us some wine?"

"Lonnie left a bottle of wine on the counter open," I replied. "I know it's from yesterday. We could probably finish that. So it doesn't go bad."

The wine bottle was almost full. "To James," Carlow said, holding out his glass. "Since this one's on him."

"To James," I replied, trying to not sound ironic and cynical. Trying to not sound like I knew anything.

We drank and then Carlow said, "Isn't that Lonnie's dress?"

"Oh," I said. "She gave me some of her old ones. Hand-me-downs."

He nodded.

"How do you know James anyway?" I asked, changing the subject.

"We went to school together," he said. "I guess I've known him since I was fourteen. That's why everyone calls me Carlow—just got used to it because we go so far back."

"What do you mean? Is Carlow not your name?"

"Last name. My first name is James, did you not know that?"

Everyone's identities were shifting underneath me. I felt stupid all over again, just like when I'd found out Lonnie's real name earlier.

"I don't really keep up with any of my high school friends," I said.

"No?"

"Moving across the country didn't help. But even before then. I don't know, maybe that's why I left. There weren't many people I grew up with I could relate to."

This wasn't true, and I don't know why I said it. I'd never lacked for friends, growing up, and had related deeply to a number of different girls. We'd had forts and imaginary worlds, secret pacts and boxes full of notes about the minutiae of our lives, dropped into lockers, just like Lonnie. Each of these relationships had ended abruptly, each for its own unimportant reason, and then we had gone our separate ways. Most of these girls were now married, still living in a small town, raising children of their own. I didn't understand them. I didn't know where I was headed, but it wasn't in their direction. Of most of my friends, I thought privately, I'd used them up.

Carlow looked around the kitchen. "I never found my book. Do you mind if I go upstairs?"

"No," I said. "William sleeps like an angel. Don't worry about waking him."

I walked up to the living room and plopped down on

the couch while he was gone. I could hear him rummaging around in the master bedroom on the floor above, then walking down the hall and doing the same in Lonnie's office. He was obviously going through her stuff. I had nothing to do with his purpose here, but instead of giving in to a feeling of defeat, I thought, *What are you going to do about that?*

I sipped more wine, contemplating how to get his attention. It sounded like he was moving books around on the shelves. I wondered if he was looking for her current journal. He wouldn't find it, I realized. I knew exactly where she kept it, inside a box of waffles in the freezer, the pages cold to the touch. I imagined her writing in it at the kitchen counter late at night, her toes curled around the footrest of one of the stools, then, hearing James descend the stairs, hiding the book quickly in the first place she could find. *I've read it.* The thought made a little private flower unfurl inside my stomach.

"Did you find your book?"

"Oh," he replied. "Yeah."

He flashed the cover of *Laughter in the Dark* my way as he sat down on the couch. I handed him his wineglass; I'd brought it up from the kitchen.

"You know," I said, my voice quiet, calm, "she talks about you."

Carlow swallowed a gulp of wine and looked at me. I didn't say anything else; I waited for him to reply.

"She talks about me to you?" he said.

"Yeah, sometimes." This wasn't true, but I reasoned the best way to get Carlow's attention was through Lonnie. I didn't look at him; I pretended to be interested in the cover of a *New Yorker* on the side table.

"Well, what do you mean?"

Since Lonnie had not confided anything of interest about Carlow to me, I pretended to be evasive on purpose. "There are some things I'd like to know about you, you know?" I said.

"Go on."

"Do you feel . . ." I paused, unsure how to proceed with the game I had in mind. "Anxious?" I said, finally deciding on a word.

He smiled. An uncomfortable smile. Took another sip of wine. "Anxious?" he said.

"Have you ever been in love?"

"Girls like you are few and far between, Elle," he said.

"I'm serious."

"So am I.

"Do you want to watch a film?" he said suddenly. "What do you like?"

I let him shift the conversation, decided not to press him. A movie wasn't a bad idea. I told him about the horror flicks I'd been indulging in as of late. I stood to switch the lights off, and settled down right next to him on the big leather couch. We picked a favorite of mine—a slow black-and-white Japanese film—a hole that swallows up men's bodies, an old woman trying to squash the blush of young lust with a haunted mask.

I figured Carlow had flirted with me to get out of answering my question. It was a way of writing me off without making me feel bad, but I felt like calling his bluff. Why shouldn't I? What did it all come down to? We were two single people, a little drunk now, in the dark.

I slouched down on the couch, casually, not caring anymore about Lonnie's dress gaping at the chest. I inched my leg over until it was touching his, just a little. He didn't pull it away; he didn't act as if he noticed at all.

Leg rubbing up against leg—it was nothing out of the ordinary, it happened with strange men on the subway all the time, but here, the bare skin of my thigh against Lonnie's lover's pant leg, the contact was charged.

After some minutes I reached over and put my hand on his thigh, rubbing.

I didn't look at him.

It was such an excellent move; I commended myself on it. We could both just sit there and watch the screen and pretend nothing was happening.

What I was thinking was, *He started it*. And also, *It's easy: you put a hand on his thigh*.

I could hear his breathing next to me.

For a moment he pressed his leg into mine a little more, and I thought it was going to work. Then, in one swift motion, he lifted my hand off his thigh, squeezed it in his own, and, a beat later, let it go.

12

That was the first and only time I thought about quitting. I told myself it was guilt. I shouldn't have been trying to steal her lover in the first place, even if she deserved it simply for having everything. She'd been nothing but lovely to me, there was no reason to try to take anything from her. But despite these thoughts I knew it wasn't guilt at all, it was the acute sting of failure, the embarrassment of it, and the thought that I'd have to face her and Carlow again.

However, when I returned to Crown Heights at the end of the weekend I found our apartment empty and in disarray. Sam was scrupulous about organization but her room was in upheaval—her clothes scattered everywhere, books strewn across the bed, the lamp from her nightstand on the floor, the bulb shattered. At first I thought she'd been home, and then went somewhere in a hurry, packing up some things and leaving me to deal with the mess, but since that was so out of character, I managed to work out what had actually happened—we'd been robbed. I checked the jewelry stand inside her wardrobe—empty. They'd cleared away her little TV, her turntable, and her speakers, as well as the one expensive thing I owned—my laptop.

I checked under the futon mattress that had come with the room, where I kept my cash. All the money Lonnie had given me so far—even though I'd hidden it inside an envelope so it looked like a thick letter—was gone. I kicked the damn futon mattress, tears pooling in my eyes. Quitting was obviously not an option anymore.

The only thing of any value they'd managed to overlook besides the furniture was our weed stash, which Sam hid inside a tea tin in the kitchen.

I figured they'd come in through the window in Sam's room, the one with the fire escape. The window was locked, but I tried pulling on it and found it popped open with enough force. It made me feel shaky—they could come back at any time.

I called the local police station.

"My place was robbed?" I said.

"Is that a question?" I already didn't like the cop on the other end of the line.

"No, it was robbed. We're missing stuff."

"Where do you live?"

I gave him my address, and heard him grunt. "We've had calls from that building before," he said. "No cameras, no doormen. What do you want us to do? Did anyone see anything?"

"I don't think so, I just got back and found a lot of my roommate's stuff gone."

"Only your roommate's stuff?"

I felt strange telling a cop about the wad of cash I

kept under my mattress. I hadn't reported my income in years—what if he asked where it came from?

"I, uh, don't have a lot of stuff."

"Where is your roommate?"

"I don't know."

"You didn't call your roommate?" the cop was making me feel worse, like I'd done something wrong. Why hadn't I thought to call Sam first? I rarely knew where she was. I thought we might be friends when I moved in but it was like we lived in parallel universes; they overlapped only occasionally, randomly. In truth, I hardly knew the girl at all. Like Lonnie, I was more familiar with her things than her person.

"Are you sure your roommate didn't just take her stuff somewhere, have you spoken with her?"

I understood this cop had no intention of writing up a report.

"No," I said. "I guess I'll call you after I get ahold of her?"

"I guess so," he said, hanging up on me.

I dialed Sam's number then, but she didn't answer. I felt too shaky and panicked to leave a message. I didn't know what else to do, so I left, thinking I'd pick up beer at the corner store. Halfway down the block I realized I had no cash for beer, either in my wallet or at home, but I kept walking anyway, surrounded by the dusk sounds of church bells and Arabic prayers sung over loudspeakers, smells of thrown-out saltfish. I felt like everyone was looking at me, though I told myself I was being crazy. A group of teenagers on a stoop yelled, "Hey, Courtney! Hey, Kelly!" as I passed.

A man approached me, thrust a pizza box into my chest. I could feel the rough cardboard against my nipples even through my bra. I jerked my head down and saw his toothless grin.

"Have dinner with me?" he rasped.

I turned and ran, the thin soles of my shoes thwacking against the pavement.

The man with the glass eye boarded the elevator with me when I made it back to the building. "Do you want to come over sometime?" I asked, still catching my breath. "Smoke pot with me like you used to do with Roxanne?"

He looked at me for a moment, trying to make out whether or not I was serious, then he laughed. "Sure," he said.

"Do you want to come over now?"

"Okay," he said.

He followed me inside and peeked into my bedroom through the open door as I shed my shoes and backpack in the hall. "I thought you said you had a roommate. Did she move out?"

"No," I said. "Sam's been sick. I actually don't really know when she's coming back."

"Did she take her stuff?"

"No," I said. "That's my room."

I didn't offer any further explanation so he didn't ask any more questions.

"We can hang out in Sam's room," I said. "She has a couch."

I led him to Sam's peppermint-striped loveseat. He looked kind of funny sitting on it, a big grown-up man in a little girl's room. "Oh no," he said, glancing around at the mess, "Your lamp."

I didn't want to talk about the robbery so I just replied, "Yeah, I need to clean that up," then left him there and went to the kitchen to put the kettle on. While I waited for the water to boil I fished out Sam's weed. I'd mocked her for it when I first moved in, for keeping it so hidden. She always cleaned up right after smoking, sealing the weed back up in one of her old pill bottles, putting it back in the tin with the rolling paper, tossing the dead ends of her blunts out the window, as if she were going to be found out somehow. I was thankful for it now.

Returning to Sam's room with a pot of tea and a thick joint on Sam's silly brass serving tray, I asked the man with the glass eye, "So, what's your name anyway?"

"Lewis," he said, and at the same time in my mind, I thought, *It doesn't matter*. The name rattled around in my brain anyway. *Lewis Lewis Lewis*. Had I ever fucked someone named Lewis before? It didn't sound familiar, but I didn't trust my memory.

I set the tray on the little coffee table in front of the

sofa. I sat on the floor below Lewis, pouring the tea into two cups, little mismatched twenty-five-cent things Sam had found at Goodwill, like all our dishes. The tea spilled, sloshing over the sides, but I didn't bother to clean it up. Lewis looked funny holding the teacup too. He was a dad, playing tea party with his little girl. It dripped onto his lap, but he pretended not to notice.

"Thanks," he said.

I lit the joint, inhaled, passed it to him, waited for the blurriness to come.

"Where are you from?" I asked this Lewis.

"Wisconsin," he said.

The state meant nothing to me and I liked that. It was just a Native American name, just a place where they manufactured cheese.

Lewis's belly stretched out a little rounded, his legs skinny below it. His hair was starting to gray, not in salt-and-pepper strands but in broad swaths. I waited to get a little more stoned before I asked about his eye.

I tried to concentrate on what he was telling me. "I moved to New York in the eighties. Lived in the East Village in one of those apartments with the bathtub in the kitchen."

"Do you know about Rev. LeRoi?"

"No, who?"

"The serial killer, he lived next door."

"How do you know about it?"

"Actually I read a lot about it, I got a little weird about

it. I like to walk by the house even though it's not in the direction of the train."

"What for?"

"I don't know. Just waiting for something bad to happen, I guess."

"You wanted to be there when something bad happened? You're the girl in the horror movie intent on solving the mystery? Following the clues while the audience yells at her to turn around, go home."

"There are certain bad things I seek out a little compulsively I guess."

I took another hit and passed the joint to him again. My heart was pounding in my fingertips, gravity pulling my hand down against his leg. I dragged my palm across the denim. What a rough texture for all of us to be wearing all the time. I thought about the inner weaving of each little thread. Time was moving slowly enough for me to feel them all. I thought, this time, it's going to be easy; I could feel every thread in his pants. I was unzipping his fly because he was hard, pressed up against the denim.

"Aren't you too young?" he asked.

"For what?"

I had his dick hard in my hand. My body was young next to his, skinny, lithe.

"For me? For this?"

It was easy; all I had to do was say, "No, I'm not." But I couldn't get the words out. I sat there for a moment, unmoving, still holding his dick. I was too high. Time was folding itself up around me.

I remembered waking up on my dad's living room floor as a kid, my shoulder aching from sleeping on nothing but a blanket and hard wood, my mouth tasting like stale popcorn. The house was quiet and dark except for the light of the television. The VCR had clicked off and the screen was bright blue.

I felt like I was waking up alone again, my father gone, the TV screen blue. How long had I been holding his dick? It was starting to go soft in my hand, melting.

"Listen," he said.

"I'm too high," I said.

"Yeah," he said.

13

It was July when I traveled with Lonnie and William upstate so she could attend an artists' retreat. We were to stay in a cabin on a lake in the Adirondacks. I remember the amazed happiness of our arrival. Yes, it was perfect—everything—the knobby Jenny Lind bed frames, the red wool blankets, the fruit pattern on the fabric skirt under the big farmer's sink. Here we could live the life we were made to live, exploring the fern-covered land, sitting around the fire together at night and reading.

Lonnie and I kept looking at each other, opening drawers. The kitchen was stocked with food already—part of the arts colony experience, I guessed. The old spice cabinet smelled so beautiful—wood and mold and cinnamon and paprika. "It's amazing," Lonnie said. "There has to be something wrong. Someone is going to rape us."

Our cabin could only be called such due to its lack of insulation—it was large, two stories, with three bedrooms, two baths, a big living room and kitchen, a washer and dryer, and a small detached garage, where we found a beautiful green canoe. The owner, who rented the house out to the artists' colony, was a sculptor, and menacing wooden animals and partially melted bottles, stretched into strange shapes, covered the walls. Past the porch, a small patch of grass led to a dock on the lake surrounded by pines.

I had been excited to travel so close to where Lonnie had spent her adolescent summers, but I hadn't anticipated how much the Adirondacks would remind me of Oregon and the Mount Hood National Forest. Tiny ribbon garter snakes slithered past us in the lawn. I remembered the texture of moss and lichen on a tree trunk, the crunch of pine cones under my shoes, the creaking sound of wind in trees, the damp cold that hardly ever went away, even in summer.

The cabin didn't have showers, but rather two claw-foot tubs. After William went to bed that first night, I soaked in the bath downstairs, next to the kitchen, and listened to the calls of the loons float across the water—a sound so eerie, so incredible, so familiar, and yet something I had managed to not think about for years.

The first morning, Lonnie had told me to sleep as late as I liked, but I woke early, even before William. I dressed and wandered into the kitchen. I put the kettle on the stove for coffee and started soaking some steel-cut oats in a pan. The loon calls had been replaced by the chirping of other birds. When I finished making coffee I took my cup outside. I didn't put on shoes; I just wandered barefoot over the cold ground, through the trees and down to the dock on the lake.

I had a friend once who used to live on a lake a little

smaller than that one. It made me sad to think about her. Once we'd sneaked out of her house at night, stripped naked, painted each other's bodies with Halloween face paint, and recited friendship oaths to each other in the moonlight. We'd intended to cut ourselves and press the wounds together, the way they'd warned us not to in school. We weren't scared of diseases, we felt the perfectness, the unsulliedness of each other's bodies, but we couldn't find a proper weapon. We'd tried the sharp tips of pine needles and jagged rocks, but couldn't manage to break the skin. That was before I had my pocketknife.

Behind me I heard the crunching of pine cones and turned to see Lonnie, in silly white long johns, rubber boots, and a big brown sweater. She was pushing the canoe across the grass between the garage and the lake, grinning, the whites of her teeth flashing in the small strips of sunlight. She'd obviously just bounded out of bed; her hair was unbrushed, tangled on the left side, as I'd seen it that first day of work.

"Elle!" she called to me when she reached the lip of the lake. "Get in!"

"What about William?"

"He's still sleeping! We'll only be out for a few minutes."

Though I felt uneasy, I hopped off the dock and into the canoe. She heaved the boat with me in it off the shore: a troubling sensation of being grounded, and then suddenly not. The little boat rocked as she climbed in behind me and I gripped my seat. We emerged from the shadows of the trees into the morning sunlight glittering on the water.

Lonnie didn't speak. She handed me a paddle and I pushed it into the water, surprised at how hard it was after a few strokes. I couldn't get the timing right, matching my strokes with hers, and we inched along, zigzagging. We hadn't gone far when Lonnie tapped my shoulder and signaled for me to put my paddle down. I laid it on the floor of the canoe and she continued to paddle. I turned to look at her, moving the paddle from one side of the boat to the other with strong, evenly timed strokes, something she'd no doubt been trained for at camp. We glided smoothly across the water and I tried to swallow my sense of failure.

There was no one else on the lake and, except the cottages peeking through the trees, no sign of human life. We docked at a tiny island, just a little mound of earth growing a handful of pines. The ground was covered in brown needles and I regretted not putting on shoes, but didn't say anything. We were in some kind of storybook now, the tiny island more like an imagined place.

Lonnie and I crisscrossed the land, separating and meeting again. She smiled and I mirrored her. Eventually we sat side by side, our backs resting against the same tree trunk, looking off in two different directions. She spoke then. "This is Rum Island."

"Named by children pretending to be pirates?" I replied.

She was quiet again, but the silence was weighted somehow, as if she were trying to work out something else to tell me. I noticed a pain and looked at the sole of my foot to find it bleeding, a little gash just below my toes. I pressed my hand over the wound.

"You know," she said eventually, "Jimmy. I still want to sleep with him. We still sleep together all the time."

I had no idea what to say. I pressed my hand harder against my foot, the skin turning white from the pressure. I wanted to look at her, but I wanted to be sure my face communicated the proper reaction. But what was the proper reaction? What reaction would make her tell me more? I thought of several emotions—confusion, curiosity, sympathy—and tried to make my face reflect them all at once, but it was impossible. When I finally dared to turn she didn't look back. Instead, she rose and stretched.

"Anyway," she said and headed back to the canoe.

When we reached the cabin, William was just waking up, babbling happily to himself in his portable crib, his blanket to his nose and fingers in his mouth.

I'll say this now—that was the only time we ever talked about her marriage.

14

The basic structure of the artists' colony, I came to understand, involved providing a group of people working with a variety of mediums private studio space during the day and then elaborate dinners together each night. You were not required to attend the dinners, should you still be entrenched in your work by eight o'clock, but they were always available.

Lonnie had failed to inform me of this dinner-party aspect of the trip and I hadn't brought anything to wear other than jeans, so she loaned me a dress that first night, one of her simple cotton affairs. "It's not going to fit," I told her, even though the dress I'd worn the night Carlow came over had been all right. "I'm too flat."

Lonnie didn't even respond, she just shooed me into her bedroom to change, shaking her head. In fact, the dress suited me. I could tell as soon as I slid it over my head. I looked at myself in the mirror in her bedroom. The bust wasn't form fitted so our difference in size was irrelevant. The fabric lay in such a way as to cover my lack of breasts. They really could've been any size at all under there. Lonnie, as if sensing I was done changing, burst through the door. “Shoes,” she said. “We wear the same size shoes, right?”

I hadn’t realized it, but we did. Of course, she would have dainty feet, despite being taller than me. She handed me a pair of navy heels and I slipped them on. I hardly ever wore heels, but these were comfortable, cradling my feet so perfectly that I didn’t feel off-balance.

“There,” Lonnie said simply, pronouncing me ready. I looked at her and found the heels had made up our difference in height. I was looking her directly in the eye. The feeling was off-putting.

“This is going to be boring,” she said.

She suppressed a grin, her lips smashed together. “Do you want to play a little game?” she said. “Between us?”

“What are you thinking?”

“Let’s tell them you’re me. And I’m you. They’ve probably never seen a photo of me—it wasn’t part of the application.”

“Why?”

“Just to fuck with them.” Every time Lonnie cursed it was surprising. Explicit words still came out of her mouth a little unnaturally, with too much satisfaction, as if she were breaking a rule. “We can make up stuff about the book you’re writing. I really hate talking about my work, actually.”

“You hate talking about your writing?”

“Every time you say what the story is about people just say, ‘Mmm, oh.’” She put a blank look on her face, in demonstration. "Even other writers. It makes me want to say, 'It's good, I swear!'"

I must have been looking at her doubtfully, though I couldn't have said no to her if I'd tried. "Please," she said, her hands on my wrists, pulling on my arms, trying to slip her wedding ring on my finger. "Please, please, it'll be fun!"

The dinners were held in a large A-frame, one wall of which was made of windows overlooking a pond covered in smelly green algae bloom. Two swans circled the green water, their white feathers coated in the stuff. Lonnie carried William with me trailing behind, trying to navigate heels through the gravel parking lot. Lonnie pointed out our host, a short old woman, with a pointed nose and thin gray hair pulled back into a tight bun at the nape of her neck. Her face was marred with deep frown lines. My heart pounded as we approached, though I felt reassured by how many times I'd tried searching for pictures of Lonnie online and come up empty-handed. "I'm Lonnie Bernard," I said. She took my hand delicately, the way my father had said was a sign of weak character.

"And this is my son," I said. William whimpered in Lonnie's arms, dipping his face into her neck. "And Elle." I pulled Lonnie toward the woman. "This is Elle, my nanny."

Tibby Walbridge looked Lonnie up and down once, and then turned to a man standing beside her and said, "I'm afraid we're short a trout."

The man—middle-aged, sipping a cocktail—did not appear to register this information. Probably because the news, that Lonnie would not receive a trout, had nothing to do with him. It had to do with Lonnie, or rather, me, because apparently it was below this woman to directly address her. I knew then a nanny wasn't supposed to be at the dinner, and I looked at Lonnie in confusion. She was smiling, as if she were too amused by our game to be offended. She passed William off to me. His little body was still tightly coiled in fear and he let out a small moan as he attached himself to my torso. I had to get him away from this woman before he started crying. Luckily, there was no need to excuse myself. Tibby promptly turned her body away from me, cutting us both off from any further conversation in an obvious and purposeful way.

I took William over to the wall of windows. Twilight was gathering outside and the huge room was reflected in the glass. For now, everyone stood in little clumps around the bar near the door, but a massive table was set next to where I was standing, by the windows. The steeply slanted walls were made of polished honey-colored wood with exposed beams throughout the room. At the back of the building doors led, presumably, to the kitchen and restrooms. The whole space was stark, undecorated, and, other than the bar and table, unfurnished. Sounds reverberated. I'd never seen anything sparkle so much as Lonnie's diamond on my hand. I couldn't help thinking it was probably worth a whole year of my salary.

Lonnie appeared behind me with two glasses of white wine. "You make a fantastic me already," she said.

"So I wasn't invited to the dinners?"

"Don't be silly. Family is invited."

I glared at her doubtfully. I felt that Lonnie, who'd never been looked down upon in her life, was failing to register the situation. "She's old-fashioned," I said. "The help can't eat at the same table."

Lonnie pushed the wine at me again and I took the glass, balancing William on my hip. "She's about to bite the big one," she said, leaning in close to my face, her breath already smelling like wine. William tried to grab her hair and she gently pushed his arm away. "She and everyone she knows will be dead soon. Just ignore her."

That actually did make me feel better, to think of Tibby Walbridge as mostly dead, though it also made me wonder if Lonnie was using me for some secret purpose. If her friendship with me, her treating me like a normal person, was something of a rebellion for her. If bringing me here was like smoking in her camp cabin after lights-out.

William was starting to get antsy in my arms, twisting his body around, wanting to be put down. Lonnie looked at me, her face close to mine. She looked hurt that I was offended. Her lower lip hung innocently from her mouth, her eyes wide. It was still strange to be standing on the same level as her. She said softly, "None of these people matter. To me, or you."

"I just feel uncomfortable," I said.

"I want you to have a good time. I don't want you to be stuck at that cabin by yourself."

"Okay."

"Okay?"

"Okay."

Lonnie took William back, propping him on her hip, and then placed her arm on the small of my back as we walked toward the bar. She was an affectionate person. She touched everyone when she spoke, but she'd never done that before, our hips rubbing together, my heels clicking in time with her steps against the polished floor.

She was delighted by our game. I could see the little surges of excitement coming over her as we introduced ourselves to the other artists.

"I'm Lonnie," I said. It became more natural with practice.

The couple we were speaking to, an attractive pair in their thirties, nodded. Lonnie's hand fluttered on my back. I could see, from the corner of my eye, her smile overwhelming her face. She could hardly contain herself. "Have you ever read Lonnie's writing?" she said.

"I haven't yet had the pleasure," the woman answered for both of them.

Lonnie's other hand was fluttering now, moving up and down like she was about to alight. "Well, how do I describe it? It's subtle, but there's something dark about it. She has amazing attention to detail."

"What's the title of your book?" the woman asked.

Lonnie and I looked at each other. "*Woman in a Double Frame,*" I said quickly, stealing the title of Carlow's painting.

"It's a sort of mystery," she added.

"I think I've heard of that," the woman replied, to Lonnie's obvious delight.

"It was a small press," Lonnie said. "Word didn't get around too much, but it had a lovely review in *Nylon*."

"That's not true," I said, thinking about how grateful I was there was no Internet service up there, so at least we wouldn't be caught in this lie right away. "They said it got a little carried away with itself."

"That's just like you, to focus on that one sentence. Anyway, they meant it in a good way. They meant the text was having fun."

There was one other woman at the colony with a child, a little boy, about five years old. The woman looked more like his grandmother; she was probably in her fifties. They arrived after us, and as soon as they walked in the boy took off running, across the room and back again, dodging the legs of guests, nearly tripping a waiter carrying a tray of fried pickles on little spears.

The woman watched him go, but said nothing about it. Lonnie whispered, "One of those couples that spends a lot of money and time trying to get pregnant—a last-ditch effort—and so the child can do no wrong."

"Oh no, do you know them?" I asked, my stomach

sinking at the prospect of being found out.

"Of course not," Lonnie said. "I know about her. She writes horrible plays." She led me to the woman, her hand on the small of my back again. We were doing a terrible job of acting like each other. A nanny would never be leading her employer around like this. "Really, really, atrocious," she said through her smile as we approached.

"Gigi Harrison," the woman said. "Playwright."

"Lonnie Bernard," I said, finding it difficult to not ironically mirror her disaffected tone. "Writer."

Another limp hand. "Pleased to meet you. This is your first time here? Did they put you up at one of the nicer cabins?"

"Oh yes, we're quite happy with it. This is Elle, my nanny."

"I've done some of my best work up here," Gigi said. "It's so generous of Tibby."

"Well," I said, eyeing Lonnie. "If I can get my work anywhere near the caliber of yours, I'd consider myself very lucky."

Lonnie's hand moved from the small of my back to my elbow, giving it a quick pinch. Carlow style.

"And who is this?" I asked. Her son was pulling on the hem of her dress, flinging it around so that I caught glimpses of her sun-spotted thighs.

"This is little Aldous."

"Mine is Billy," I said, touching his head, using Lonnie's nickname for him.

"Ah," Gigi said, then frowned. "But you are far too young to have a baby!"

Lonnie grabbed my arm. "Excuse us for a moment, Gigi. Lonnie, can you help me with something?"

I nodded, and she led me toward the back of the room and through a sliding wood door. I'd thought she'd just wanted to escape Gigi, but when we got inside she passed William to me, then gathered her skirt around her waist and pulled down her panties—light pink lacy ones. "I really can't stand that woman," she said, squatting over the toilet. I wasn't sure where to look. Politely turning around might've made me feel more comfortable, but then the fact that she'd dragged me in here with her made it seem rude somehow. I remembered the night of her party, how she'd followed me into the bathroom to smoke a joint while I peed. Maybe she was one of those girls who really hated to be alone; one of those girls who thought all girls should go to the bathroom together. I listened to her piss splash into the toilet, moving my eyes around the room, trying not to stare at her or avoid looking either.

"I bet you have a really nice dad," she said, suddenly. I didn't understand where it had come from.

"I guess I do," I ventured.

"Mine's a fucking ass, like all these people." She flushed the toilet with the toe of her flat. "You should drink more wine," she said. "Really stuff yourself, get loaded. Let's take everything we can from these people."

I thought it a weird thing for her to say, considering how everything was always handed to her—whether here or at home. She was really getting into character.

She wiggled her panties back up under her dress.

We emerged from the bathroom to find dinner was starting—everyone making their way over to the huge table. We filled up our wineglasses before following the crowd.

There were too many place settings; it was obvious immediately. I wondered if several people had chosen to have dinner in their cabins. I wouldn't blame them.

"Is everyone here?" someone said.

Gigi, the seasoned attendee replied, "Yes, not everyone comes to the dinners."

I counted fifteen people, including William and Aldous, but the table was set for twenty-five. Tibby Walbridge made her way slowly toward the head and everyone else found seats around her, leaving a long section of the table empty. I wondered if the servers would have to wash each of the untouched plates, bowls, spoons, forks, and knives. I took William from Lonnie and sat next to her with him on my lap.

Tibby Walbridge looked at me and said, of Lonnie, "No, she can sit down there." She gestured to the empty end of the table. "With the children."

Lonnie's mouth hung open. I flushed, seething, but was unsure how to react. Lonnie put her hand on my shoulder, and scooted her chair out. She leaned over me as she took William, her hot breath in my hair. "This bitch."

She didn't look at anyone as she made her way to the other end of the table and selected a seat at the corner. I would've liked to meet her eye. In fact, I'd never felt more endeared to her than at that moment, as she accepted the isolation that should've been mine. But even as I watched her walk—her head held high, William's little arms circled around her neck—feeling such pride and utter devotion, I was also aware of a sharp envy. I didn't want to sit with these people, especially without her. Even when we traded places I still somehow drew the short stick.

There was a long pause in the conversation before polite chatter started up again. A few minutes later Gigi approached Lonnie, dragging Aldous to the seat next to hers. He sat for a moment, his whole face red, tears brimming in his eyes, then ran back to his mother. I couldn't blame him. Tibby Walbridge didn't address his continued presence in Gigi's lap, and, despite his unrelenting pulling of her hair and patting of her cheeks, Gigi kept a bored look on her face, as if he weren't really there at all.

We were served cubes of some kind of fish in a red sauce as an appetizer. "Sea lamprey," Tibby announced. "A French delicacy and locally overpopulated. Doing our part to even things out."

It felt like rubber in my mouth, but I ate it all quickly, along with the bread, intending to follow Lonnie's directions regardless of my stomach. When I finished my wine the waiter refilled the glass.

The man next to me leaned over and whispered, "They're parasites, primordial. Their mouths jawless, full of teeth. But"—he picked his last chunk up with his fork and my full stomach lurched—"hardly any bones."

The woman who'd claimed to have heard of my imaginary book started discussing her own work—an installation project that required a group of women to walk around speaking one-word sentences to one another while holding mirrors directly in front of their faces.

"And what do their bodies look like?" Gigi said. "I feel it is an important question."

"Ah," the woman said, pausing. "I am using the white young naked female body."

Gigi nodded seriously, though in her lap Aldous giggled at the word "naked."

The trout arrived after the lamprey, served whole with tiny potatoes and a tomato salad. Though I felt sick, I looked the waiter, a young man, probably my age, in the eye, thanked him loudly, exaggeratedly, but no one took any notice. At the other end of the table, he leaned over and said something quietly to Lonnie.

"Oh," I heard her reply. "It doesn't matter, the baby and I will share."

I'd never eaten a whole fish before and had no idea what to do with it. The sight of its gooey cooked eyes disgusted me. The other guests grinned and giggled, complimenting Tibby on her selection.

At the end of the table, William wrinkled up his face at the fish, reached out as if to poke it, and then quickly drew back his hand, scared. Lonnie fed him potato. I didn't know if I was supposed to cut off the skin or eat it all even if it turned my stomach. I used my knife to snap off the head, as I'd seen the other guests do. William suddenly started crying, a sharp, piercing wail. Lonnie scooped him up and walked outside.

I tried to catch glimpses of Lonnie and William on the porch as I dissected the body of the trout. I didn't do a very good job. My plate was soon covered with scales, and I kept catching bones in my mouth. I crunched them between my teeth.

"In the film a man is playing a card game—it's not exactly solitaire, though he is playing it alone." The man sitting next to me was speaking now. "But he's in a swimming pool, trying to play on the surface of the moving water. The cards are obviously floating away."

I didn't know what he was talking about, though I related to the man in the film, as I suffered down more and more fish.

"And you," the man turned to me, "your book. It has been receiving wonderful reviews?"

My mouth was full. "Mmm," I said, chewing bone. "Mm-hmm." They all waited for me to go on. My three glasses of wine were hitting me, which made Lonnie's words make more sense. None of these people mattered. "I was really inspired by these obscure, sixteenth-century

Italian erotic dialogues," I said, thinking of a book I'd found in Lonnie's office.

"You know, the history of the body." I lifted the phrase from Carlow.

I felt something scratching my foot and peeked under the tablecloth to see Aldous running his nails over my skin.

Everyone nodded. Gigi squinted at me. "Are you thinking about the male gaze?" she said.

I shook Aldous off my leg. He didn't look up—I was nothing but a pair of disembodied legs to him. I heard him scamper over toward someone else, and jammed another glob of fish into my mouth, chewing in earnest. Was I thinking about the male gaze? Should I have been?

I nodded at Gigi. I could feel my face flushing. Lonnie was crazy for sending me in here. All I could think about was the ending of the movie *Sisters* where conjoined twins are on an operating table in the middle of a swimming pool while an audience looks on. The nurse pulls a meat cleaver out from underwater. It's passed down the line of onlookers, slowly, with reverence, until it finally reaches the hand of the doctor.

"In what way?" Gigi said. "Are you giving the erotic dialogue a multiplicity of views?"

"Yes, exactly," I said, taking another mouthful of trout, not knowing in the slightest what she meant. I kept picturing that doctor's hand reaching up with the meat cleaver.

The man next to me picked up the conversation with a series of names that held no meaning for me. I nodded along with everyone else, relieved to have someone else speak and terrified the conversation would circle back to me, but it never did.

My decimated trout plate was eventually cleared away and we were served thick wedges of gooey chocolate cake. I matched little Aldous bite for bite. He glared at me from across the table, stuffing the confection into his pink maw with a frantic combination of fork and fingers—chewing openmouthed, sucking the remnants off his stubby digits. I swigged more wine, my stomach tight and painful.

When people finally started to trickle away from the table I slipped outside. Lonnie and William were sitting on the far edge of the porch, by the back entrance to the kitchen. William ran to me when he saw me coming, but Lonnie didn't turn. She was wearing a large black sweatshirt over her dress, the sleeves pulled down around her hands. I picked up William and noticed a half-eaten peanut butter sandwich on crusty bread in his hand. He held it to my face, offering me a bite.

"No," I told him, feeling sick. "For you."

The waiter was crouching next to Lonnie, in the middle of telling her something I couldn't hear. She laughed, her head thrown back.

I cleared my throat as I approached. "Are you ready?"

She looked up at me surprised, registering my presence for the first time. "Oh," she said. "Time to go?"

I nodded and they both stood. The waiter introduced himself. "I hope it's okay I gave him a sandwich," he said. "Thought he might like it better than the fish."

I realized Lonnie had continued to pretend he was my baby. "Of course," I said.

Lonnie unzipped the sweatshirt and handed it to him. "Thanks," she said, kissing him quickly on the cheek.

"Are you coming back tomorrow?" he asked.

"Sure," she said.

I didn't have to look back to know he was watching her leave.

I tried to keep all that food down, but when we got back to the cabin the sickness overcame me. Thinking of the lamprey, I vomited in the downstairs bathroom while Lonnie put William to bed.

15

In the middle of the night Lonnie crawled into my bed. She whispered, "It's scary," to me in the dark with a little laugh, and I felt her body curl up, legs to her chest, timid.

"It's okay," I whispered back, and my assent allowed her to unfurl, the sheets rustling around us as she settled herself into sleep.

I don't know how to tell about the kind of pain I was in. I didn't understand it myself. I still felt I hated her, though I fingered the ends of her hair as she slept, thankful for the lack of sensation there. The room was filled with a sort of static I wasn't used to. The old wooden dresser, the cedar chest at the end of the bed filled with extra blankets, the wavered glass in the windowpanes—everything was alive and crackling. The whole room was filled with objects sleeping—breathing lightly, like Lonnie, unaware of my existence. I put a foot on the floor trying to steady my head, and then quickly drew it back up again, still nauseated by the dark space between the bed and ground. I couldn't have slept if my life depended on it, though I was also entirely incapable of rising from that bed.

I don't know what time it was when Lonnie stirred.

Her body jolted and I heard her exhale. I closed my eyes, embarrassed to still be fully conscious, but I felt her sit up, the blankets rustling around her legs. When she grabbed me by the shoulder, mumbling, "Let's keep this between you and me," I opened my eyes to see her gripping the silky edge of the blanket, her eyes large and blank, roaming a room we were not in. I realized she wasn't awake at all. A moment later, she wilted back down, her face landing even closer to mine on our shared pillow—the warm wet air from her half-open mouth smelling of sour wine.

Only when dawn broke, the pink sun seeping through the breathing windowpane, and Lonnie rose for a glass of water in the kitchen, did I finally nod off for a couple hours, my head aching, my muscles weary from struggling to stay motionless so long.

My body somehow never felt tired after that sleepless night. I played with William all day, and planned an elaborate dinner, stretching pizza dough on the counter. I liked the cocoon Lonnie and I had wrapped ourselves up in. I couldn't wait for her to come back from the studio.

What was she actually *doing* out there anyway? She hadn't brought her computer at all, just a pile of books and a cheap spiral notebook I'd never seen before. I didn't really view Lonnie's writing career with any seriousness. Since I knew we were here because of her father, since she rarely worked at home, since I hadn't been able to find a single publication online, since she'd said to me in the bathroom when she was high, "I don't ever *do* anything anymore"—what else could I conclude?

She was late coming in from her studio that evening. I'd had to put William to bed when he started falling asleep in my arms. The sun was setting when I heard the screen door slam, but in fact it wasn't Lonnie. The waiter from the night before wandered into the kitchen, carrying two brown bags. "Mid-week grocery delivery," he said, then, noticing my surprise, "Sorry, the door was open."

"Oh," I said. "That's okay, thank you." I peeked in one of the bags—fresh produce.

"I'm Alex," he said. "I met you and Elle last night?"

I nodded, remembering that Lonnie had given him my name. "Of course, I remember."

"Have you been getting good work done?" He glanced at the pizzas on the counter. "Doesn't look like you're coming back for dinner tonight."

"No," I said. "Just been getting a lot of writing in, you know. Sometimes being social disrupts things."

I was hoping he would excuse himself at the comment, but he didn't seem to get the hint. He just bobbed his head. "A lot of people feel that way," he said.

The animosity I felt toward him was unfair. He'd been kind to William, and had to put up with working for Tibby Walbridge. I should've been on his side, but his obvious interest in Lonnie put me off in a way Carlow's and James's didn't. I may not have found her first, but I sure as hell found her before he did.

Lonnie came in then, the screen door slapping behind her. She quickly set down her stack of books when she saw Alex.

"He brought us more groceries," I said in explanation.

"Thank you," Lonnie said, greeting him with a kiss on the cheek.

"William's asleep," I said.

"He should stay for a drink," she looked at me. "Right?"

"I brought some stuff," he said.

What could I do but nod?

We cut the pizzas into equal parts and Lonnie poured gin and tonics. She'd packed the big bottle of gin in her suitcase. "Mother's ruin," she said, holding up her glass. I took a sip, but it made me feel a little sick, made me remember my sleeplessness the night before.

"Oh!" Lonnie said, jumping up from the table after only a few bites. "Look what I found in this house!" She ran to a built-in cupboard next to the table and pulled out a Ouija board. "We have to play! All we've been doing is trading tips on curling our hair and painting each other's nails. Do you want to turn this into a real teenage sleepover?"

Though Lonnie and I hadn't actually traded any beauty advice, unless you counted my borrowing her dress, I nodded, pleased by the lie she'd wrapped our experience up in, even if it was just for Alex's sake.

"How do I know I can trust you two?" Alex said.

"Doesn't someone just always move the pointer?"

"It's called a planchette," Lonnie said.

"Every time I've played nothing has happened," I said. "I guess I've never played in a haunted location."

"Or with people who took it seriously." Lonnie nodded. "You have to respect the board."

Alex glanced at the animal sculptures above the mantel. "This house is definitely haunted, but I still think you're just going to fuck with me," he said.

Lonnie glanced at me sideways. "Let's do a test of trust then," she said.

Before Alex could answer she dashed upstairs and returned with an eye mask. I tried to remember, back on my first day of work, if she'd been wearing one when I walked in on her sleeping. It made the moment the night before—her eyes darting around the room of her dream—feel more intimate. Maybe even James had never seen her quite like that.

Lonnie dangled the mask in front of Alex.

He raised his eyebrows, but he was smiling. "What are you going to do?" he said.

"We're going to lead you on a walk through the woods," she said. "When you make it back to the porch you'll know you can trust us."

"Should we leave William?" I asked.

"He'll be fine," she said. "He's sound asleep."

"That's it?"

"That's it."

I thought the blindfold seemed unnecessary, not just because the woods were pitch-black at night, but because it was already obvious this boy would've let Lonnie lead him off a cliff, even if he could see where he was going. Nevertheless, I found myself excited by the game, excited to be in on the secret of where we were going with Lonnie.

Alex let Lonnie guide the sleep mask over his head and tighten the Velcro closure in the back. She had to stand a little between his legs, leaning over.

"It's not good enough," she said, looking at me, thinking. Then she ran to the kitchen and returned holding up a roll of duct tape.

"Isn't that mean?" I said.

Alex quickly lifted up the mask, but Lonnie slapped his hand away. "It falls off. Just a little insurance. Don't worry, I won't get any in his hair."

She ripped a few small strips off the roll with her teeth and placed them around the mask, under his eyes, along the bridge of his nose, and on his forehead. She gave his cheek a little pat. "There," she said.

The three of us made our way outside, Lonnie grasping Alex's hand, and Alex slow and unsteady on his feet, reaching out with his free arm, feeling for obstacles.

The moon was a shard in the sky, hardly illuminating our path. "Pick up your feet," Lonnie said. "You can't trip if you pick up your feet."

We marched through the woods surrounding the house, Lonnie holding on to Alex's hand. I was relieved that she didn't take us too far away from the cabin—I could still see the lights on the main level. I tried to focus on our distance from them, always keeping track of how to find my way back. We circled around the house and then Lonnie positioned Alex right on the edge of the dock. "You feel the wood boards under your feet?" she said. "You're back on the porch."

Alex began to peel off his blindfold. Lonnie giggled, clasped a hand over her mouth. "Trust me?" she said, through the slats of her fingers.

A confused smile spread across Alex's face as his eyes adjusted, as he made out that slice of moonlight bouncing off the lake.

"Trust you?" he said.

Without pausing long enough to think, I pushed him, hitting the center of his chest with my shoulder. He reached for me as he stepped backward, but it was too late. The dark water swallowed up the thin slip of his frame, the spattering sound echoing across the landscape, quieting the loons. Lonnie pounced on me, her hands around my shoulders, her mouth at my ear. She yelped, laughed, and then fell completely silent as we waited for Alex's reemergence. Nothing happened for too long.

Lonnie's body began to vibrate against me. Though we looked at each other, it was too dark for me to make out anything but the shadow of her features, the blurry white of her teeth.

I hadn't meant anything by the push—it was a

joke—but I had failed to take into account how deep the water was, or whether there were rocks below. I didn't move in disbelief. It couldn't be that easy to kill someone.

I think if Lonnie had said something or moved to the edge of the dock, if she'd jumped in after him or even run screaming back to the house, I wouldn't have remained inert so long. As it was, with her clinging to me, the pulse of her breath on my face, I felt protected, like we were in this together, like it wasn't really my fault.

I suspected even if I hadn't pushed him in she would've—why else had she led him here? Why had she placed him so close to the lip? I'd only anticipated her actions.

I don't know how long we stood there before we heard the lapping of water and saw something crawl onto the little beach to the right of the dock. We knew without being able to see that it must be Alex—he must've swum underwater, trying to scare us—even though it looked more like a wolf or some other hunched creature on all fours, emerging onto the mud, gasping for breath.

"Fuck you guys," he sputtered when we ran to him. "Neither of you jumped in after me?"

Lonnie knelt, her knees in the water next to him, pulling on the collar of his shirt.

"We knew you were faking." She laughed, then added, "You fucker," with her usual hesitancy, her overzealousness for obscenity.

He pulled her into the water, the reflection of the moonlight splintering around their bodies. She didn't scream, but accepted the cold—the cold that shocked me as I joined them, throwing off my shoes and wading in, anxious not to be left out. Everything on the bottom of the lake was soft and slick. Mud and the slippery stems of cattails squeezed between my toes. There were no rocks in this area after all.

Following a brief tussle with Alex, Lonnie swam away, leaving a trail of waves behind. Watching where we could no longer see her, I reflected on how fucked all of this was. Alex thought she was the single one. He thought he had some kind of chance.

"Elle!" he called. It was jarring to register my own name, not directed at me.

We were just past the dock, up to our waists. He waited only another moment before taking off after her. I ducked underwater, trying to get used to the cold, but my scalp prickled with it, my jaw chattering. I crossed my legs, used my arms to move my body toward the bottom. I felt grass brush against my back. I had to keep moving my arms to stay down there, had to fight against my body's buoyancy. I let all the air out of my lungs slowly and then just sat, feeling my chest pound.

I thought I might take a glob of mud to throw at Alex—or maybe Lonnie, whoever returned first—but the clump I pulled up mostly disintegrated by the time I broke through the surface. I was left with a single stone—a little convex, a smooth triangle. I liked the way it felt in my palm, so I held on to it.

Alex came back first, panting, shaking water from his ears. "She's fucking fast," he said. "I lost her, you think she's okay?"

I didn't have to answer. All either of us could do was wait.

There was the sound of water, the lapping of motion, but it could've been wind on the surface or the nocturnal loons, diving for food. I knew she was doing it on purpose. I thought she might've made it all the way to Rum Island, and was hiding out there as a child will hide from her mother inside a rack of clothing, for the sheer pleasure of another's panic.

"She got jealous when you pranked us," I said. "She wanted to do it too, and do it better."

"You don't seem like her boss," Alex said.

"We're friends," I said.

He probably nodded, but I couldn't see him.

Lonnie came back, of course, charting a straight line in our direction, though we couldn't see her until she was very close. Alex went to dunk her, reaching for her sides, her belly, until she screeched, clutching at me, asking me to save her.

I didn't care about their exchanges of revenge. I wanted to get out of the water. I didn't want to lose one another in the cold and the dark anymore.

I started thinking about the girls LeRoi had chopped

up and put in the lake upstate. Divers collected them in a fried chicken bucket—a detail so absurd, so small and random, and yet it was repeated again and again.

"I'm crazy cold," I said, moving toward the shore, with those slow-motion underwater steps. "And we should probably check on William."

"You're right," Lonnie called, dashing out of the water behind me, still splashing and pushing Alex.

I set the stone on the dining room table and went to find towels. When I returned Lonnie was holding it, turning it over in the dim glow of the corner lamp. Her dress was pooling water on the wood floor. "Did you bring this in from the lake?"

I nodded, handed out the towels.

"I don't think that's a rock," Alex said.

"What do you mean?"

"That's somebody's kneecap."

Lonnie dropped it, and it banged down on the table next to the sad remainders of my homemade pizza. All that work and we'd hardly touched it. "It's too small!" she said, but she stepped toward me like she was afraid.

"Look how white it is!" Alex said, picking it up. "And just the right shape."

I didn't know what my own kneecap looked like exactly. I reached a hand down, but touching it gave me a sick feeling. It wasn't possible, was it? We couldn't be anywhere near the LeRoi property? I tried to remember the name of that lake, but I don't think the news story had specified. I longed to look it up on the Internet but the only service at the cabin was an old corded landline.

"Have you ever heard of Rev. LeRoi?" I found myself asking. When they shook their heads the whole story spilled out—the nuns, the church, the proliferation of offspring, the murders. I was nervous, or maybe just excited, to finally have a reason to talk about this thing I'd grown a little obsessed with. I could tell I was talking too fast. Lonnie's eyes were getting wider and wider. "I don't know where the lake was," I said, "but I think it was in the Adirondacks."

I thought for a moment she would share in my fascination but then she said, "Lonnie." It took me a moment to understand she meant me. "Enough. Stop."

Alex rubbed his hair until it stood up on end, either unperturbed by my story or acting macho for our sake. He looked so skinny and baby faced in the soft light. I'd assumed he was my age, but he could easily have been as young as twenty, the difference between those ages feeling very wide.

"You're freaking me out," Lonnie said as she dropped her dress to the ground with a nonchalance that annoyed me. Disrobing in front of this boy was too much—how desperate for attention could she be? We'd been away from the city and her men for only three days.

She was wearing a little white thing we used to call a training bra, though I now saw them in stores for women—two triangles of lacy fabric that concealed the state of one's nipples but did nothing in terms of support. She wrapped her scantily clad body up in a towel and said, "Well, Alex doesn't trust us, but we found a kneecap in the lake that apparently might be from a victim of some local serial killer so I think there's nothing left to do but contact some spirits."

We set up the board on the living room floor and Alex built a fire in the fireplace. Each of us put four fingers on the planchette. Lonnie touched Alex's hand. "Lightly," she said. "You don't even really have to touch it, just hover your fingers over."

We followed her instructions. The pads of my fingertips barely brushed the plastic. "No laughing," Lonnie said to Alex, though he wasn't even smiling. "It's not a game. It's not a joke."

"Of course not," Alex said. "Though it's manufactured by Hasbro. It's not a game."

Lonnie turned to me. "We're going to have to do this after he's gone, aren't we?"

"Boys never take it seriously," I said, flashing Alex a disdainful glance.

"Okay," he said. "I'll be serious. What can we ask? Let's just do it."

Lonnie gave him one last doubtful glance, and then looked down at the board. She let out a deep sigh, which unraveled the fold of her towel over her breasts, but she didn't move her fingers. She didn't seem to notice. "Are there any spirits in this room?" she asked. "If anyone's here, please feel free to contact us. This is a safe space. We're only here to talk."

I tried to draw my attention away from Lonnie's body, onto the board, tried to concentrate on her words. I thought, even if nothing happened, even if the Ouija board was not a means of communicating with the other side, Lonnie would still be able to tell I wasn't trying.

"Give us a sign you're here," she said.

The game piece veered left suddenly and all of us jumped. Lonnie smiled, exhaled. "Good," she said. "Thank you, we're so happy you're here. Can you tell us what you'd like us to call you?"

The planchette moved to the letter "S" and stopped.

"Okay," Lonnie said. "S."

I thought about how she referred to everyone by initial in her journal. I tried to judge how close her fingers were to the planchette, but it was hard to tell. "Can you tell us more about yourself, S? Can you tell us what year you died?"

The pointer spelled out "7–4."

Lonnie and I looked at each other. "Are you moving it?" she asked. I shook my head, the truth.

"You guys, this is freaking me out," Alex said. "You're not moving it?"

"S," Lonnie said, ignoring Alex and maintaining eye contact with me. "We want to talk to you. We want you to feel safe. Can you tell us, was your death an accident?"

The planchette moved to "No."

"Was your death because of an illness?"

"No" again.

"S, did somebody hurt you?"

"Yes."

"I'm so sorry, S. Can I ask if you're okay now? Are you all right where you are now?"

The pointer moved sharply down and then back and forth along the two words at the bottom of the board: "Good bye good bye good bye."

"We lost her," Lonnie said. "She's gone."

"This is fucked, you guys," Alex said.

"I wasn't moving it," Lonnie said.

"Me neither."

"Do you believe in ghosts?" Lonnie asked, leaning toward him.

"No," Alex said. "No way."

"What do you think just happened?"

"I think one of you was moving it."

"What about you?" Lonnie asked me. "Do you believe in ghosts?"

"I don't believe or not believe," I said. "In anything. There could be a whole mess of shit we don't know about, right? I guess I don't really believe in a soul, though, so I don't think about ghosts in any traditional sense."

"You don't believe in a soul?"

"Well, I think we're just animals, you know? I think the soul is a word we use to talk about something non-concrete, like love or hope. Love doesn't really exist in the way we talk about it. It's a chemical reaction, it's hormones, it's society's expectations and evolutionary code telling us we have a better chance of survival if we're not alone."

"I don't believe I'm just a body," Lonnie said. It came out quietly, so I felt bad.

"Maybe you're not," I said.

"You think that was somebody really talking to us?" Alex said.

"Yes, that was somebody."

"You want to try it again?" I said.

We placed our fingers back on the planchette and Lonnie began the same routine, asking if anyone wanted to talk. After a pause the pointer moved to "Yes." When Lonnie asked for a name our fingers spelled out "W-I-L-L."

"That's our baby's name," Lonnie said, personable even with ghosts. "What a great name. Can you tell us where you are, Will? Are you somewhere in the room with us?"

C-R-E-S-T

I glanced around and noticed, for the first time, a family crest, carved from wood on the wall right above us. It was close enough for a person, a real person, to reach down and touch the board. Something about knowing the exact location, right next to us, put me on edge.

"Will, can you tell us what year you died?"

1-9-7-4

"Fuck," Alex said. "That's the same year as the last one."

"How old were you, Will?"

2–2

"Why the hell were they so young?"

"Will, can you tell us how you died?"

"No."

"Okay, you don't have to tell us if you don't want to. What would you like to tell us?"

The pointer swam around the board, running over all the letters, pausing briefly at "A" and then "Z."

"A. Z.," we chanted out loud, reading the dictation. "A. Z. A. Z. A. Z."

"Does that mean anything to you?" Lonnie asked.

"Maybe he doesn't know what to say," I ventured.

A-Z-A-Z-A-Z

It was moving fast, and my fingers were hardly on it at all. Alex visibly lifted his hands up, but it kept going.

"I don't want to play anymore," he said.

The planchette stopped. We took our hands away too. "Don't you want to find out what Will wants to tell us?" Lonnie looked at us.

"It's just nonsense and numbers. We're not finding out anything." Alex waved his hands around, his eyes narrowed at me, as if any of this had been *my* idea. "You think we can actually do something? You pull this game board out like, what, what do you think is gonna happen? You think this is important somehow? You think the ghost is gonna have you solve some little mystery like you're Nancy Drew or something? You think these are real people?"

I was crying—sudden big embarrassing tears. I couldn't remember the last time I'd cried. I'd gone all those weeks starving to the point of pain and hadn't even cried then. Why now? Why over some stupid game? I hated Alex, hated how his obvious fear was coming out as anger at us. I hated the way he felt he had the right to control the room—the right to call it quits whenever he wanted. I also hated the fact that he was right—we could move this pointer around all night, but what did it matter? What the hell did AZ mean?

"Oh my God," Lonnie said, noticing my tears. "Elle—Lonnie."

She'd given us away, and was laughing at the mistake, but Alex didn't even seem to notice; he was all worked up, his face red, distracted by himself. "Even if they are real people, or were—you think you actually matter at all to them?"

"Fine," Lonnie said, annoyed now, her voice tightening up, "Fine, stop playing, nobody said you had to play."

She got up and ran to the kitchen, bringing me back a beer. Alex looked at me wide-eyed, as if for the first time. I wiped my nose, against my hand. The tears kept coming; I'd accepted the embarrassment, so now I couldn't stop them. I clutched the cold can of beer in my hand—it was a Budweiser, Alex must've brought it. Lonnie cracked the can, but I couldn't get the resistance right, my hand wavered and we spilled a fair amount on the rug. She rubbed it into the weave, like a child.

"I'm sorry," Alex said. "I wasn't trying to be mean."

I sucked beer down. I knew the appropriate thing to do was apologize for my overreaction, to tell Alex it wasn't his fault, that my emotions were a mystery to me, but I couldn't get any of that out.

"I think we all need more alcohol," Lonnie said, swatting at the game so the planchette skidded across the rug and the board folded up on itself. I was hoping she would say, "I think you need to leave," to Alex, but more alcohol would help too.

"Yeah," Alex said, getting up. "I brought a lot of beer."

I leaned against the couch and Lonnie put her head on my thigh, a move I guessed she wouldn't have pulled if Alex weren't watching. We used to do that in high school too—leaning on each other in hallways as if our bodies needed holding up, exemplifying the kind of touch we were capable of.

"So, have you ever seen a ghost?" Alex said, handing Lonnie a Budweiser. The way he said it, you could tell he expected her to say no.

"In my dad's building," she said, sitting up just enough to spill a little beer into her mouth. "Where I grew up. There are washing machines in the basement, and I'd sometimes go down there with my nanny. We used to wash the towels and sheets down there because we only had a small machine in our apartment, and the dryer took forever. Every time I was in that basement, since I was a kid, somebody tried to hold my hand. It was a kid—the hand was the same size as mine when I was little, but when I was twelve or thirteen I noticed it felt small."

"And you looked and nobody was there?"

"I never looked."

"Never?"

"I haven't been down there since probably high school but no, I didn't look at my hand, I always just stared straight ahead."

"Because you were scared?"

"I don't know how to explain it. I always had the feeling that was what I was supposed to do."

"So, you think, what? People's souls are just hanging around? Or, like, only when they can't rest in peace?"

"I don't know," Lonnie said. "I think maybe the past is sort of superimposed on the present. Or the immaterial world. And there's overlap sometimes, but I don't know why."

Alex lay down on the floor. I was thinking about all those times in high school we'd parked next to cemeteries at night, wandered around among the graves, waiting for something to happen. All the horror movies I'd watched. All the times I'd walked past the LeRoi house. Nothing ever happened to me, but of course, something would reach out for Lonnie.

"Sometimes I think of dreams as overlap too," Lonnie said. "Sometimes they're obviously just your mind jumbling up your experiences, but other times they feel like you've slipped into something you maybe shouldn't have? Something that maybe doesn't really have much to do with you?"

When neither of us responded she said, "These things are impossible to talk about anyway."

She got up then, and went to put on clothes. I missed her while she was gone; I worried about her upstairs without really knowing why. The house felt so isolated. I missed the city, missed the idea of my neighbors next to me, even if I couldn't hear them—when had isolation started to scare me? She returned, of course, in her robe, carrying the baby monitor and an armload of blankets. The three of us spread out on the floor in front of the fireplace. Lonnie curled her body against mine. "Did you have a fireplace growing up?" I asked quietly.

"No," she said, the words in my ear. "And I missed it my whole life."

We fell asleep nested together like that. For all his childish bravado, I think we'd frightened Alex; I think he was scared to leave. Or maybe he was hoping for sex—hoping our affection toward each other would spontaneously trickle over to him, though he made no move to wedge himself between us. He probably didn't know how.

It was still dark when the phone rang. The fire had long burned out and the big living room was cold. I rose without fully waking to answer the ringing. It was only when I reached the familiar sound that I realized the time, the place, the year. I hadn't spoken on a landline since I moved out at eighteen. This was not my phone, not my kitchen, and whoever was on the other end was not trying to reach me.

I picked up the receiver anyway—it seemed wrong to let it ring while William slept upstairs. My palm cradled the object. How many hours had I spent talking on a phone like this growing up? It was funny now—I'd had to do it in the kitchen, waiting for my dad to turn on the television in the other room to ensure he wouldn't be eavesdropping.

"Hello?" My voice came out full of the static of sleep.

No one replied. "Hello?" I said again, my voice clearer now.

Someone on the other end was breathing.

"Carlow?" I said. I don't know why, but I sensed it was him.

He mumbled something that sounded like "Lonnie?" but I wasn't sure.

"No," I said uncertainly.

Then there was the cold blare of the dial tone.

16

It was hot when I woke the next morning—the living room sticky and humid. The weather had changed overnight and a streak of sunlight burned across my legs. I could hear William crying through the monitor. I sat up, and found Alex sitting too—shirtless, his skinny torso emerging from a pool of blankets. Our eyes met, but I didn't say anything, just dashed upstairs to lift William from his crib. When I carried him down I found Alex was gone.

"So," Lonnie said, cuddling William on the ground. I expected her to say something about Alex, but she didn't seem to even register his disappearance. "There's kind of something I forgot. Don't be mad at me."

Her mouth was in the middle of a sheepish smile-frown. "What is it?" I said.

"I'm supposed to do this reading. At the end of the week. Well, *you're* supposed to."

I glared at her. "What am I supposed to read?"

"I have a short story," she said. "It's not very long. I didn't not tell you on purpose, I swear. I just forgot about it, but don't worry, we can totally blow it off. I don't care what any of these people think. We can just call Tibby and say you're sick or something. It's no big deal."

Of course my first thought was to agree to never go back to that horrible A-frame, but then I realized this might be the only opportunity for me to access Lonnie's writing. If I told her I'd do it she would just hand the story over.

I said, "I dunno, maybe I could do it," thinking I could take it back later, just trying out her reaction.

"Really?" she said, squinting at me.

"Yeah," I said. "Maybe."

She smiled then and awkwardly pressed William between us in a hug. Her hair still smelled like pond water—that muddy mineral scent.

"That's going to get my dad off my back so much," she said. "You have no idea how annoyed he'd be to hear I bailed."

She still had her head on my shoulder. "You don't have to do a good job or anything. I'm not looking to impress him. I just wasn't looking forward to any angry emails."

Lonnie's story was about a woman who married a man with a twin. She then gave birth to twin girls, making her the only singular member of the family.

> *Karen thought of Tom now the way she had once thought of her husband, with blind endearment. The two men were so similar, it was impossible to delude herself into thinking her life would be*

much different if she were to swap one for the other; still, sometimes she thought about DNA and wondered—if she had met Tom first, if they had fallen in love and gotten married, if they had conceived at the exact same time, would they have had the same children?

Karen had not expected these particular girls to come out of her. They were far more silent than she had anticipated. They contented themselves by lying in piles throughout the house and whispering to each other. Even as babies they'd been that way. Karen remembered taking them to the playground shortly after they'd learned to walk. She'd expected them to run around wildly, to chase after them, but they stood sucking the collars of their tiny coats, watching the other children with big eyes. Karen picked up a large stick and ran it along the metal fence that encased the playground, making loud clanging sounds. She shouted, she climbed the jungle gym, sat down atop the metal slide and banged her boots against it, the noise ringing out across the park, making the other mothers turn and stare. She grinned, to show the girls it was okay. They stood below her, looking up in fear, clinging to each other.

She'd taken the girls to doctors, but instead of agreeing with her that there could be something wrong, the doctors had smiled, delighted that they could drink water from heavy glass tumblers without spilling, that they could write their names already at the age of three, that when prompted delicately, they could utter eloquent full-sentence responses to a few basic questions—albeit their voices were so quiet the doctors had to lean down and sit very still in order to hear.

My first thought was *Isn't this a little obvious?* A woman considers swapping out her husband? Couldn't she come up with anything else?

Tom and Ralph sat next to each other on the couch and Karen, in an armchair across the coffee table, studied the brothers as they spoke. Ralph shaved his beard occasionally; his chin and cheeks were still visible below the scruff. Tom's beard was neat and trimmed, but also thick, he hadn't shaved for years. Their voices were a little different; Ralph's a little lower and scratchier, perhaps affected or from smoking. There was a slight difference in their height, though you couldn't tell when they were sitting down. Her own twins were also slightly distinctive in stature. The doctor had told her it was because they'd shared a placenta, and the nutrients had gone to one before the other.

The differences in the brothers' personalities were harder to pin down. They had separate lives—separate jobs and cities—but if you transplanted one with the other would their reactions be any different? There was no way to know. It seemed to Karen that Tom was more polite. He held doors for her, allowed her the space to walk ahead of him should they meet a narrowed sidewalk. He apologized for interrupting and quieted others so she could be heard. He looked at her with interest. These aspects were probably not actual variance, however, but just the things that tended to fade over the years, within a marriage.

"Look!" said Tom, pointing to the arched window at the front of the room. "It's snowing!"

Karen looked. Flurries of white flew past the glass. The city was quiet outside, but she could hear a distant siren somewhere, the meow of a sad stray cat. She could hear Tom's neighbors through the wall behind her, preparing dinner in their own house, the thuds of other people's noisy children dashing up and down the stairs.

Tom departed to the kitchen to give the turkey a last baste and Karen followed. "I'll help," she said, hoisting herself up. Above the sofa was a rectangular mirror framed in gold. Karen caught sight of herself for a moment—her hair flat from her winter hat, her complexion dull and pale, the matching gray shadows under each gray eye. She didn't look old yet, but she could see what she would look like later, when she was old, when all the shadows deepened.

The kitchen was small, a little yellow space at the bottom of the house, lit up blindingly bright by fluorescent bulbs. Tom stood at the strip of counter space watching a thermometer in the turkey rise. Karen had only intended to offer to help carry out plates and flatware, but instead she wrapped her arms around Tom, feeling the soft flannel of his shirt and the pearly buttons running up the front, feeling the beginnings of a pudge developing where his taut belly used to be, feeling the hard edges of his hip bones near the waist of his corduroy pants. The pudge attracted her most. It was a sign of time passing, outward evidence of the decline she felt. The softness drew her hands there soothingly; the softness telling her decline was a gentle thing, gradual, supple even; it wasn't going to hurt her. She breathed in the scent between his shoulder blades, pine soap and turkey fat. She dropped her hands as Tom turned around slowly. His eyebrows were furrowed, but he was smiling. "Karen?" he said.

She forced a laugh. The faux-laugh became real almost immediately as she realized the simplicity of her solution, how easy this action would be to explain away, and soon she was clutching the counter. "I'm so sorry," she said between convulsions. "I must be a little drunk. On an empty stomach, you know. I thought you were my husband."

I had a hard time looking up from the stack of papers when I was done. I pretended to be reading for much longer than I actually was. I didn't know what to do with the fact that I liked the story—that I somehow felt deeply sorry for the woman in it, though there was no reason to feel that way.

A thick envy welled up. Stronger envy than when I thought of her and Carlow together. It made me wonder what I could've achieved, with everything she was handed. I don't know why exactly, since the only thing I wrote were lists and maps—endless notes for a nonexistent project, a project of which I had no concept. Her talent made me certain somehow that I could've eclipsed her, if only I'd had the time and resources.

She must've been able to tell that I was just scanning the same sentences over and over. "Is it that bad?" she said.

I looked up and saw her son crawling on her. She ignored him, though he was pulling her hair hard enough to make her head jerk to the right. Her face was filled with a genuine sort of shame I wasn't expecting. That expression made it impossible to tell her anything but the truth.

"I like it," I said.

Her face didn't relax. "Really," I said. "I think it's very good."

"Shut up!" she said.

"No?" I said. "I won't?"

She laughed then, in a way I'd never heard before—a sort of startled yelp that caused her to clasp a hand over her mouth in embarrassment.

"My opinion should mean nothing to you," I said. "Why would you be nervous in the first place?"

"I never stop being nervous," she said. "It means so much to me, it's the most important thing, even though I always let everything else get in the way. I never share it with anybody, not James, not Carlow, not anybody."

I smiled, my feelings of envy transforming so easily into a sort of happiness. As always, I was happy to be in on one of her secrets.

"Also, you're a writer, aren't you?" she said. "You're always scribbling in that notebook of yours. And I always see you reading when Billy naps."

I thought I'd been careful to hide the notebook from her. I took it out only when she was gone, or in the office with Carlow. It unnerved me to know I'd slipped up without even realizing it.

"I read a lot just because I'm bored," I said, but she nodded with her head tilted as if to say, *Keep telling yourself that.*

17

That night we decided to get drunk. Or, rather, Lonnie decided to get me drunk. I didn't understand her aim. I assured her I was perfectly capable of reading five pages in front of everyone regardless of my level of inebriation, but she lined up four shots on the counter before we left the cabin, did one herself, and then pushed the others toward me. I'd never taken a shot of straight gin before, but it was the only alcohol we had in the house. Dutifully, I tossed them back all in a row. The juniper flavor reminded me of pine trees.

We were late arriving at the A-frame and I stumbled in loudly, tripping on the threshold, nearly laughing, catching myself just in time to notice Gigi, framed by the wall of windows, in the middle of some kind of one-woman performance. Lonnie had put William in a fancy wrap and he was already asleep against her—his eyes darting back and forth under his eyelids in the midst of a dream, his fingers drooping out of his mouth, slick with saliva.

There was no formal dinner that night and the big table had been replaced by rows of chairs. Lonnie and I tiptoed over to the bar, where glasses of wine were set in neat rows. I already felt warm and light enough but

I took the glass she passed me anyway, and told myself to pretend to drink, putting the wine to my lips without swallowing.

"Don't be nervous," Lonnie whispered to me.

In fact, I felt calmer than I had at dinner earlier that week, partially because I knew now they all accepted my false identity but also because it seemed far easier to just read something than to attempt to discuss work I hadn't done.

Lonnie and I watched from a pair of chairs in the back row as Gigi scratched at her face in some kind of trance, repeating, "My cunt, my country, my cunt, my country."

Though I actually found the performance arresting, when I glanced at Lonnie she crossed her eyes and hung her mouth open in a terrible look of stupor. I choked a little, trying not to laugh, even if I thought she was judging Gigi too harshly.

When it was my turn Lonnie grinned and squeezed my arm. Tibby Walbridge pulled over a microphone stand and started talking about the great things that were expected from the release of my book. *Was Lonnie working on a book?*

I rose when the room started applauding, realizing how many more people were in those chairs than there had been around the dinner table the other night. Either more had arrived or many had forgone dining with Tibby entirely. Though my heart wasn't racing—I was too drunk to be nervous—my legs wobbled. I tried to concentrate on walking but couldn't be exactly sure where my raised foot was going to land. I managed to make it to the microphone and found, miraculously, that I was still holding Lonnie's story. I unfolded the paper and cleared my throat.

I had intended to just plow through the piece, but as I stood there in front of everyone it occurred to me that I should perhaps relish this moment, when I was Lonnie Bernard—young writer, effortlessly beautiful, universally desired, daughter to all manner of privilege.

I looked out at the crowd—looked at them smiling at me, and for a split second mistook the situation entirely. It was like a flashbulb went off and suddenly everyone seated before me was familiar. I saw Lonnie's mother and father, though of course I had no idea what they looked like. I saw her old girlfriends from Marymount, her boyfriends, camp counselors, nannies, and teachers. They weren't wearing uniforms or any other identifying articles, but I recognized their faces as Lonnie would've. They seemed to recognize me too. They were just staring blankly, waiting for me to start speaking. I was drunk, of course, but it seemed far less like an inebriated fantasy than a real, if momentary, lapse of some kind. I thought about Lonnie's belief in ghosts as a temporary overlap between worlds. The image was gone as quickly as it had arrived. The room returned to normal. The experience had scared me, and I wondered if that was what dispelled it.

"Thanks to Tibby Walbridge," I said, my voice shaky, feeling sober now.

The strangers in front of me clapped politely.

I looked down at the paper, thankful it was there, thankful to have Lonnie's words to guide me through the rest of my time at the microphone. Though I tried to add expression, tried to concentrate on the paragraphs and sentences, the meaning behind them, it was impossible. Each individual word was separate from those surrounding it in my mind. I knew the story, and seemed to be reading it, but I didn't comprehend the meaning at all that time around—I was just reading a long list of words. I was, however, thankful my hand wasn't shaking the paper too violently. I was thankful the waver in my voice was minimal.

Monday morning the girls went back to school. Karen poured them two glasses of cold milk and buttered a pile of bread. She combed the knots from their silky hair and helped them into navy dresses. When she buttoned the second twin's coat, she tapped a fingernail against the child's thin wrist. "You're not a doll, are you?" she said. "You're not made of porcelain?"

The girl blushed—two circular pink spots engulfed her milky cheeks. "My girls are so pretty," Karen said.

As they made their way out of the door Karen

grabbed her winter coat and a pack of Ralph's cigarettes, even though she hadn't smoked since college. "I'll walk with you," she said.

It was a short walk, only to the corner, but the biting air felt good to Karen. Her lawn was powdered with thin patches of snow and the street had rivulets of slush. There were a few other children at the bus stop. Two were in the twins' grade and one was a year younger. Mary, mother of the younger one, stood in a black wool jacket that tied around the waist, making her look thin despite the layers.

Karen brushed Mary's arm. "Hi."

"Hi," Mary replied.

Karen took the cigarettes from her pocket. "You know," Mary said, "it's my day to wait. You don't have to be here."

"I know," Karen replied and held up the cigarettes. "Ralph doesn't like me to smoke in the house."

She shrugged and Mary nodded. Karen realized then that she didn't have any matches. She dug deep in her pockets, feeling the wads of used tissue and a bundled pair of cotton gloves, knowing there was nothing else. "I should quit, though," she said, looking at the pack in her hand.

Mary nodded again.

"I guess the snow has started," Karen said.

Mary turned to her. "Do you mind?" she said. "If you're here, do you mind if I go back in the house?"

"No . . . no," Karen replied, flustered.

Mary gave her son a quick kiss on the head and dashed away. Karen watched her retreat.

One of the children, a boy with missing front teeth, tugged on Karen's coat. She smiled down at him. "Missus?" he said. "Are you in love?"

Her twins stood behind him, watching, giggling into their mittens. Karen touched the boy's warm soft cheek. "Of course," she said to him. "Of course I am."

The boy ducked away, grinning.

After the bus came and the children waved goodbye to her, Karen stood on the walk for a long time. She looked around her neighborhood. The houses had been strung with strands of twinkle lights over the weekend—the only thing blooming in the snow. If she walked for fifteen minutes in a straight line to the north she would be in the woods. But she didn't move. She took out a cigarette and perched the filter between her dry lips. When she exhaled her breath came out in a thick fog from the cold.

When I reached the last word I looked up. All those strange faces were staring in a manner that completely unnerved me. They looked confused more than anything. Then they suddenly began to clap. I had no concept of how well or awful I'd read, had no concept of how the writing had been received. I folded the papers and returned to my seat to find Lonnie gone. Though I suspected her absence was because William had woken and she hadn't wanted to disrupt the reading, it still made me anxious.

I sat through another writer and then a slideshow of artwork, not paying any attention, before we were all finally released to get more wine and partake of the appetizers coming out of the kitchen. I stood, intending to leave immediately to find Lonnie, to ask her if she'd caught any part of my performance, but was instead surrounded by a throng of people.

They complimented my work. They wanted to know when the book was coming out. They wanted to know what it was about, how far along I was, if I knew so-and-so or had read such-and-such. They wanted to know where I had gone to school and whose classes I'd taken. One woman wanted to know where I'd bought my dress. I gave them half-hearted answers, a mixture between complete ignorance and blatant lies, then emerged onto the patio, my legs still shaky from the alcohol, weak from not having eaten. Someone handed me a cigarette. They were all smoking, so I was smoking too. I hadn't smoked in a long time, and I struggled to remember what I was doing, how often to tap off the ashes, where to put my hand to avoid catching myself on fire. It seemed like a dangerous thing to be holding with that amount of alcohol inside me.

I was laughing at someone's joke though I hadn't understood it. Gigi was talking about how I was a mother too, and how that was the real impressive thing about my art—that I'd managed to continue making anything at all. Though I wasn't deluded into thinking I actually was Lonnie, into believing any of those people, as she spoke—my shoulder pressed up against her armpit in a way that made me feel sick—I kept thinking: *Where's my baby where's my baby where's my baby.*

I found them later, after I'd been served a handful of tiny toasts and little fried things on sticks and was sober enough to excuse myself and make my way to Lonnie's car. Lonnie had laid William in the back seat where, I could see because the door was open, he was curled in a little ball next to his car seat. Meanwhile, Lonnie and Alex were side by side on the hood, their heads against the windshield, fireflies flitting around them, like some kind of gross romance movie. I cursed myself for not leaving sooner, for not even thinking about Alex. I could hear their low voices whispering and laughing together.

My heels crunched over the gravel, too quick for me to worry about getting caught on the uneven surface. Lonnie popped up from behind Alex's body as I approached. "Hey," she said. "How'd it go? I had to leave, Billy was about to cry."

Her casualness annoyed me. "It went great," I said, looking at her mouth, trying to make out in the dim light coming from the open car door, whether or not her lips were swollen from kissing.

"Hi." Alex offered me a little wave. I ignored him, though I was conscious of my rudeness. "I'm sorry," I said. "You got me way too drunk. Can we go?"

Lonnie slid off the car hood. "Of course," she said.

Alex followed her and they exchanged a long hug. I lifted William and put him in his car seat. I wasn't particularly gentle and he woke and started crying as I buckled him in. I was glad—his cries dragged Lonnie into the car behind us. The interior lights switched off when she shut her door and the dash lit up green. She turned to me in the dark, ignoring William's tired crying. "Are you okay?" she said, her hand on my knee.

"I don't like Alex," I told her. "He's a creep."

She laughed. "He's just a boy."

It made me feel bad, the way she said it. I was acting like a teenager over what? Why didn't I feel the same way toward Carlow or James? Ostensibly they had a lot more over me than this waiter from the middle of nowhere. Lonnie's attraction to them was logical though, fitting to her character. I didn't understand why she was giving this waiter the time of day and my lack of understanding made me angry. Or maybe I was just jealous. I was the nanny. I was the single one. It should've been me he liked.

She didn't push me on the issue. She just turned the engine over and said, "Anyway, just one of those people we'll never see again."

Lonnie drove us all the way back to the city the next day. I was sweating and aching and fell asleep in the passenger seat for half the ride. Eventually we stopped at a gas station and bought coffee in Styrofoam cups. We let William wander in a patch of grass for a few minutes before resuming our trip. Lonnie lifted up her sunglasses and squinted at me. The heat was oppressive again, now that we were closer to home. "You read a lot better than I could've," she said. "You weren't nervous at all."

"I thought you missed it."

"I only missed the last paragraph. Anyway, am I crazy or was that really fun? Screwing with everybody?"

"Ask me when this hangover wears off," I said, though I knew, even then, the fact that Lonnie had thought of the experience as fun was enough to rewrite everything in my mind. Something ridiculous was happening to me.

18

The entry I'd been waiting for. I'd anticipated her saying something basic like "We have a new nanny named Elle. She seems okay with Billy." I tried not to get my hopes up too far. I didn't wait for her to say anything like "She's our best nanny yet."

When the entry came, it wasn't in reference to my work at all. Though it wasn't horribly insulting, it made me feel gawky and awkward, to see myself reflected through her eyes. I have been dreading writing it down, though I remember it word for word.

> *Elle is a strange person. I didn't really know her until we went away. I still don't really know her, though lying next to someone for a while makes them feel closer even if you don't learn anything. Here is what I know:*
>
> *She is probably very lonely.*
>
> *She feels uncomfortable talking about men and sex. I have no sense of whether or not she's ever slept with anyone—ever.*
>
> *She never talks about her friends.*
>
> *She moved across the country in order to leave*

everything behind instead of seek anything out.

There's a lot she doesn't tell me.

She doesn't give much up, but I like the way she holds herself. I like the way she hunches over a table, the volume of her voice, the way she eats. She's not a little fluttering girl, though she looks practically malnourished. You can tell something about the way she was raised, that's it. There's a certain kind of childhood that spits out a certain naïve, anxious, occasionally blundering but ultimately charming person. She eats everything, that's exactly what it is. You should've seen her at this dinner. I watched through the window as she just kept shoveling it in. I just want to keep feeding her.

Her writing inspired a certain amount of resentment in me. I had friends, or at least I felt I did, though we'd never been close and I hadn't seen any of them for a long time. I decided to invite Sam out for a drink one night. She sat with her shoulders slunk inward, her back hunched as if she were trying to take up less room than she did—her posture a permanent apology. I'd had a lot of friends like that growing up. I suppose they made me feel good by comparison, made me feel confident and effervescent. I used to think girls like Sam looked up to me, but it's just as likely that they were judging me all the time.

The loud music of the bar covered the silences that fell between us so I felt grateful for it.

"Are you seeing anyone?" I asked, when we'd worn out the subject of her work.

At first it felt like an imitation of interest, but I quickly realized I was hungry for it—this interaction.

"No," she said. "Not right now."

She smiled, but that was it, that was all she was going to say.

We'd never had these kinds of conversations. We'd always been capable of leaving well enough alone. She didn't follow up with reciprocal questions. Maybe she was not as awkward as I imagined, but rather just incredibly self-involved. Why didn't she care?

"I've been thinking lately, I don't want to wear makeup anymore," she said.

Sam was never someone I'd known to wear makeup in the first place. "Once I wore eyeliner," she said. "And I found it blurred all over my face later that night. I can't do it."

She really did have a bad habit of touching her face constantly. When I thought about it too much everything about her disgusted me. I pictured her hands on the sticky bar, the subway pole, and now fiddling with her mouth—the lips natural, but too pink somehow, not the right shade for her face. "It just seems wrong though," she said, "posturing that way."

I wasn't wearing much makeup, though I'd taken to

painting the cat-eye swoop across my top lid like Lonnie. I'd spent a long night in front of the mirror perfecting the delicate technique on the quivering canvas. It was annoying to have her pick out this little detail I'd struggled over and label it as posturing.

We'd lived side by side for years, Sam and I, and in the end there was nothing there but that—just a shared address, an unwanted intimacy. I had nothing to say.

"I wish we could be friends," I muttered, though I hardly meant it. What I really wanted was for her to be someone else. I didn't really want anything from her at all.

All around us people were laughing, shouting over the music, grabbing onto one another. It all seemed obscene, being outside of it. A couple next to us started to kiss—lapping at each other's mouths. A bunch of monkeys at the zoo.

"We *are* friends," Sam said.

"Just better, I mean," I stumbled. "I mean, I'm sorry."

Later that night the sound came sharp through my open window: a woman's scream. Though it woke me, I was sure of what I'd heard. My back shot up straight, the sheet falling around my waist. I waited, but heard nothing else, nothing distinct. I strained my ears with anticipation and wondered if that faint rustling was hurried footsteps or merely pigeons on the roof. When I couldn't stand it anymore I walked down the hall.

"Sam," I whispered into her dark bedroom. "I heard a scream."

"I didn't hear anything," she said, groaning. "Go back to bed."

"It was a woman's scream."

"It's a bad neighborhood," she said, dismissing me.

I couldn't go back to sleep. Instead, I checked all my jacket pockets and eventually fished out a loosey. I rarely smoked but there was sometimes one stale cigarette floating around my things, left over from an unremembered moment of indulgence or anxiety. I pulled on a pair of shorts, shoved a matchbook in my pocket, and ran down the stairs and out the front door of my building.

Across the street a group of men were sitting on plastic buckets, smoking too. They said nothing but laughed as I walked by. It seemed like a bad omen, but I hurried past anyway, heading toward the tall LeRoi house.

Every window was dark when I arrived. It was three a.m. and the street was quiet save for the scurrying of rats back and forth across the sidewalk. I was beginning to doubt myself. Had I dreamed that scream? Was I making up an excuse to visit the house at night? Was I just aching for some imaginary ghost to reach out and hold my hand? I sucked on my cigarette, promising myself I'd turn around just as soon as it was out.

"You my neighbor?" The voice made me jump. I turned to see a figure emerge from the dark doorway. I tried to see if he could possibly be the oldest son—if he was in his forties, handsome like his father. A yellow beam from a nearby streetlight bounced off his forehead but he was too far away to see in any detail. I could only make out his frame—tall and lanky.

"Sort of," I said, gesturing across the street, in the opposite direction from my real building. "They don't like us to smoke in front of the building so I took a walk. Tenant's association." As I said it I realized it was true.

"Is this a church?" I asked.

He didn't answer, but said instead, "You go to church?"

"No," I replied.

He didn't respond, just nodded.

"It's late," he said. "You're pretty, you know? You shouldn't be out here."

"Why?" I asked, my voice shaking as I said it.

He stood and turned to go inside. "Get home safe," he said, and I swear, the way he said it sounded like a threat.

My heart pounded the whole way home. I felt the interaction must foretell some violence. I clenched my sweaty palms together, expecting something to detach from the shadows and swallow me up, expecting to turn and see someone following me. I felt deflated when I reached my front door without incident. Even the men on the plastic buckets had gone home. I was alone on an empty street. In the distance the glowing lights of a late-night bus approached.

19

As it turned out the violence that night with the scream predicted had nothing to do with me. I was working my usual hours when a text came through from Lonnie asking if it would be all right for her to come home late. I agreed, having nowhere else to be. I'd already put William to bed when I heard the downstairs door open and assumed Lonnie and James would shortly come up to greet me in the living room, but instead I'd heard only silence, so I went down to investigate.

She was sprawled on the ground, wearing a sheer white button-down and little black panties. I glanced toward the front door and saw her dark pants on the floor, in the same uncomfortable position as her legs, the left knee bending the lower leg outward, as if they were still a part of her body, despite the distance. My mind rapidly fired everything I knew about Lonnie but nothing added up to the inert body in front of me. Was it just drunkenness or something self-inflicted? Had she taken drugs before? Had she seemed depressed? Shouldn't there have been a warning sign?

I crouched beside her, pressed up against the cupboard under the sink. I pushed hair away from her face. Her skin was warm, I noticed with relief. I couldn't manage the courage required to touch her neck and feel for a pulse, so instead, I put a finger under her nose, waiting for wisps of air.

Then, as if by miracle, her eyelids flew open. Her hand reached out and grabbed the flesh around my waist with a force that startled me. "Elle," she said and then louder, moaning, "Elle!"

She'd returned from the dead with a terrifying vengeance and my name on her lips. I scrambled up, her nails leaving red marks on my hip bones, and backed away.

Her breathing was shallow and raspy, and after her eyes opened, they wouldn't close again, though she was still completely motionless in every other way.

Her mouth opened and closed slowly, but she wasn't forming words, just vague soft sounds, like a baby. I was confused and terrified. Had she been out alone? I ran upstairs to find my phone, and typed out first James's, and then Carlow's number, one after the other, but I was too disoriented to call either.

I ran back down the stairs. She hadn't moved. "Lonnie," I said, bending over her again. "I'm going to call 911," I said. "Okay?"

She said something that sounded at first like nonsense, but I leaned closer and she tried again. "So confused," she said. And then, "So cold."

"Lonnie," I said, touching her face, slapping her a little. "Where were you? Did you take something?"

"No," she said, but I didn't know which question she was answering. Slowly, she blinked her bloodshot eyes. "So cold," she repeated.

I ran up the stairs again and brought a pillow and throw from the couch. I wished I could move her. I tried, briefly, but even her head was heavy with dead weight. I struggled to push the pillow underneath—her face plopped onto the velvet fabric with a startling thud.

"Okay," I said, tucking the blanket around her. "Okay. You're going to be fine."

I felt self-conscious, as I said it, like she could tell I had no idea what was going to happen to her.

I kept looking at my phone as I sat next to her on the kitchen floor, stroking her hair while she breathed in that harsh, raspy way. Her eyes never closed, though they didn't move either, like she wasn't really seeing whatever she was looking at. I imagined having to slide my fingertips down over her eyelids to close them, imagined her dead. For a moment I could see myself stepping into her place somehow—comforting James in his grief until he accepted me as William's rightful mother, as his next beautiful wife. I'd never really thought very much about James until then. He was rarely home during my hours. I'd often wondered whether he was also having an affair, if her dalliance was just a response to his.

The chaos of James returning home, supposedly from a late business meeting, interrupted these fantasies as well as Lonnie's and my private moment together. "She just passed out," I said. "She made it home, but can't seem to move."

"Call 911!" James yelled at me. He grabbed my phone from my hand but then shoved it back at me when he failed to unlock the screen. "Why haven't you called yet?"

"She just got here," I said, my voice shaking. "This just happened."

I didn't know what to say to the man on the phone. "She just came in the door and passed out."

"She's unconscious?"

"No," I said. "She's conscious, but she can't move. She's having trouble talking."

"Yep," he said. "She was at a bar?"

"I don't know," I said. "What do you mean 'yep'?"

"We'll send someone out."

When the paramedics arrived they just nodded, like they'd seen it all a million times. One shined a little light in her eyes, pulled up the lids. "Yep, they're dilated."

"Were you drinking? Were you at a bar?"

Lonnie didn't answer.

They turned to me. "She was roofied. Happens all the time."

"Does she need to go to the hospital?"

"We can't really make that call. We'll take her if you want, but likely, she'll just come out of it soon. She's still conscious so she might not have gotten a whole dose. She'll probably be sick tomorrow though."

James said, "No, no. She would kill me if I took her to the hospital."

She did seem to be rejecting the idea of it, moaning in a raspy, awful way. I knew about her last experience there, for William's birth, from her journal, but I didn't say anything.

James signed a paper stating he was turning down further treatment and the paramedics left shortly after. I felt bad for calling them, since they really hadn't done anything. "Can I get you something?" I asked, feeling shaky and awkward. "Coffee?"

They shook their heads, having more important places to be, of course.

"Here," I grabbed one of Lonnie's green apples and shoved it at one of them, questioning my own motives as I did so. "Take it, take it."

He waved his hands in front of me, refusing, and shut the door.

Then James and I were left alone with only the sound of Lonnie's breath. Neither of us spoke for an uncomfortable beat. I rubbed the waxy apple skin against my palms. We both just looked at her there on the ground. I felt thankful to James for returning in time to make the decision about the hospital.

"Let's get her into bed," James said eventually, and we struggled together, nearly laughing from the difficulty, of getting the dead weight of her up two skinny flights of stairs. I had her ankles, those smooth bony parts, connecting her tiny limp feet to the rest of her. Her feet were cold as ice bumping into my sweaty arms as we walked.

Upstairs, we shrouded her in the white bedding, pulling it right up under her chin. James rinsed out the toothbrush cup from the bathroom and tried to get her to sip some water, but it mostly just dribbled down her chin. There was nothing to do then but sit there, the two of us on the edge of the bed, and look at her as her breathing slowly returned to normal. I was filled with the urge to go down to the freezer and pull out her frozen journal, to leaf through the cold pages right there in front of both of them, to reread the entry about William's birth. James would never know what it was. So long as I didn't flash her handwriting in his direction he would think it was my own notebook. But I didn't have the guts. Instead I just sat there studying her face. Her eyelids, streaked with tiny blue veins, were finally closed, though her eyes couldn't stop moving beneath them. Her mouth moved sometimes too, her lips parting and coming together again, still emitting an occasional guttural rasp. I expected James to tell me I could leave, but since he didn't I assumed he liked my silent presence there next to him; he must've found it comforting. I guess we were both just waiting for her breathing to fully return to normal.

Finally James spoke. "She said she was at a bar? Alone?" He sounded confused and doubtful.

"Yes," I said, though I actually couldn't remember

whether or not she'd answered that question. Then William started fussing and I went up to soothe him back to sleep. As I came out of the nursery, James cornered me in the hallway. His tie was askew, his dotted socks peeking out from under his slacks.

"Is he asleep?" he whispered.

"Yes," I said.

He slinked past me and I watched through the open nursery door as he knelt by William's crib, looked at his little face through the slats in the soft strip of light from the hallway. I'd spent hardly any time with James at that point. I hadn't really thought about him other than to worry what would happen if he found out about the affair. He was arguably more attractive than Carlow—his jaw and cheekbones cut more sharply, his hair thicker, his shoulders wider.

When he came back I was still standing there. I didn't know where to go or what to do at this point. "Listen," he said, a twinge of desperation in his voice. "We're going to the Hamptons for a couple of weeks at the end of August. You have to come with us. I mean, you don't have to but will you, please?"

I nodded. "Okay," I said. Of course I would follow them anywhere they asked.

He put a warm hand on my shoulder. I noticed his lips were bruised with wine. "We'd be lost without you," he said, an odd thing for someone who'd spoken to me only a handful of times to say.

"No," I replied.

He shook me a little. "Yes," he said. He pulled me in for a hug then, and kissed the top of my head, where my hair fell in a part. I don't know why, but I leaned my head back, bringing my face up in front of his. I'd like to think I did it simply because he'd done something unexpected—kissing my head. It's a natural reaction to look at someone when you question them, but in truth I probably did it so his lips could find mine in the dark, in case they wanted to, which they did without further hesitation. His skin smelled like cedar. His mouth tasted sweet, more like chocolate than wine. He whispered something to me, his voice deep and soft. It was an apology. Then he kissed me again. I kissed back so he wound his hands under my skirt, feeling the seams of my underwear. It was an old pair, full of little holes like everything I wore under my clothes, but he didn't let on that it mattered. I pushed my hips into him, hoping to feel his erection against me.

He pulled away then, brought his hands up, and cradled my face between his palms. I probably looked like a deer in the middle of the road—that wide-eyed look of dumb shock; that look that people mistake for innocence and stupidity. Actually, the deer were there long before the roads, wending their way over the same corridors for generations. People don't understand on those dark country roads, why they don't get out of the way, but the deer probably just feel the same way.

"Give me your address again," he said, breaking the silence between us. "So I can order you a car."

At the front door he pulled out his wallet. "I almost forgot to pay you," he said. "You have to remind me. Don't let me get away with that."

"I wasn't thinking about it," I said, though it wasn't true.

He counted out a stack of fifty-dollar bills. "I'm giving you extra," he said.

"Why?"

"I'm just giving you extra," he said, shoving the money at me.

Lonnie was sick the whole next day. I came to watch William even though it was a Saturday. I wondered if James would try anything else while Lonnie was incapacitated, but he was distant and locked himself up in the office when he wasn't bringing the garbage pail of Lonnie's vomit back and forth from the bed to the toilet. Lonnie couldn't get out of bed to make it to the bathroom. Maybe he felt guilty. He probably should've.

"My legs don't work," Lonnie said when I peeked in to check on her while William napped. "I can move them now, but they won't hold me up."

"You really scared me," I said. It was the same garbage pail I'd taken her gum out of and put into my mouth, I realized.

"I feel like such an idiot," she said. "I don't remember anything. It's all a blank."

"You can't blame yourself," I said. "What's the last thing you remember?"

"I was just having one drink before I came home. I never drink alone, but I needed it. No one talked to me. Nothing strange happened. I remember leaving but then that's it."

"It was only one drink?"

"I have this pain in my hand," she said. "Right down the middle. It won't go away."

"You were poisoned."

"No," she said. "It's in my hand but it's in my mind."

I sat down on the bed next to her, and she grabbed my arm. "Elle," she said. "Thank God you were there. I just kept thinking about when I had William. There was a time when they left me all alone in the room and I tried to get up but passed out on the floor from the pain. It's so scary to be alone."

Her skin was still as ashen as the night before, her face totally devoid of its usual blush. Her eyebrows furrowed, as with pain. I leaned down, and without letting myself stop to think, kissed her once, full on her sour mouth, then got up and left. We never discussed the gesture, but I felt better about James after that.

On my way home, I found a small bar with a banner advertising hamburgers over the door. It was as dark inside as it was outside. A few old men were sitting at the counter, hunched over their beers. I could feel them staring at me as

I walked over to a table and sat down. A waitress appeared, an older woman with heavy makeup and a low tank top revealing wrinkled cleavage. Her face was very sallow, as if she hadn't set foot outside the bar in many years. There was a blank look in her eyes that told me she wasn't really seeing me even as she said, "What can I get you?"

"The hamburger," I replied. "Rare. And a whiskey."

As she walked back to the kitchen to put in my order the men at the bar yelled to her, "Barbara! You didn't even say hello!"

She ignored them, but they were at her again when she came out with my food. "Are you deaf or something, Barbara? We're talking to you!"

She put my burger, whiskey, and check down at the same time, then picked up her step a little to get back to the kitchen. The men didn't speak when Barbara was gone, but they did turn on their stools to watch me eat. I didn't care. The burger was seasoned perfectly, with a thick ripe tomato and blood dripping off the lightly toasted bun. I became completely absorbed in eating it.

When I was done, my stomach stretched tight with food, I stuffed a wad of money into the bill book and left the bar. I probably tipped that waitress a hundred bucks. I thought of something my dad liked to say: "Only the rich are stingy."

I can see Lonnie walking out the door of her brownstone, leaving it unlocked, and driving away. I can see her at a bartending job in some other, smaller city, collecting cash tips, living alone, getting old and sallow like that waitress. She would learn to distrust attention from men, since so much of it would be unwanted. She would go home and turn the TV on for company. This is more or less what happened to my own mother, what I imagine probably happened to the LeRoi woman who'd abandoned her daughter if she was still alive. Though it enters my mind often, I don't like thinking of Lonnie this way.

She might've left with Carlow, but I didn't like that ending either. Their lives wouldn't have ended up so different, and anyway it wasn't what she wanted, it seemed to me. She never spoke about him, in her journal or coded in her fiction, as anything so incredible. He was merely a remembrance of past excitements. In the Hamptons, I even felt she might be trying to pawn him off on me.

I try to give her another story. It's hard to imagine one that doesn't revolve around men—being desperately in love with them or sick of them or ruined by them. What I can see is her alone in a room at night, that little electric clock from her office glowing on a bookshelf as she scribbles something in a notebook. She doesn't know whether or not it's any good, but that doesn't matter, that work comes later and is less important. The main thing is getting the words down in the first place, the movement of her hand, watching the filled pages multiply. When I picture this, though, I'm never really sure if I'm seeing her or myself.

20

I needed soup dumplings that night with the same specific urgency that I've needed every meal since I stopped puking every hour in the first trimester. Jimmy drove me down to Chinatown. We couldn't find a restaurant with an empty table, but an old man gave up his chair so I could shovel the hot dumplings into my mouth at a table—though I was surrounded by strangers, with Jimmy behind me, trying to eat standing up. I was in quite a lot of pain, and kept stopping to make terrible faces, then would go back to eating.

Afterward we bought a bag of longans and I started peeling them open as we walked. Jimmy said they looked like eyeballs and refused to try any. Then I felt something wet and worried my water was breaking. I made Jimmy walk me back to the car and sat on the side of the road with the parking light on, trying to maneuver into a position that would allow me to see into my underwear. It was blood. I was suddenly really scared. I knew you could sometimes bleed but it seemed like too much. I bled right through my dress, I could see it on the seat. I started crying and Jimmy tried to calm me down.

We didn't have our things with us, and the hospital was all the way uptown, but Dr. Leland told us to come in right then so Jimmy called C to bring us the suitcases. I told him to call somebody else, but he didn't listen. The pain was bad by the time we arrived at Mount Sinai, but I was only three centimeters dilated, so they told us I should take a walk around the block. I told them it simply wasn't possible, but everyone kept saying, "Of course it is, of course it is," and Jimmy dragged me outside and into the park.

I was clinging to him when C showed up, carrying our bags. He was very sheepish. I remembered that my dress was all bloody—it seemed cruel of the nurses to send me on this walk with a bloody dress and cruel of Jimmy to invite C to come see me this way. Then a contraction hit, before we'd all exchanged two words, and I suddenly didn't care about any of it—where I was or who I was with. What the hell do either of those men matter? C's sheepishness disgusted me. I vomited up soup dumplings at the edge of the East Meadow. I was unable to crouch down because of the pain, and I ended up covered in it.

C left, no doubt horrified. Jimmy carried our bags in one hand, and supported me with his other arm. Painted in blood and vomit, they finally admitted me.

It was a relief to be in the hospital bed for the first hour or so—a welcome change from everywhere else I'd been that evening. Then the back labor started. Pain layered on top of pain. Dr. Leland said I was progressing nicely; I'd already dilated two more centimeters. He wanted me to try to wait and see if I needed the epidural. I felt then that the hospital was staffed by a series of clowns. I told him he was crazy, and had better order the epidural as quickly as possible.

I started screaming a lot of mad things when he left—about going back out to the park to have my baby alone since no one was helping. Jimmy tried to tell me they knew what they were doing, but I said I'd like to spend hours cutting open his body so he could see what it was like. Resultantly, everyone left me alone for some time. I was in so much pain on the bed that I tried to stand up, but ended up sort of stumbling down to the floor and passing out.

No one came in. I woke up and my vision slowly came back to me. I was sort of on my side, but I worried I'd crushed the baby. I called the nurse, who helped me back into bed and said the baby was fine. I was shaking very badly at this point; when they finally brought the epidural in, they had trouble getting me to hold still for long enough to administer it.

As it turns out epidurals don't do a thing for back labor. My legs were icy cool, totally numb, and my belly too, but my back didn't stop throbbing, not for a minute, which seemed erroneous since that's where they put the damn thing in. I kept telling them something was wrong, that it wasn't strong enough, but they just said that was as good as it was going to get.

I couldn't tell you how long things took from there. I sort of sank into the pain, once I knew there was no possible way to make it go away. I felt like it was a little space I inhabited. Other people existed outside of it, moving around, but they couldn't reach me. It was like being very high—that feeling of existing in multiple dimensions. I sort of oscillated between my own little pain world and then the world of everyone else would rise up for a moment before I went back under alone. I tried to think about how I'd wanted this. It was me who'd wanted the baby, me who'd convinced Jimmy on that train in Bali that it would be better to do it soon. He'd said, "You're getting at least five years ahead of me here."

Everything was so mixed up. I lay there, the nurse pushing her knuckles into my back as I moaned, and tried to imagine what I was thinking on that train. I'd been drinking a lot of red wine. I wanted to make love all the time. It had all been very romantic. How absurd.

The baby came, of course. William was born. It was very early in the morning. Jimmy was holding one of my legs, which I didn't want at all, but the doctor told him to go there and no one was in any position to argue. The doctor told me to look down with the last push and I watched his head come out, then the rest of him, which just slid down, slippery like a fish, in a way that horrified me, making me realize how much of my body had come apart by then.

That's the point where most women probably stop telling their birth story, but for me, the next part is even worse. I thought I'd feel very strong afterward, but I was just immediately very tired. I didn't even care about holding William. It's scary now to think if we were in the wild, no society, just him and me experiencing all that pain, I might've left him in the woods to starve the way some animals abandon their young.

They said I had to deliver the placenta, but I couldn't feel anything to push anymore. I thought I was trying but they said I wasn't. They told me I had to try harder. When it still didn't come the doctor had to remove it by reaching his hand all the way up. I guess they usually put a woman out for it, but they only upped the dosage of the epidural for me. I don't want to think about his hand inside of me. I tried not to look but it was impossible, the nurses were holding me down, my eyes roving everywhere, trying to escape the unbearable pressure.

It feels dumb to talk about childbirth as trauma, but that's how it felt. I couldn't use my right leg properly for the next month. They'd struck a nerve with the epidural, they said, and feeling would probably fully return "eventually."

I keep doing things I think will make me stronger, but it doesn't work.

I skipped a few pages, as she had, and continued:

I've never loved anything more fiercely. This love that is not really like love. It feels markedly close to fear. I've never feared for anything more. I keep waking up while he's sleeping, gripped by panic that he's going to stop breathing; that it's going to be my fault. I wish I could put him back.

21

The Southampton family house was long and low, the shingled roof rising in several curved pitches from the surrounding beach grass like an extension of the landscape. It had been built in the Gilded Age, they told me, and handed down through Lonnie's mother's side of the family. The rooms—like Lonnie's drawers, the boxes, the closets, and the cupboards—never-ending, filled with so many forgotten unused things.

Horse stables with no horses in them. Servants' quarters, which no longer housed servants. Maids came and went inconspicuously, when the family wasn't home. They were not a part of the fabric of the house itself, they merely removed the dust when you weren't looking. It must have been a fantastic amount of dust. The house was built so that members of the family would never have to see or hear one another unless they desired it.

At the top of the house was the nursery—not just a bedroom, but three of them, designed for the sort of large family that had fallen out of fashion. The bedrooms ended in a vast playroom, filled with half-inflated balls, old squeaky tricycles, a smattering of child-sized chairs, and a stage at one end for spontaneous performances. There was a secret cupboard underneath the stage big enough for two small children to fit comfortably inside, or, less comfortably, a skinny woman and her small charge. Lonnie's name was carved crookedly, sloppily, in one wall of the cupboard, deep enough to be traceable with a finger, even in the dark.

We arrived in the evening, by car. They didn't make me find my own way by train, but let me ride in the back seat, like I was a second child. The air was cooler the farther we got from the city, though still filled with moisture. We rolled the windows down and I felt I could eat mouthfuls of the breeze.

We didn't say much on the drive. William was subdued by the view out the window, and we all appreciated the silence.

"You know," Lonnie said at one point. "My hand still hurts. This sort of ache right down the middle."

"Have it looked at" was James's only response.

Between the wealth and Lonnie's criticisms I'd expected her father to be a large villainous man. I pictured him, bearded, behind a huge oak desk in a bow tie. The man who answered the door in Southampton wasn't anything like that.

Robert was small and thin, bordering on delicate. It was as if all his virility had gone into producing his daughter, as if she had sucked the life out of him. Lonnie kissed him on each cheek, her face betraying no sign of emotion. "What are you doing here?" she said. "You didn't tell us you were coming."

"You definitely picked a rough time for me to make it out." His voice was soft and sweet. "I'm trying to imagine you didn't do that on purpose."

"Daddy," Lonnie said, her voice stern despite the childish nickname.

I couldn't help thinking, *What do you call a man with no arms and no legs in the water?*

"You're here now anyway," Lonnie said. "How long can you stay?"

"Through next Monday."

"You'll be here for the Labor Day party!" James said.

"I just want to see my grandson. Where's William?"

I carried him over. Robert was shorter than me by a few inches and leaned in close enough that I could smell the mothy old-man scent coming off his skin. William regarded him curiously, his hand on my breast.

"This is Elle," Lonnie said. "Our nanny."

"Hi," I said.

Robert didn't look at me. He was studying William's face, furrowing his brows. He didn't touch the baby or speak to him, he only looked and then, turning toward Lonnie, said, "More and more like a Thomas," declarative, approving. I guessed that was Lonnie's maiden name.

"Now," he said, turning his attention to me. Our faces were practically touching. "Tell me about yourself."

I laughed nervously, unsure what to say. The sentences that flashed through my mind had no business being related to this man. I didn't like being put on the spot, but I did like the way his attention moved from one thing to the next purposefully—the way he directed his focus entirely.

"I'm from Oregon," I managed.

"You are taking care of our most prized possession," he said, ignoring the information I'd offered.

"Yes." I tried to use my voice to convey an understanding, but it was hard, with only that one word. And equally hard to come up with anything to say after.

"I received nearly two hundred résumés when I posted about needing a nanny on that website," Lonnie said. "I can't believe I found her."

"I didn't know that," I said, caught off-guard by the confession.

"It was fate," Lonnie replied, smiling.

"I hope you know how much we appreciate you," Robert said, his face still close enough for me to smell the piquant mint of his breath, one hand on my shoulder. "I hope you know how important you are."

It wasn't long before Carlow arrived—walking through the front door unannounced. I don't remember knowing he was vacationing that same week, but it seemed inevitable; of course he was there as soon as we arrived. "You have a house?" I asked.

"I converted a boathouse down the shore into a studio. Made it livable. I get more work done out here than in the city."

He was excited, bouncing from one foot to the other. What did he have to be excited about? If anything, it would be harder here, to get her alone. Much harder, in fact, with James not working, with Robert around. Is that what excited him? The challenge?

Lonnie, on the other hand, was subdued and cold as she cooked dinner. I blamed it on her father. On the patio, she tossed back two glasses of wine very quickly and said to James, "If we're going to go through with the party, we'd better start inviting people. It's already so late."

"Do you want to?" he said.

She just looked at him, didn't respond, and instead cursed the big fancy grill.

"He's so particular about his steak," she said to me, as if I were somehow judging her. "He always complains when James cooks them."

The pool had an ethereal look in the late evening twilight, like it might float away at any moment. I ran after William to stop him from coming close to the edge. He was up past his bedtime, overtired and high-strung.

Robert, tumbler of scotch in hand, meandered around the lawn, inspecting the fantastic array of purple and white blooms that surrounded the pool while Lonnie cooked. Whenever I dared to take my eye off William my gaze drifted to him. It was possible that he was a reasonably nice man and she was just immature, of course. Possible she'd just never gotten over the usual teenage resentments, when you had to find something wrong with your parents in order to form your own identity. It was also possible his presence became more overbearing the longer one was around him. I was braced for either possibility, braced to lose a little respect for one or the other.

"The nasturtiums didn't bloom this year," Robert yelled across the pool to no one in particular. "My favorites!"

We ate at the dining room table that evening. The room was larger than the one in Manhattan, and flanked by inlaid mirrors. The chandelier above the table sparkled, and in the reflection, sparkled again.

Despite Lonnie's difficulty the meal showed no sign of effort when it arrived at the table, plated with mashed potatoes and thin grilled asparagus. James clamped a fancy baby seat to the table for William so he sat next to me, suspended in a mesh basket, his skinny legs dangling. He was happy with the seat because it placed him closer to everyone else than his usual high chair. He banged his plastic spoon against the tablecloth gleefully until I took his hand gently, brought it down to his plate, and whispered, "No banging."

Robert complimented the food. He didn't seem capable of complaint or insult, but Lonnie didn't react, didn't seem pleased to have pleased him.

"Try your wine, Laurel," he said. "I bought that in Italy."

Lonnie said nothing but lifted her glass. Robert started talking about a painting he'd seen in Rome. "I had to consider who goes in our history books," he said. "Warriors. Ruthless conquerors. America never gets anything done in comparison to these ancient kingdoms." His voice was light and mocking, his face amused. "They had leaders who just said, 'We're doing this and I don't care what the serfs think.' The serfs don't know what's best for the country."

Though it was obvious he wasn't taking his own words seriously I still felt anger bubble up and over. "I'd hardly say the powerful do either." It just came out. It was the same tone my dad used when he told off someone he disagreed with—a lighthearted scoff. Everyone stared at me, waiting for more. It was only then that I realized I shouldn't have interjected, shouldn't be having the conversation at all. We'd hardly spoken up to that point, I'd told him what—the state I was from?—and I was a guest in his home, eating his food, disagreeing.

"The French Revolution," I said, stumbling, grasping for something, anything, to back myself up. "You know, didn't we sort of learn that the women marched because they couldn't afford bread?"

I didn't actually know that much about the French Revolution. I'd read Lonnie's copy of *The Red and the Black* for the extramarital love affair, without understanding much of the political references. I didn't even know if it was really hunger that spurred the Women's

March on Versailles or if that was just a cliché I'd picked up somewhere.

"Astute observation, Ella," Robert said, smiling at me. Then he didn't say anything else. I felt like a puppy who'd been thrown a little scrap. It wasn't enough—where was the rest of it?

"Speaking of rulers, in fact, we have an announcement, don't we, James?" Robert said, changing the subject.

James nodded. It seemed to me he was purposefully not meeting Lonnie's eye. Robert said, "I've decided to make James here senior partner."

Lonnie showed no reaction, so I said, "What does that mean?" to cut the silence.

Robert said, "I'm going to be running the business with James. And when I retire, I'll hand it down to him, though of course"—he looked at James—"I'll still be the primary shareholder."

"Oh," I said. "Congratulations, James."

"Thank you, Elle."

I chewed my steak slowly, took tiny sips of wine. Lonnie looked miserable across the table from me. I wanted to find a way to show my allegiance, but I couldn't reach her. She didn't look up.

I discreetly peeked under the lip of the table. Her feet were curled under her chair, her ankles crossed. I could reach them if I scooted forward a little, my ass on the edge of my seat. In one swift motion I gave her a sharp kick in the shin. She jumped, looked up. As I met her blank eyes with a smile, William started to wail. He'd dropped his spoon on the Oriental rug beneath the table and was mourning the loss. Everyone turned to me. Robert, I noticed, wore an amused smile.

"Sorry," I said, bending to pick it up. It left a smear of food in the wool pile of the rug. I tried to wipe it up with my napkin but only succeeded in pushing it deeper into the fibers.

Reunited with his spoon, William happily began to bang the table again. I sat back up, pressing his arm down again, holding it to the table and saying, "Shh, William, no."

Tired of being rebuked and conscious of his sudden command of attention, he yelled at me, a high-pitched screech.

"He has something to add." Robert laughed.

22

When I put William to bed that night, he had a hard time falling asleep. "Let him cry," Lonnie said. "He needs to get used to the new house. He needs to know the rules aren't different here."

But I couldn't leave him all alone in that huge attic space. I kept thinking of lonely little Lonnie, crying herself to sleep in the same room, the long night in the quiet of the country. I rubbed his back as he cried in his crib, humming a little tune. Lonnie was probably right, I probably kept him up longer, drew out the crying, but I didn't care, I didn't want him to be alone. When he finally dozed off, sucking his middle and ring fingers, nuzzled into his faded old blanket, I wandered back downstairs. Everyone had left the dining room. I had to look for them, as if we were playing hide-and-seek. There were three sitting rooms and a library on the first floor alone. I finally found Lonnie and Carlow on a pink silk sofa in the library, her feet on Carlow's lap. Robert sat in a green wingback across from them, fingers curled around a tumbler. James, I guessed, had gone to bed.

"William's asleep," I said, settling into a chair across from the sofa. "Finally."

Lonnie smiled at me. She didn't move her feet. Carlow had a hand over them. It was nothing, but it was dangerous between the two of them. He could run his hand right up her leg at any moment.

"Nothing's happening here," Lonnie said. "Just all these stuffy parties. I don't know why we keep coming."

"Perhaps to see your father?" Robert ventured.

Lonnie sighed. "I'm not saying anything about *you*, Daddy."

He took a swig of his liquor, then smiled at her as he brought his glass down. "I'm sorry, my darling," he said. "But I don't get to see you nearly often enough."

Robert looked very old and very tired, his eyes sunk deep into his skull. He said, "Elle, do you want to have children?"

I hated this question. I felt the urge to lie, to say of course, I can't wait, just because I was working as his daughter's nanny.

"I don't know," I said, choosing my words carefully. "I have a hard time wrapping my mind around the idea, to be honest. Of course, I've just never had the money to really consider it anyway," I said.

"You're smart. You're going to be moving forward. You'll have money soon."

I wanted to argue. It wasn't an upward trajectory for all of us. Money didn't just naturally come with age for some the way it had for him. I was already getting paid top dollar for my career and it was only enough to make ends meet for me. There was nowhere else to go, and it certainly wasn't preparing me for success in another venture. Likely though, he was only trying to be polite.

Lonnie said suddenly, "To not have children is to live always in fear—of pregnancy, of what it would be like, of regret. To have children is to live with fear for the children, for the rest of your life."

Carlow sighed and interjected impatiently, "You're going to meet some perfect guy, Elle. And none of this will matter." He turned to Lonnie, "Isn't that right? Isn't that what happened?"

I couldn't make out her reaction; her face was turned away from me. I thought, *Are we starting this already?* I had every expectation of this trip escalating toward a breaking point for their love triangle. That's why they needed a new house—all those extra rooms—to guard against the encroaching claustrophobia. Something was closing in on us.

23

The difference in light from the night before was extreme. The sky was cloudless and the sun, even in early morning, washed everything out except the lush green of the grass around the house and the frothy blue of the ocean.

William was delighted with the sand, running it through his tiny fingers, charmed with his own inability to hold it. He was equally enchanted with the waves lapping the shore and the blue expanse in front of him. We all watched him stare and grin. I thought of a story I'd read in one of Lonnie's books. A man goes to a beach and suddenly cannot tell the difference between the organic and the inorganic. Everything around him breathes and grows.

The day ahead of us felt long.

Robert had stayed back at the house, claiming to lack patience for sand. I hoped Lonnie would be happier without him. On the beach she changed into a bathing suit by pulling the top of her sundress down to her belly. I didn't look at her breasts before she covered them. I looked at James watching her. I looked at Carlow trying not to watch her, his head turned uncomfortably to the side, as if he were just absorbed in the landscape.

The sundress slithered off her hips and she stretched her arms over her head, lengthening the whole of her body. She left us to swim while I fed William cheese and crackers from the cooler. When she returned, dripping, she inhaled more than her share of our food, but none of us said anything.

There is something engrossing in watching a beautiful woman eat ferociously—wolflike—salami grease and peach juice on her chin. I hadn't seen her really eat in days, I realized. It was a relief. We all tried to conceal our interest, looking up to catch glimpses of her gluttony only every third time we desired to do so. I thought about her watching me eat in the Adirondacks—the journal entry about it, how that had been enjoyable for her. I didn't know where she'd keep the journal at this new house, or if she'd brought it at all, and I felt lost without it. I longed to be let back into her mind.

William, stripped down to his diaper, fell asleep soon after lunch. We'd forgotten the beach umbrella and I couldn't leave him out in the noonday sun, so I gathered four sun-bleached sticks and, twisting them down into the sand around his towel, tied Lonnie's dress to their tops, making a shady canopy above his little form.

Carlow lit a thick joint and we all passed around Lonnie's iced thermos of Pimm's. Lonnie fell back on her towel, exhaling smoke. James and Carlow sat cross-legged on either side of her. No one moved for a long time. I watched the men. The weed was making it hard for me to see them as their proper ages. I watched them oscillate between two young children, shirtless and barefoot, dressed in navy shorts, and two half-naked feeble old men. I looked down at my own skinny legs, dotted with swollen mosquito bites, and realized this same dichotomy was true of myself as well. We were all lacking the center of our lives.

Though no one spoke, I also had the sensation we were sharing feelings, as if the location had transformed the three of us into some sort of hive mind. I could sense their lust and frustration. They had been distant with each other for a while now. I never saw them talk when Lonnie wasn't around. I could feel their growing mistrust. There was a constant churning introspection in my brain, but also a sense of vacuity, like the process of melding our thoughts together slowed down the machinery. Only Lonnie was separate from this evolution, still singular and unparalleled, as esoteric as she'd been in the city.

Slowly, I stood and walked to the water, the sand hot on the arches of my feet. I imagined James and Carlow could feel the heat too. I was conscious of the untruth of this fantasy in surges, doubt drifting across my mind like the waves engulfing my feet at the shoreline and then receding. Each retreat filled me with dread. The ocean sucked back its water and took fragments of myself with it.

"Don't leave me with these people," I murmured when the tide returned. "I'm not like them."

But as the water washed away from me I failed to remember how. I thought about the Greek mythology we'd studied in high school. Staring at the ocean, I thought: *Yes, the never leaving, that hypnotic pull out to sea. Of course it could be embodied by a woman.*

24

A little girl approached William and me one morning when he was digging in the sand on the beach. It was early and no one else was up yet. The girl was wearing a bikini, which looked funny, with her back arched and child-belly ballooning out between the top and the bottom. Her skin was deeply bronzed, though a white line of flesh emerged on her shoulder when the strap of her top slipped down. The sight of her made me realize how long it had been since I'd seen a tan child. All those hours at the playground, but kids were always coated in zinc sunscreen now, streaks of white all over their bodies protecting them from the sun.

I looked around for her parents, but there was no one else on the beach that I could see. Where had she come from?

"Where are you from?" she said, parroting my own thoughts back to me. I didn't know how to answer the question. "The city," I said eventually.

"Where are you *staying*?" she said, sighing a big exasperated sigh.

I pointed up to the roof of our house, peeking through the trees. "That one," I said, then, imitating her tone, "Where are you *staying*?"

She pointed farther down the beach in an indiscriminate direction.

She had big ears, this little girl, or maybe not so big, but the kind that stuck out. She seemed to know it; she had a habit of tucking her hair behind them, then untucking it and then tucking it back in, her arms always moving up and down as she spoke. I wondered if her mother had told her not to tuck her hair behind her ears. She couldn't have been more than seven; she seemed too young to recognize a feature she didn't want to accentuate.

"How old are you?" I asked.

"Six and three-quarters," she responded. "How old are you?"

"Twenty-six."

"Wow."

"Is that old?"

"Are you a teenager?"

"I'm older than a teenager."

"Wow."

"What's your name?" I asked.

"Sienna," she said.

"My name is Ella and this is William."

"Are you his mommy?"

"Yes," I said, the lie feeling natural for some reason. "Do you have any babies?"

She giggled. "I'm too young for babies!"

"Oh!"

"Can I tell you a secret?" she asked, leaning in toward me.

"Of course!"

"I don't want any babies. Ever. I think they're *disgusting*."

I laughed. "I think that's great."

She sat down in the sand next to me, her legs bent to both sides in the shape of an M. I'd been told to correct children when they sit like that, that it wasn't good for their spines. But I said nothing to this little girl. She seemed to know best what was good for her. I'd sat like that as a child constantly anyway. My spine was okay as far as I knew. "Do you know any stories?" she asked me.

"Sure," I said. "Why do you ask?"

She rolled her eyes. "I want you to *tell* me one!"

"Let me think," I said, tapping my chin with one finger.

"Wait," she said, shoving her hand in front of my face. "I don't want it to be one of those stories about how I shouldn't do something."

"How you shouldn't do something?"

"You know, about how no one will believe you if you lie. Or, like, how if you don't help make it, you'll never get any bread."

"You don't like cautionary tales," I said.

"What do you call them?"

"Cautionary tales," I repeated.

She rolled her eyes again. "It's just not true," she said. "Something bad doesn't always happen."

"In fact, you're right," I told her.

She threw her arms up dramatically and flopped back onto the sand. "*Thank you,*" she said. And then, sitting back up, "I think you're nice. Will you be here tomorrow?"

"Yes," I told her. "Tomorrow morning."

She stood, untucked the hair from behind her ears, then tucked it back in.

"Can you think of a good story and tell me then?"

"Sure," I said.

She stumble-ran away down the beach.

When I returned to the house Lonnie was perched in an alcove by the kitchen, on an antique chair, the crescent of the telephone receiver cradled to her cheek. It was a position I would see her in every morning from there on out, planning every detail of the Labor Day party.

There were general misgivings from the men as early as that morning. James paused in front of her—her robe sliding open, the end of a pen in her mouth—and made a questioning face. Lonnie mouthed the name of someone—whomever she was talking to—and he mouthed back, "Why?" holding up his hands.

She didn't respond, but turned away from him, toward the wall, letting loose a boisterous laugh into the phone. "I don't believe it! I don't believe it!" she screeched.

She twirled the curly cord of the telephone around her finger, speaking like a teenager to everyone, not just guests but caterers and florists too, punctuating her whispers with laughs, screams, and fits of giggles. It made me uncomfortable, to see her oscillate so wildly between the depression her father's presence conjured and the glee speaking to anyone outside the house seemed to cause. It made Carlow and James endlessly curious. They lingered in the hall or around the corner in the kitchen as she spoke. She had some kind of internal logic about the guest list, though Carlow and James could not figure out what it was—and hounding her over the lunch table (she had begun skipping her usual coffee and fruit entirely) proved ineffective.

"Did you invite the Cunningham twins?" Carlow asked.

Her coquettish face—chin tilted down, looking up at him out of the side of her eyes.

"Ex-girlfriends," James said, "should maybe be off-limits."

Carlow held a finger in the air and said, "Not that either of the Cunningham twins are ex-girlfriends per se, but I'm not exactly looking to speak to them again either way."

"*You* want to plan the party?" Lonnie said, the flirtatious tease of her expression quickly erupting into a pinched anger.

It stopped both men short.

She took the phone off the hook and shoved it into James's stomach. "Be my guest."

We all watched her stalk out of the room. No one followed her and no one apologized.

25

The following morning Sienna was waiting for me as William and I walked toward the water. She was playing in the ocean, her hair stringy, her ears sticking out between the frizzy strands. She turned when she saw us and a big wave hit her from behind, knocking her over. I caught my breath, but she reemerged, crawling toward us, a long piece of seaweed caught on her shoulder, laughing on the wet sand.

"Well?" she said, approaching us, dripping, shucking off the seaweed.

I handed William his shovel and bucket. As he got to work on a hole, I told her, "Once upon a time, there was a little girl. Actually, she looked a lot like you. She had brown hair too, and brown eyes. She was lying in her bed in the middle of the night, trying to fall asleep. Just as she started to drift off she heard a sound. It went"—I whispered—"*rap-rap-rap.*"

Sienna's whole demeanor changed as she listened. Her eyes were wide, her body completely still. I was a little surprised how quickly I'd drawn her into the narrative.

"She lay in bed, thinking the sound would stop, but it didn't. She heard it again. *Rap-rap-rap*. She was scared now. This little girl, though, she was not the kind of little girl who would just call out 'Daddy!' or 'Mommy!' in the dark. She was the kind of little girl who would get up and see for herself what was making the noise, even though she was afraid. And that's what she did. She climbed quietly out of bed and *slowly* tiptoed across her room and *slowly* opened the door to her bedroom."

I mimed creaking a door open. My voice was as quiet as I could make it with the roar of the ocean behind us. The key to a scary story is to tell it in an almost-whisper, like a secret. Even William was transfixed now, staring at me, unmoving.

"She heard the sound again and it got louder. It went *rap-rap-rap*. She looked around her living room. The room looked different in the dark—all the furniture was lit up by just the moon—but everything seemed to be in place. So she tiptoed ever so quietly to the kitchen. She could still hear the sound going *rap-rap-rap,* but it didn't sound like it was coming from the kitchen. So she tiptoed to the hallway. The sound was louder there. It went *Rap! Rap! Rap!* She tiptoed down the hall. She stopped in front of the closet. The sound was very loud there. *RAP! RAP! RAP!*"

Sienna was curling inward, hunching her shoulders, clenching her fists. I almost felt bad, watching her fear. I had the urge to reassure her it was nearly over, but instead I continued.

"She *slowly* turned the knob on the closet door. The

door creaked open, the sound getting louder and louder. *RAP! RAP! RAP!*"

Sienna's eyes were little moons, her mouth hanging open a little. "Do you know what was inside?" I asked her.

She vigorously shook her head.

"The wrapping paper," I said.

She crumpled, pulling her knees in, covering her face with her hands, shaking her head. "That was a dumb story!" she said, giving me the same reaction I used to give my dad when he told it to me.

"Yep," I said. "It was!"

"I want a better story," she said. "I want you to think of a better story."

"I might need more time," I told her.

"I'll come back tomorrow," she replied.

26

The next day there was no time to meet Sienna on the beach. We left early: James, Carlow, William, and I, with Lonnie lagging behind—first to finish a telephone call, and then to shove last-minute necessities into a big straw bag—and boarded a sailboat. "A keelboat," James explained. "Scientifically impossible to tip over."

I hadn't realized tipping over was a concern. I'd never been on a boat before. "Just watch out for the boom," they all told me. I sat with William by the rudder all the way in the back, as far as possible from the boom, as we departed. James steered, one arm hanging on the ropes that moved the sails, his tan leg draped over the rudder.

It was foggy on the water when we left, but the low clouds burned off by mid-morning and we all shed our sweaters. William was delighted with the sun, the seagulls, the waves lapping the sides of the boat, the sensation of movement. I held on to the straps of his tiny life vest, scared he was going to topple over the side. He kept sticking his arms out, trying to touch the water. I imagined him falling, and my having to dive in after him.

At high noon we were in a bay, surrounded by an empty, rocky beach. The wind died down here, and

Carlow lowered the sails. Lonnie inflated a yellow tube and tossed it into the water. William tried to jump in too as she dived after the ring. James lifted him, struggling, from my arms. "You can go swim with her," he said to me. "I'll take the monster."

"Okay," I said, though I felt nervous for some reason as I stripped off my shorts. It wasn't that I'd had any lack of exposure to water; I swam in lakes and rivers all over Mount Hood growing up, but I hadn't actually been swimming—swimming where my feet weren't grounded in murky mud—in a long time.

I felt suddenly like I had done so little in so many years—my twenties, my teenage years too, full of meaningless work and endless drinks. I was shaking a little with the prospect of trusting my body to keep me afloat, to propel me across the distance to where Lonnie had both arms linked over the big yellow ring. She yelled at me, and though she was far away, her voice traveled across the calm surface of the water, against the rocks surrounding us: "Come on!"

I took a moment on the edge of the boat to tie my hair into a ponytail; then, unable to find another reason to delay, I placed my arms into a V over my head and dove in.

The water was warmer than I expected, nothing like the waves on the Oregon coast—icy even in August. I let myself sink for a moment, remembering the way the water pulled me down when I was motionless, and then, kicking, the way it held me up when I moved. Breaking through the surface, I squinted in the sun, inhaled sharply, and charted my path toward Lonnie.

When I reached her I hooked my arms over the ring, resting my chin on the slippery plastic. We looked at each other, smiling, happy to be meeting here. The weight of my body spun the ring around and we circled like that, bobbing in the rippled water, our legs dangling down together, brushing against each other. I tried to imagine what Carlow would do with her in my position, out here alone for a moment. I imagined pulling my knee up between her legs.

"He's cute, though, right?" she said.

"Carlow?" I replied.

She grinned, water dripping off her nose. "You think Carlow is cute?"

I had no idea how to answer. It occurred to me she could've been talking about her son. "Sure," I said. "I mean, objectively, of course he is."

She laughed. "Objectively?" she said. "But is he cute to you?"

I guessed it would be more insulting if I said her lover was unappealing so I said, "Yeah," as casually as I could muster.

She grinned. "I wonder if he likes you," she said.

"Isn't he . . ." I trailed off. Had she forgotten what she said to me on that island upstate? Had I somehow gathered the wrong meaning from her words? She did know that I knew, didn't she? Was she trying to get rid of him? "Isn't he taken?" I said.

She grinned again, her only answer, that flash of her teeth in the sun. "What kind of men do you like?" she said.

I didn't know what to say. I thought, *Traditionally? Whoever's interested. Currently? Whoever's interested in you.* I said, "All men."

She laughed. "I might know a few guys who fit that description."

She sank down then and popped up in the middle of the ring, very close to my face. "Let's swim to shore," she said, waving at James. "Come to the side, help me push this stupid thing."

I did as I was told, holding on to a blue handle on the side of the ring and swimming alongside her. Our progress was slow, swimming connected like that, with me able to use only one arm. It took us a long time to reach land. When we did, Lonnie slipped on an algae-covered rock, splashing back into the water, the yellow tube comically bouncing off her. She laughed, though she had skinned her knee and blood started trickling down her leg. She ignored the wound completely, just letting the blood pool. The rocks on the shore spiked steeply upward. After climbing the first few sun-soaked boulders it was impossible to go any farther. We sat down, water dripping off our bodies, collecting on the jagged surface of the rocks. Lonnie used one finger to smear the blood from her knee into the shape of a heart.

"Do you know how to French braid?" she asked. I nodded and she pulled out the band holding back her hair.

"It's so tangled," she said. "Just yank it around. Don't worry about it."

I couldn't help worrying, though. I worked slowly so as not to hurt her, gently pulling the wet locks apart as I moved them from side to side.

There was a time in my life—it was long ago—when girls had been the center of everything. I tried to pinpoint when that had ended. Was it kissing the boy with the red sweatshirt that had done it? For some reason, what came to mind had nothing to do with boys at all. It was a slumber party in a tent in my friend's backyard, a year or maybe two before my first kiss. A round of truth or dare, where a little smooth-faced brunette from another school, I don't remember her name, told us her best friend made her have sex with her.

None of us knew what to say to this baring of her most intimate secret. Nicole, intensely Christian, said, "That's bad!"

"How does she make you?" someone asked.

I remember her vague, uncomfortable reply: "She talks me into it. She says it will feel good."

I ventured to ask, feeling stupid, "How do two girls have sex?"

It was explained as "just rubbing."

The following morning the little dark-haired girl pushed me into the bathroom and shut the door. She leaned in close to my face and whispered, "Do you like that girl Nicole?"

Since I secretly hated Nicole, I grinned and said, "No, I can't stand her."

She grinned back and we emerged from the little room to a semicircle of scowling faces. They probably thought she'd tried to kiss me. I never saw that girl again and I remember feeling sad about it. Had I liked her because she had a secret? Because it felt good to be in on it? Or had I liked her because she brought the idea of sex into our child-world? Though chronologically it wasn't, this particular sleepover somehow seemed the culmination of all adolescent sleepovers.

I also remember someone daring me to strip naked in that backyard while the other girls squirted a cocktail of condiments from the refrigerator at my body. This was so far from any of the other dares I remember performing, I feel certain it was her who'd come up with it. I had to be hosed off afterward, trying not to wake up the parents with my cold-water screams.

Lonnie hugged her knees to her chin as I braided her hair, holding her feet in her hands. "It's better over here," she said. "Just the two of us. They drive me crazy, you know? Sometimes I feel like telling them both just to leave me alone."

"They do?" I asked, wanting more. "How so?"

She shrugged off the question, though, and mumbled, "Let's maybe not go back," then didn't say anything else.

I could see the men out in the water. I never stopped being conscious of the fact that they could see us too.

Back on the boat, everything seemed to have shifted along with the position of the sun. Lonnie held William in her lap, whispering into his ear, pointing at birds and fish and other boats. He was tired and rested his head against her breast, falling asleep as the salt-heavy wind whipped his hair around.

I shakily made my way around the boom and along the rope that circled the deck. Sitting up there next to the flapping sail, waves splashing my legs when we swayed and surged, I was aware of everyone's eyes on me. It's funny—being watched—the way it makes you feel outside your body, like looking at a good picture of yourself, wondering—hoping—about what other people see. It was nothing like walking around Crown Heights. It was entirely pleasurable. I imagined what it would be like to be James, discovering my taut young body. I remembered his mouth on mine the day Lonnie was drugged. I found myself wondering if he would ever kiss me again, if he was waiting for his moment, or testing me to make sure I was on his side, that I wouldn't say anything. My arms were tired after the long swim to shore, and in the sweltering heat of the afternoon sun, my bathing suit drying against bare skin, I felt deluded by my own body's strength. As if I might be headed somewhere other than eventual death. I thought, *Lonnie must feel this way all the time.*

27

When I saw Sienna on the beach again the next morning she shot me a dirty look, then ran to the water like she intended to ignore me. I watched her in the waves, splashing and laughing, flinging water as if invisible companions surrounded her, as if she were trying to make me jealous.

When she finally approached, she didn't quite look at me. "I'm sorry I wasn't here yesterday," I told her. "I had to go on a boat ride."

She still didn't look me in the eye, but she lay down next to me, her head almost, but not quite, touching my hip, sand immediately coating the wet tendrils. "Anyway," she said, with the flippant tone of a teenager, "I kind of wanted to *talk* to you."

"I kind of wanted to *talk* to you too," I said, imitating her.

"Do you know," she said, looking up at the one tiny white cloud in the sky, "someday, a long time from now, I'm not going to be alive anymore?"

"Well," I said, "that's true of us all. You know, that's something that happens to everybody."

"But what's going to happen to us?"

"Well," I said, "different people have different ideas about that. Have you asked your parents? What do they say?"

"They told me if I'm good I'll go to heaven."

"What do *you* think about that?"

She paused for a long time, narrowing her eyes at the little white cloud. Finally she said, "If we just go to heaven, why are people so sad when someone dies? What do *you* think?"

"Well," I said, feeling strangely excited by the conversation. I didn't have to answer to this little girl's parents. I could tell her whatever I wanted. I could tell her the truth. I said, "I don't know. It's not something we can research. No one can come back from the dead and tell us what it was like, so I just don't know."

"But," she said, "what's going to *happen*?"

"Maybe nothing," I said. "Think back before you were born. What do you remember?"

"Nothing."

"I don't know what will happen when we die, but I think it might be nothing, just like before we were born."

"I don't want it to be nothing," the girl said quietly.

I thought about telling her, *We must face all of life's unknowns with courage*. I felt like telling her, *Within nothing there is no fear, no sadness*. I felt like telling her, *That's why you have to appreciate what you have now.*

Instead, I just said, "I know," daring to give her a little pat on her bare belly. "I know."

28

Carlow's studio was completely empty save for a wooden table and one old rolling chair, the stuffing peeking out of a rip along the seam. The walls were white, with big windows on opposite sides, looking out on a path that cut through the trees and down to the ocean. The floorboards were painted white too, giving the whole space the impression of a blank canvas. In one corner a ladder stretched up to the wooden beams that cut across the vaulted ceiling.

"I expected more . . . paintings," I said.

The table had a gridded cutting mat and a stray X-Acto knife, but otherwise the space was void of art supplies as far as I could tell. There were drawers under the table; I guess he kept his paints in there.

"I keep most of the ones I don't sell back in the city. I have a few downstairs I can show you. I don't like to be surrounded by my old work."

I stepped into the middle of the room. The windows that faced away from the ocean showed an expanse of lawn and then a large Edwardian house, which the studio had probably belonged to at one time. Carlow was standing by the door. The sun was setting outside and he fiddled with the lights so a bright bulb lit up over my head. He was looking at me, his face tilted a little in contemplation. I felt uncomfortable, unsure why I was in that empty room.

Carlow had come over for dinner earlier that evening and as we ate Lonnie said, in front of me, "Why don't you take Elle out? She does nothing but work and read alone in her room. We can put Billy to bed once or twice."

Carlow gave Lonnie a long look, probably wondering if she was trying to get rid of him. "Um-hmm," he said finally, then, "Okay."

"Take her to see your studio," she said.

"Can I see the paintings?" I asked.

He ignored the question. "Do you want me to photograph you?" he said.

I thought it was a weird question, a weird way to ask. Why not *May I photograph you? Would you mind if I photographed you?* As if he'd be doing me a favor instead of the other way around.

"I thought you weren't interested in photography anymore," I said, trying to decide if Carlow looking at me through a camera lens would be something I wanted or not.

"I'm not really," he said. "I don't go around photographing women. I just wanted to all of a sudden."

It was true, at least as far as I could tell, that he didn't photograph women. Beyond *Woman in a Double Frame* there were no other realistic depictions of women—painted or otherwise—in his online portfolio. Most of the bodies he looked at were chopped up and genderless. I wondered if that's what he wanted to do to my body. I was interested in what parts he would extract from the whole.

"What do you want me to do?" I asked now, hovering in his studio.

"Sit tight," he said. "Let me get my camera."

He came back holding two camera bags as well as a white stretch of fabric.

He studied me a moment before setting them down. "It's much easier if your face doesn't look so tense."

"My face looks tense?"

He went about unzipping the camera bags. "Yes," he said.

He squinted up at me from his kneeling position. When he rose, he put a hand in my hair, pulling it back, his face so close to mine I could feel his breath on my forehead. He walked over to the table and extracted a heavy-duty paper clip from the drawer, then spent a long time arranging my hair inside it. I wasn't sure where to look as he worked. I could feel sweat pooling under my arms and along my upper lip. I hoped he wouldn't notice as he pulled pieces of hair over my face, brushed them away, and pulled them back again. "It's hard," he said. "Posing."

I said nothing.

"I don't want you to wear that," he said, snagging his finger on the neckline of my shirt. He handed me the white fabric, which, unfurled, revealed itself to be a thin slip dress. I wondered if it was Lonnie's. He was crouched by his cameras, so I unbuttoned my shorts, thinking he would politely load film or screw on lenses as I changed, but he kept looking up at me. All traces of his smirk were gone, though his face maintained its innocent, full-cheeked appearance, the eyebrows drawn up like an unsure little boy's. There was nowhere else to go, so I peeled off my shorts in front of him, trying to meet his eye, as if that would help me understand what was happening. He wasn't looking at my face, he was watching my body. I took off my shirt, then bent to pick the dress up off the ground.

"No," he said. "You'll be able to see your underwear through the fabric. Take it off."

I paused a moment, trying to work things out in my head. Did he regret turning me down back at the beginning of the summer? Was this his way of coming on to me? I was as confused by the prospect as I was excited. I wondered, even more than when James had kissed me, if I should feel remorseful out of loyalty to Lonnie, but my curiosity overpowered any sense of shame. I told myself it was because she was disloyal, sleeping with Carlow in the first place. She should understand that no one really belongs to anyone else. Besides, after our conversation in the water, it was almost like she was giving me permission, like she was trying to pass him off. Why else would she suggest I visit his studio? She must have known what would happen here.

I dropped my panties and unclipped my bra, letting them fall to the floor. He stood, walked over, and handed me the dress. "I want to get your face," he said, leading me to the window. "Look at your reflection." I did. I thought I looked good—my complexion tawny from boating the day before.

"You keep a lot of tension in your mouth," Carlow said.

I gave him a pout. "No," he said, touching my lips. "Don't try to make any expression. Forget about them. Look at your nose. Your nostrils are a little asymmetrical. I like that, that's interesting."

He snapped a photo. I'd never thought much about the shape of my nostrils before. I didn't really want my face to be interesting—it almost seemed like an insult.

"Lean your head back," he said, touching my chin.

The shutter clicked. "Now look at me."

He leaned around the camera, put his face in the loose hair near my ear, pressing his rough cheek against my jawbone, then moved back behind the lens again. The shutter clicked. He smiled. "That was a good one."

"I want to watch you move around the room," he said. "Take your time."

He backed away and I hesitated, wondering what to do in that empty space. I realized I'd liked his directions; I felt far more uneasy without them.

I walked over to the table, touched the edges.

He smiled, said nothing, put his face behind the camera.

I sat on the table. I felt I had to make something happen in order to hold his interest. I took the X-Acto knife and poked the pad of my index finger, just a little at first, idly cutting through the first few layers of skin, then harder, until blood came. Carlow moved closer, looking at me through the eye of the lens. I smeared it across the hem of the dress. The shutter clicked. I peeled the dress up, gathered the skirt around my waist and he moved closer still. I lifted one leg up on the table, leaning back on my elbows. The shutter clicked. I shucked the dress off entirely and lay down on the table, my limbs splayed over the sides. He leaned over, photographing my torso on top of the green grid, close enough for me to smell the citrus of his cologne.

"Get up," he said, backing away. "Go somewhere else."

I moved toward the ladder, scaling it up to the ceiling beam. I lay my body out along the beam and let my arms fall open. The wood was the same width as my back and I felt like I might fall if I moved at all, so I spread my legs, putting one on each side of the beam, feeling more secure that way. Carlow stood below me, his foot between my legs. I could hear the shutter. I imagined my arms and feet cut off by the beam in a way he'd find interesting.

He climbed up after me, standing at my feet, hunched over with the angle of the ceiling, looking down at me and snapping the shutter button. I could see the eye of the camera open and close. Then he pulled a flash out of his pocket and the light blinded me. I closed my eyes. I didn't feel sexy exactly, though it was what I'd intended. I felt more dizzy than anything, high up on that thin beam, unsure how to get down without falling.

When I opened my eyes he offered me a hand to help me sit up, so I could climb back down.

On the floor again, he loaded his camera back into its case.

"That's it?" I said, standing in the middle of the room, looking at my naked reflection in the windows.

"That's it," he said, giving me a little half smile.

"Was that not what you needed?"

"If it wasn't what I needed we'd keep going," he said.

After I'd dressed, he walked me back to Lonnie's along the beach. It was too dark to see each other. He passed me a flask by pressing it into my stomach, so I could find it. The air was damp and cool, and I was cold, but it felt good—a natural cold, not manufactured by machines. I hadn't felt that since the Adirondacks.

I took off my shoes and carried them. The sand was damp and as we walked little sparks spread out around my feet. The water crashing on the sand had a ghostly glow about it.

"Noctiluca," Carlow said. "Does that happen in Oregon?"

"Yeah," I said. "I don't think I've ever seen it this concentrated, though, where you can see it in the water."

"There must be some kind of bloom right now."

"We used to bring those ground bloom fireworks to the beach at night," I said, "light them, and throw them in the water. They don't burn out right away, they make the water glow for a minute. It seems really obnoxious now—we were just throwing trash into the ocean."

"My parents had a summer house in Michigan for a while when I was growing up," Carlow said. "The Upper Peninsula. The house was near Lake Michigan, past these dunes with all this marram grass. When I was eleven my parents had a party to go to and they left my little sister and me home alone for the first time. We decided we were going to do all of the things my parents never let us do. We were drunk with power, I guess. We decided to light a bunch of matches—that was one of the rules, you know, we were never allowed to actually light matches, we had to let my parents do it. Well, we knew it was dangerous, and we weren't looking to burn the house down, so we decided to go outside. We ended up burning up about three miles' worth of beach grass before the fire department came and put it out. It was kind of devastating for the landscape; we were on the news."

"Oh my God! That's terrible!"

"My parents didn't leave us home alone again for years, I can tell you that."

I laughed and took another sip from the flask.

"You know, Elle," Carlow said. "I like you a lot. You have only one flaw."

"Oh yeah? What's that?"

"You think you're different."

"Different from what?"

"Different from whoever you're with. Any room you walk into, it doesn't matter what room—you think you're different from everyone there. You're trying to be different."

"And I'm not?"

"No," he said simply. "Not really."

I didn't know what to think about this insight. It was beyond me why he felt he had the right to offer up any sort of criticism about my personality, at that moment or any other. I wanted to say something about how I'd started out the summer by not eating for two weeks, but it was an exaggeration.

"Do you photograph Lonnie?" I said instead, suddenly.

"No," he said. "Lonnie won't let me."

The statement made a painful lump develop in my stomach. I guessed that meant I shouldn't have either.

We were approaching the back of the house; I could see the ghostly lights of the pool in the yard. "Did you call us when we were upstate?" I said.

"No," he said.

"Really? You didn't call the cabin? In the middle of the night?"

"No," he said again. It bothered me; I knew he was lying. It also bothered me that he didn't say "Thank you" when we parted.

29

The next morning a woman I'd never seen before approached me before breakfast. "You are Elle?" she said. "Mr. Thomas would like to see you."

I was giving William his bottle. "I will take the baby," she said. "Only for a moment. He's in the far wing." She pointed down the hall.

I assumed she was a cleaning woman—she was dressed casually, in white orthopedic tennis shoes. I followed her to a door at the end of a long hallway I'd never been down before and handed William over with some trepidation.

Everything smelled like eucalyptus—vaguely medicinal. The door opened to reveal a bathroom, where Robert was sitting on the lip of the tub in a navy robe, his skinny legs crossed. It was hard to see with all the steam and it was cloyingly hot.

"A touch of a cold," he said, gesturing around the room. "Forgive me." His voice was hoarse, his throat filled with the clogged sound of phlegm.

"It's okay," I said, though I couldn't have been more uncomfortable with the intimacy of the location.

He coughed for a long time, as if for emphasis. "I'm

supposed to sit in the steam. Horribly boring. Hard to even see the pages of a book."

"I can imagine," I said, though in summer, any kind of sickness felt far off, hard to remember. He looked pretty awful in his robe; they can put it off, but the rich are not completely immune to aging. He was trying to sit up very straight but having some trouble perched like that, his skinny wrinkled neck sticking out at an angle, his jagged collarbone emerging above a few sad tufts of gray hair and brown age spots. "As I have no intention of wasting your time, I'll get straight to the point. I don't think you're the best fit for this family."

Despite these words, his tone didn't change at all. He was using the same syrupy-sweet voice as he had at our first dinner, when William had screeched at the table. The heat of the room became suddenly painfully apparent to me. It was probably eighty degrees outside, full humidity, and we were sitting in a sauna.

"I don't want you to take this personally. I'm sure you're perfectly capable of doing your job and would be an excellent fit with another sort of mother."

He couldn't have twisted the knife into a more delicate spot.

"Another sort of mother?"

"You don't understand my daughter."

I felt sick. I understood that all the money really came from this man, that Lonnie was not the one who wielded any power in the family.

"I think I know her pretty well at this point," I said, my voice not nearly as calm as his, though I was trying my best to control it. "I consider her a friend."

"You see," he said, shaking his head. "That's exactly the problem. She doesn't need a friend. She needs someone to take charge—someone to teach her how to be a mother. My daughter is a clumsy, spiteful, directionless embarrassment. She's spent her whole life trying to make men love her. She doesn't have the faintest idea how to do anything else. I gave her every opportunity—every single thing she's ever shown any interest in, I've encouraged. I never pushed her in any direction she didn't want to go. But all she did was flit from interest to interest, from person to person. She has a weak character, no self-control, no discipline. She can't see anything through."

My body was tense, ready to argue, but everything he was saying was true. And I hated her for all of it, but, also, he'd left out the part where she'd made me love her. I didn't understand what any of this had to do with me or my job, regardless of its veracity. I was about to blurt out as much when he said, "And you." His eyes met mine, unblinking. I wanted to look away but I didn't let myself. "You came here from some little nowhere town—and what do you think? You think you can somehow understand where she came from? You think she deserves empathy? Losing her mother so young, you think, that must've been hard—it must've had an impact. You're too nice to really see her.

"Are you close with your mother, Ella?"

It seemed like a power play to use my real name instead of calling me Elle like everyone else—had he been doing that the whole time? I couldn't remember. I didn't want to answer, but I couldn't let us just sit there in silence. I knew he could wait for the answer much longer than I could wait to give it to him. I also felt if I lied he'd somehow know. I didn't trust my voice. I stood still in the doorway. I felt like a child being lectured standing up like that—why couldn't he have taken me somewhere to sit down? To the library or his stately home office, not this hazy bathroom? "She left," I said, trying to keep things simple.

"You lost your mother too?"

"I didn't *lose* her," I said. I didn't want to tell him anything else, but he just sat there, steam swirling around him, waiting for me to finish. "She walked out on my dad."

I cursed myself for giving away so much. I didn't know how, but I suspected he'd somehow find a way to use it against me. "I had my dad," I said, unsure why I was still talking, telling myself to shut up. "I would've chosen to live with him anyway."

"Well," he replied, nodding thoughtfully. "That *is* different."

I thought he was going to say something about being thankful for my father; it was the direction this conversation had always gone in the past, but instead he said, "There's no resentment when someone dies. It's a clean break. You can mourn them without all your other emotions getting in the way. You don't have to sit around for years and wonder why she doesn't return, if you could've done something different to make her stay."

"What are you getting at?" I said, angry now, anxious to see what he was planning to do, but also not wanting to continue this conversation at all, wanting to leave this sick old man to die. It started to disgust me, breathing in the steam surrounding us. It was starting to feel like tendrils emanating from his body, connecting us somehow. And yet, I was also aware that all he was actually doing was pointing out his daughter's privilege—the very same trait I'd initially hated her for.

"Let's get it straight," he said. "You're the only one who's had it hard. You probably can't afford to buy new clothes, there's probably a safety pin holding your bra strap in place."

I cringed. It was nightmarish for him to be thinking about my underwear. "Don't delude yourself," he continued. "She's not to be empathized with. Her inability to do anything but appreciate her perfect storybook life shows nothing except a lack of moral character."

I wondered then if he knew about the affair. If he was somehow angry at me for helping her cover it up, for letting it continue. It upset me to think about someone else knowing the secret. It felt like everyone was pulling her cold journal from that absurd box of waffles—James, Carlow, Robert, even the housekeeper Pilar, and God knows who else.

I was on the cusp of blurting something out—some kind of defense or argument—every muscle in my body was tight and rigid despite the billows of heat, ready, but I didn't know what to say. The words wouldn't come. He started coughing again anyway, a long endless stream of hacking that prevented any response.

"I don't have the authority to do anything about your employment," he said, finally, meekly, when the coughing stopped. "I'm not a threat to you. And I know you're not asking for my advice. I just think you should go back to the city and find some nice hardworking family to help out."

"You're right," I said, turning to the door, not believing for a moment that he wasn't a threat to me. But before I walked out I said, "I'm not asking for your advice."

30

After my parents' divorce, the first thing that changed at Mom's house was that she stopped eating very much. She drank glass after glass of white wine with dinner, which had become small cuts of light fish and a pile of carrots instead of the cheap cheese and sausage and boiled broccoli we used to eat. She made me cut up the carrots—telling me I needed to get used to using sharp knives, to get used to doing things for myself.

One night she asked me, "Have you ever heard of an anglerfish?"

I shook my head.

"They're a type of fish that have a lure coming out of their head, like a fishing lure, to attract prey. They can eat things that are almost as big as them. There's a species that live in the bottom of the ocean and when they mate, the male fish, which is smaller, attaches itself to the female like a parasite and they fuse blood vessels. The male then gets smaller and smaller, losing his organs, including his brain, until all that's left is some sperm, which fertilizes the female's eggs."

"That's disgusting," I said, poking the white flesh of the fish on my plate.

"It's amazing," she said. "Imagine a whole society of nothing but female fish, able to self-perpetuate."

"But the guys are there," I said. "They're just parasites."

"Not unlike human men," she replied, picking up her fork again and pointing it at me. "There's a lesson here."

The next thing that changed: she started bringing men home to dinner. I remember a long line of them, one after another. I started to hate eating at her house. I hated the way she'd ask me to show off for them—

"Tell us about what you're learning in school," she'd say.

"Nothing good," I'd reply.

"Ella is very bright," Mom would say, giving me a look.

The food was more filling at least. We ate peppers stuffed with ground beef and onions or thick creamy casseroles—the kind of food she used to bring to parties, to impress people. She'd stopped eating meat at this point, though she cooked it for us. She nibbled on slices of cheese and more of those stupid carrot sticks as we ate, drinking rum and Coke out of a tall water glass. "Do you want a sip?" one of her dates asked me. I looked at Mom, but she just giggled, so I took his glass and swished some of the drink in my mouth. It burned the back of my throat, but I didn't make a face, knowing they would laugh at me.

Mom cleared our plates, stacking them and taking them into the kitchen. While she ran water in the sink that man said to me, "Look under the table."

I bent over and squinted in the shadows. I could see his penis dangling from the fly of his pants, a reddish pink color, surrounded by thick black hair. I couldn't help but think of the parasites dangling from the anglerfish. I sat back up and he winked at me, putting one finger to his lips and saying, "Shh."

I used to think my mom was very sophisticated; she wore her hair curled into a swirl on top of her head and sat up very straight. She had been to Africa, on an archeological dig in college, making her one of the few people in town to have ever left Oregon. She seemed stifled in our town, and told stories about her coworkers that made me picture them like apes. When I was younger we had met one of them at the bank, and I had been surprised to find him fully capable of carrying on a conversation.

It wasn't like she left without saying goodbye. I used to say that to myself a lot, trying to count my blessings, trying to tell myself that I mattered enough at least for a goodbye. And it wasn't like she didn't tell me where she was going, or give me her phone number, her new address. But she did leave. She left and she never came back, and she never asked me to join her and she only called a few times, for a while. Then that stopped too.

31

"Your nanny doesn't know what the hell she's doing," I heard Robert say later that same night. I was coming downstairs after putting William to bed, carrying his dirty clothes to the laundry room, but I paused outside the kitchen, peeking around the corner of the arched doorway to see Lonnie sitting with her knees curled up to her chest at the little breakfast table. I couldn't see Robert. I ducked back around the corner and strained to hear Lonnie's reply.

"She's been great with William," she said quietly. "He loves her."

"He's growing up with no boundaries. You're making the same mistake I did at first, hiring these young girls because you think they have energy, but then you watch your kid embarrass you."

"There is no way for him to embarrass me," Lonnie said.

"You say that now. He's a baby. But you start them out this way when they're young, and soon they'll be uncontrollable. He can already walk and talk, it's time to worry about it."

"You want me to find someone like Lada? I hated Lada."

James came up behind me then. "Don't worry," he said softly. "Why don't you go out for a while?"

I nodded, though I would've preferred to keep listening. Though I was terrified of being let go, I couldn't make myself resentful of Robert—like Lonnie. The fact was, I thought with a sinking feeling, I *didn't* know what I was doing. My job was mostly following William around, pulling his tiny hands away from electrical sockets and breakable objects, waiting for him to go to sleep so I could look through his mother's things. I was a terrible nanny. It wasn't exactly shame or self-reproach I felt then, however. At that point I regretted nothing; I just didn't want to have to leave.

I decided to walk into town by myself. I wasn't clear on how safe this was, but I set off anyway—walking along the highway. At first there was a considerable shoulder, with a view of the ocean at twilight, but soon the shoulder tapered off and I found myself hugging the metal railing that separated the road from the bay, ducking out of the way of tree branches and turning sideways to make myself thinner as cars passed me, honking, at rapid speeds. Eventually, I gave up and flagged a cab down.

"You try to walk?" the driver said. "It's not good to walk. You have to drive."

"It's not very far," I replied. "But the road isn't made for walking."

"You could get hit," he said. "You are lucky."

The cab had a strong cloying smell, some kind of sweet incense. A Virgin Mary icon swung on the rearview mirror. The driver handed me a business card when we stopped. "You call when you want to go back," he said. "You don't try to walk. Luck is like lightning."

"Okay," I said weakly, taking the card.

Main Street in Southampton was a line of small Colonial-style shops and restaurants, sidewalks in good repair, well-pruned trees, American flags waving. In other words, nothing like the small town I grew up in. Nothing like the vacant strip-mall towns of the rural West.

I walked down the sidewalk, past well-dressed families out to dinner—little perfect groups of four, the children better-looking miniatures of the parents—past jewelry shops and kitschy housewares and windows of pastel dresses.

I passed a teenage couple in the window of a candy store, sharing a milkshake. I went inside and lingered behind them, looking through a rack of postcards, waiting to hear what they would say to each other, hoping for an interesting distraction, but they just sat silently, passing the milkshake back and forth, staring out the window with vacant faces.

In a bin of random trinkets I found a little box, the size of my palm, with tiny decoupage daisies on top. I clicked open the miniature latch and found a tiny oval mirror inlaid in the lid. It was an out-of-place item, among little rubber balls, booklets of fake tattoos, and plastic children's jewelry. I thought I might give it to Sienna.

The man at the counter said, "Only this? You want candy too? You want a bracelet?"

"No," I said. "Just this."

"You want chocolates?"

"Just this," I repeated.

He shook his head, but wrapped the box up in tissue paper and put it in a little paper bag for me.

I wandered across the street and into an airy French restaurant with wicker chairs and white tablecloths. There were a few open stools at the bar and I took one of them.

"Gin and tonic, please," I told the bartender.

He replied, "Can I see your ID?"

I pulled it out and he stared at it for a while, then looked at me as if trying to work out whether or not it was real. Whenever this happened I felt deeply uncomfortable, as if I really was pulling one over on everyone, as if I wasn't an adult in some essential way that all the other people drinking were. Finally, he passed it back and went to fix my cocktail.

The man sitting two stools over turned and said, "You don't look old enough to drink."

They were ganging up on me. It didn't have to do with my age, though, but rather the fact that I was dressed in cheap simple clothes, with no jewelry or expensive handbag. Like a teenager, or, in their world, like a child.

"I am," I said simply, meeting his eye. He looked away.

"His grades aren't very high," a woman behind me was saying. "I'm worried about him dragging her down."

"Anyone," a man replied, "is going to drag her down."

A television in the corner was running a news story about the LeRoi woman's daughter. The sound was turned off, but I watched the closed captioning. LeRoi wasn't lying, as it turned out: the girl's mother saw the news report and made contact. The two adult women met, on camera, both crying, both carrying flowers. They sat together awkwardly on a sofa and the mother explained that she had been trying to keep the daughter safe; she knew it would be dangerous to try to leave LeRoi. She said she tried to look for the daughter later, but to no avail, until she saw her on TV. She handed the daughter her birth certificate.

The way the mother carried herself was wrong somehow, though I couldn't pinpoint it. Her tears seemed fake; she was too pulled together. Shouldn't she just be absolutely breaking down? As I watched, I developed a theory that she'd never wanted to see the daughter again, not really. She'd left her intentionally, and not because of any danger, though it did give her a convenient excuse. She hadn't looked for her, hadn't wanted to revisit any part of her life with LeRoi, but when she saw her daughter's pathetic face crying on TV, when she knew friends would've seen it too, she was left with no option but to come forward.

I stared at that image, thinking, *Why did she go with him in the first place?* She must have been weak in some way. LeRoi must have sniffed out that weakness. He must have seen that for this woman, life was nothing more than trying to soak up anything pleasurable all at once, as fast as she could. If he gave her parties, drugs, sex, he could do whatever he wanted.

I couldn't relax, couldn't get Robert out of my head. I had an awful feeling, every muscle knotted. All these people around me seemed like they were operating on some other level, the same way those tourists at the Met had when I'd lost Lonnie for a few moments earlier that summer. No one else was paying any attention to the news—nobody cared. I nervously checked my phone, worried that someone was calling to fire me, and found I'd somehow turned it off without realizing it. I had no idea how long it had been off—I hadn't had the urge to use it in a while. I pressed the POWER button and it illuminated bright blue and buzzing—vibrating over and over in my hand as more and more messages popped up on the screen. My stomach sank. Something had happened. "Aunt Wendy" came up again and again. "Missed call, Aunt Wendy."

The last time my aunt had called me was the night my parents decided to split. I'd been at a friend's house, applying cherry lip balm, when my friend's mother handed me the phone so Wendy could tell me she'd be picking me up, that my parents needed some time alone.

I stepped onto the street, leaving my drink at the bar the way I knew Lonnie would disapprove of now, and dialed my voice mail. "Ella," her voice came through. "Where the hell are you? Please call me."

In the next message I heard her fumbling with something, breathing heavily, "Ella," she said. "I hope this is your number. You need to call me when you get this."

I pressed CALL BACK and listened as a phone, somewhere far away, rang and rang. It went to voice mail so I hung up and tried again. On my third call, she finally answered. "Hello?" she said. I could already tell the connection was bad. Her voice broke halfway through the word, replaced by that strange electronic static.

"Aunt Wendy," I said. "It's Ella. What happened?"

"Who is this?" she said.

"Ella," I said. "Wendy, it's me."

The line was silent.

"Can you hear me? It's Ella."

"Ella?" I heard her say, relief in her voice.

"Yes. Can you hear me?"

"Ella," she said. "I don't know if you can hear me, but your dad had a heart attack."

I didn't know what to say, but I thought she might hang up on me, thinking she'd lost the connection, if I stayed silent so I said, "My dad?"

"Ella," she said.

Silence. Then one long unbroken sentence, "I don't know if you can hear me, but I think you should come home."

"Is he okay?"

Then silence again.

And more silence.

"Wendy, is he okay?"

"He's okay," her voice finally came through. "He's asking for you."

"I'll come home," I said, wondering as I said it how I would possibly manage the trip.

"What? Ella, I can't hear you."

"Wendy," I said, but then the connection cut out.

I navigated to my bank account on my phone, already knowing I'd spent every extra penny I'd earned paying off old credit card debt. There was no way for me to get home from here. It wasn't just the money though; it was the idea of leaving itself—of leaving now, of leaving Lonnie. I thought, *Maybe if he were dead*. I guess I didn't really believe there was any way for him to not survive.

I typed a text. "I heard you," I said. "I'm so sorry. I can't afford to travel home last minute. It's not possible. Please tell Dad I love him. Let me know how he's doing."

I pressed SEND and then stood there for a long time, staring at my phone, waiting for a reply.

She finally wrote back, "OK."

I walked back into the restaurant and finished my drink.

Staring at my aunt's two-letter message, I remembered what I'd told Sienna about death with a sick feeling. I'd thought what she needed was truth, but in fact a child survives on stories. She even knew this, she'd been asking for one directly from the start—not a morality story, but a story that broke open the world, that made ordinary things into something more potent, something that gave her instructions, spells, treasure maps. The truth of it didn't matter; it mattered only that for a few moments she could believe she was in control of the forces of the world, that she might remember that feeling of possibility and power.

32

I traversed that same stretch of highway again, tossing the cab driver's card into the ditch, and reached the house in one piece. Upon my return, the general mood surrounding the pink sofa was low. William was in bed, and Lonnie, visibly drunk, was perched on the lip of the couch, drink in hand, James prone beside her, looking tired or bored. Carlow, his back to them, was absorbed in something on his phone. I was reminded of coming downstairs from Lonnie's bathroom during her birthday party, finding them all stoned, feeling separate from it all to the point of seething. I decided not to mention my dad.

"Where's Robert?" I asked.

"He went to bed an hour ago," James said. "And since then Laurel has decided to drink all the liquor in his house as if she were a teenager."

I didn't know why he was using her real name, the first time I'd ever heard him do so, as if she were in trouble.

"Elle," Lonnie said, registering my presence for the first time, "Let you get me a drink." She laughed, tried again. "Let me get you a drink."

"I could use one," I said.

"*She* could use one," Lonnie said, standing, pointing at James and then Carlow's back.

"Should I not have encouraged her?" I asked, when she disappeared.

"It doesn't matter," James said. "There's no stopping her anyway."

She returned carrying two highball glasses, filled far too high with scotch or cognac, something brown and straight—one for me and a refill for her.

We clinked glasses. "Never let a lady drink alone," she said. The alcohol smelled mossy and strange.

"I want to tell you," she said, putting an arm around my shoulder, pulling me awkwardly down to the rug in front of the sofa where we sat side by side, "about my idea. My book idea. Because I'm going to write a new book. I'm going to scrap the old one. I wasted a lot of time upstate with those people. But I have a new idea, a better idea."

"You were writing a book?" I said, the wrong thing to say. She frowned and reached out as if to hit my face, but only managed to graze my cheek with a couple limp fingers.

I tried again, "What is it?"

"I want to write the mystery we made up. The one named after Carlow's photo. But I want the mystery never to be solved. Or for the woman to not actually exist."

"How deconstructionist," James said.

"Is it?" Lonnie said.

Though I actually felt like telling them both to shut up, that none of this mattered, I tried to cover up my anger and anxiety. Tried to act normal. "What does that mean?" I asked.

"Words don't signify what we think they do," Lonnie said, still slurring. "We can only understand 'now' in relation to 'then,' so we can never really understand time. James doesn't really get it." She whacked him on the arm.

"You kids," Carlow said, "you kids and your lack of guilt."

Lonnie and I both whipped around. "What the hell are you talking about?" Lonnie said.

Carlow didn't look up from his phone. "You can just sit around talking about the unknowable like fact. No God anymore. You lucky kids."

I didn't know where he got off.

"Bullshit," Lonnie said, and I thought she was going to call him out on distracting from the conversation at hand, but instead she said, "I feel guilty all the time."

"Can't you just deconstruct your guilt?"

"You know I still believe in God." It came out small from her mouth, a quiet little sting of a sentence. "I'm Catholic." No one responded. Lonnie tilted her head back to down the rest of her drink, and went to get another.

It was at that point, when she returned, that Carlow started to record her, pointing his phone in her direction, holding it steady and not saying anything.

I can picture the video in my mind as if I'd watched it

repeatedly, though I never saw it. Something about the act of him recording made everything sharper, higher risk. She was sloshed, wobbling, her eyelids at half-mast. "Bedroom eyes," my dad used to say, like a femme fatale's in an old film. Her mood had changed when she returned to the room; she was trying to be funny, trying to shuck off the uncomfortable religion discussion. She said, "I have a hard-on for it anyway."

She thudded back down on the floor next to me. "The way we have to eat Christ's body," she said. No one else said anything, the camera made us self-conscious, but Lonnie remained unaffected. She slumped into the sofa, not even glancing at Carlow, not even curious. The dead air of the recording hung around us, thick and warm. Time elongated. I found myself picking on my cuticles. I hated what Carlow was doing, both because of the unnatural way it affected the room and also because it wasn't fair. It wasn't fair for him to have this weird souvenir, to be able to watch it whenever he wanted. To make it right there in front of James.

"You hung your sheets up on a windy day," Lonnie said after a long silent pause. "You hung your sheets up to dry, but the wind took them. You lost three sheets. Three sheets . . . to the wind."

Her finger twirled in the air as if imitating the flight path of the sheets.

"It's a nautical idiom," James said.

"In our house," Lonnie continued, ignoring him, "we

have four sheets. We have four beds so we have four sheets."

"We have more sheets than that," James said.

"Which house?" Carlow said.

"We still have one sheet left." She held up her drink. "One more sheet."

"You should maybe know that sheets are lines."

"Shut up, Carlow."

Worried now, I stood, walked over to James, and whispered, "How bad is she?"

"About as bad as I've seen," James said.

"What? Ever?"

"Yeah."

It took only one more drink for her to pass out, half a drink really. Carlow joked, "Half a sheet, must have been William's crib sheet."

The three of us stood over her inert body on the floor beside the couch. She looked small, her ankles and wrists so skinny. One of her shoes had come off and the smooth thin knob of her heel was the same pink as the sofa. She was slumped against the silk cushions, her hair falling in her face. It was a good position to be in; she wouldn't choke on her own vomit, it would just fall neatly next to her.

I felt the urge to talk about her, standing there, staring, flanked by her men, but what could I say? We all knew her in vastly different capacities, but no one of us seemed to understand more than any other. We just looked at her for a long moment. Carlow put his phone back in his pocket and then turned and left the room without saying anything.

In the wake of his abrupt exit, I had the sudden terrible urge to tell James everything. I might've said it too—"Don't you know he's sleeping with her?"—if James hadn't calmly placed his hand on the small of my back and said instead, "Come on, she'll be fine."

We walked upstairs together. He kept his hand on the small of my back, all the way to my bedroom door. It's a polite little gesture, and yet a man could lead me anywhere with his hand there.

"I haven't been in this room in a while," he said, following me through the doorway.

I needed a distraction, and I felt interested to see where he was going with this. I was able to recognize the pattern easily enough—any time his wife was dangerously incapacitated his attention turned to me. His intentions were obvious, but it's always amusing to see how men smooth over transitions.

I stood in the middle of the room, by the foot of the bed, as he walked around, examining the pictures on the wall, the view from my window. I didn't feel nervous. The whole scene felt inevitable, as if I were watching a dream I'd had play out in real life. I guess I'd known it was going to happen since he'd kissed me in the hallway. I smiled when he looked at me, to let him know it was okay, and he stepped over, very close to my body.

He'd been drinking too; I guessed they all had before I'd arrived. I could smell it on him, mixed with that cedar-scented aftershave or cologne.

"You're very pretty," he said, moving a lock of my hair away from my face. And then he said, "You know how pretty you are, don't you? You must think about it all the time."

I could've corrected him, explained that in fact I only thought about how pretty his wife was all the time, but an answer was not necessary. An answer wasn't what he was looking for.

The person Carlow had been right about lacking a sense of guilt was me, to some extent. It was all that isolation of my childhood. All those times I rode my bike down the hill at my dad's house in the rain alone. It was the lack of expectation that I would ever do anything at all. There was another version of myself in my mind—fat, sitting on a porch somewhere, swatting flies, probably cancerous. She never left town. Nobody felt disappointed in her. Nobody gave a shit. And my old friends, teachers, neighbors, even my own mother didn't give a shit about me in New York either, not advancing my career, not marrying, not having babies. If anything they probably thought my moving here was pretentious, like I thought the world owed me something more than I'd been handed. Some people were probably disgusted with me, and I liked that, I liked their imagined disgust.

33

The way James was with me didn't have anything to do with Lonnie. He stripped me and turned me over to rub my back, moving his hands up and down the muscles on either side of my spine, his erection brushing between my legs. And then, when I rose and turned back around, he surprised me by slapping my face. It smarted where he hit me, along my cheekbone. I hadn't been slapped in the face since childhood, when my dad was at his wit's end. Though I would never hit a child, I felt then that I'd deserved it. I was the child, he was the adult, and I'd failed to listen to his words. I don't remember what I was doing, but I knew I was being unreasonable, more so than usual, as it wasn't a regular occurrence. Now, as an adult woman, the sting confused me. Was the slap punishment, as it had been in childhood? I was being bad, sleeping with another woman's husband, but it seemed to me he was being just as bad, if not worse. I had the urge to slap him back. I brought my hand to his face, but too hesitantly; he grabbed my wrist and in a swift motion, pinned my arm to the bed. I fell back. Held down like that I felt like crying, though it also seemed like some kind of erotic joke. I struggled to figure out what role

I was in—he smiled at me as if to say, *We are playing, doesn't it turn you on?*

I didn't cry, though I also didn't raise my free hand to hit him. Even when he whispered, "You want to hit me?"

He was testing me. I brought my hand to his jawbone and stroked it gently. I was wet, the whole summer of sexual frustration coming over me. I choked down a sob, also conscious of the fact that if he touched me, touched me at all, I would come, it would take only a few seconds. He didn't let go of my wrist, but moved his mouth down to my tits. I was aware of their smallness compared to Lonnie's again. Even though I fit into her dresses, it still seemed a deficiency. As if he could read my thoughts, he said, "Look at these little-girl tits."

He bit my nipple, hard enough to make me arch my back. He wanted me to be a teenage babysitter, some kind of innocent virgin ten years younger than I actually was. He slapped my breast, lightly at first, and then, when I showed no reaction, harder. He wanted me to cry as much as, if not more than, he wanted me to come.

The word "debasement" came to me, but it didn't seem to apply. To debase myself would be to have sex with someone I didn't really want. Someone I didn't want like this. It seemed I had never wanted anyone as badly as this. I wanted James, and I didn't care if he wanted me to act as a symbol of his own cliché rebellion, his own teenage babysitter sex fantasy. I wanted him for reasons equally as strange. I wanted Carlow more, but I wanted James too.

I wanted the cock that had been in his wife inside of me. He had one leg between mine and I inched down, trying to rub against him. He slapped me again and I retreated. I was being indulged, the poor little match girl, in front of the daydreamed feast, and also punished for eating.

I reached my hand out, feeling for his cock instead. He let me hold it. He straightened his torso as I did, still pinning my left arm down, but looking down at me as I jacked him off. “Fuck me,” I said, and then repeated it, begging. “Please, please, please.”

Ignoring me, he came on my stomach and then collapsed next to my writhing body, finally letting my arm go.

“You want to fuck me?” he asked, and I nodded my head like an eager child. “You have to fuck my wife too. You want to fuck my wife?”

34

I've always found it strange, the way we traverse the world of sex and then return as if nothing happened. The way one can do something as simple as chew scrambled eggs afterward, calmly, as if one were a different person.

William woke in a good mood and I took him to the beach after breakfast, carrying the little box from the candy shop, wrapped up, inside my towel. But, though we waited all morning, Sienna never appeared. I worried her family had gone back to the city. It made me feel unreasonably sad, thinking about her gone. I unwrapped the box from its tissue paper and popped the lid open and shut while William dug in the sand.

When eleven o'clock rolled around I knew the others would be waking, so I picked up William with our towels and carried everything back to the house.

Lonnie was perched in her usual spot at the telephone in the hall. I could hear her laughter as I brought William in through the French doors that led to the back patio.

"Come over." She laughed. "No, I'm serious, it's tonight."

Carlow was sipping coffee in the kitchen. "Is she inviting more people?" I asked. "Isn't it kind of late? Kind of rude?"

He smiled at me, shrugged.

I brought her a cup of coffee and a kiwi, halved, with a spoon. "Thank you," she mouthed, flashing me a big smile. She didn't appear hungover at all. She was wearing her robe, and I wondered when she had woken and returned to her room. I wondered how close I'd cut it with her husband.

By the time James came downstairs I'd put William down for his nap and was lounging on the pink sofa with a book, though I wasn't actually reading. James looked at me, then came over and grabbed my foot, wanting to sit next to me. I moved my leg up over the back of the sofa and pulled the other in toward myself. He put a hand on my knee, watching me, running the other hand through his hair.

Lonnie was still on the phone in the hall. We could hear her laughing and saying "No! Stop it!" to someone on the other end. The doorbell was ringing; the help had started to show up.

In the hallway I could hear Robert, interrupting Lonnie's call. "Put some clothes on," he said, answering the door. "For God's sake. And tell your nanny to do the same."

I was still wearing my lacy beach cover-up, but I didn't realize he had even seen me all morning. The couch faced away from the front door, my foot was the only thing visible to him.

James ran his hand up my leg, glaring at me with

mock-seriousness, and whispered, "Put some clothes on, Elle. For God's sake. This is obscene."

I smiled, though it wasn't funny. I was unnerved by Robert, on edge. Everything felt like it was coming together and falling apart at the same time.

"Do you feel at all bad?" I asked him. I wanted him to tell me no. I wanted us to feel the lack of guilt together.

He said, "There's something going on with her. The night she was roofied—she never goes out drinking alone. Also, I called her late one night when you were upstate and she answered, asked if it was Carlow. As if *he* were the one who'd call her late at night."

So he was using me as revenge. My stomach knotted up but I said nothing.

Lonnie dressed me up, as she had in the Adirondacks. I wore a dress of the same Alice blue as her school uniform with a thin black sash under my breasts. Lonnie spent a long time putting my hair in hot rollers, and when she pulled them out it fell around my shoulders in perfect waves.

"Who taught you all this?" I asked, referring to what color lipstick to use, what dress to pick for which occasion. My mother had never given me any advice in these matters. She had the same reaction to anything I tried on in front of her—neither affirmative assent nor disagreement—she said, in the same tone as Carlow had accepted the request to take me to his studio, "Mm-hmm."

“All what?” Lonnie said absentmindedly, tugging at my last hot roller. Before I answered, though, I guess she gleaned what I was talking about and just said, “Oh, you know, you pick it up along the way.”

Lonnie had been just as bad off as me, I realized, since she’d lost her mother at a young age. Maybe the lack of a female role model had made her pay closer attention when aunts or girlfriends gave counsel. Maybe it had perversely benefited her in that way.

The gesture of smoothing my hair while looking at my reflection in the mirror gave me a peculiar sensation. It was affectionate, but also corrective. I thought about Sienna’s tic, tucking and untucking her hair from behind her ears. I wondered why she lavished me with this sort of attention. I liked being the recipient of her touch, but it made me feel like a doll as well—just a prop in whatever game she was playing.

I sat with her as she did her own hair and makeup and put on a white dress. We’d passed William off to James and it felt good to be rid of him, to listen to music on Lonnie’s bed and watch her dust her eyelids with glitter at the vanity.

“You have to stop doing that,” Lonnie said, looking at me in the mirror. I was lying on the bed, my knees curled to my chest, revealing my underwear. I hadn’t realized that I was also scratching at the mosquito bites all along my legs. I paused for a moment, but only long enough to register how terribly I needed to continue. Lonnie turned, studying me.

"You don't have any?" I asked.

"I'm too bitter."

I shook my head at her, unable to stop. Lonnie grinned. "One," she said, starting the same routine she used with William when he ignored her. "Two. Three."

I kept scratching, because the bites were not yet at the stage of pain that would cover the itch, but also because I wanted to see what Lonnie would do. She made a dash at me, grabbing the hand closest to her. I relinquished it and continued scratching with the other. She struggled, laughing, to reach the hand she'd missed but I pulled it under my back when she came close so that she had to roll me over in order to reach it. She won, eventually; gripping both my wrists so tightly it hurt and I had to sit up, to follow her body, in order to avoid further pain.

"Look!" I screeched at her. "You don't understand! You just have to scratch until they burn! There's no other way!"

We stared at each other for a long moment and then she dropped my wrists, forcefully, so they hit my lap, and went to the bathroom for a bottle of alcohol and cotton balls. As she wiped the stinging stuff over where I'd broken open the skin she said, "If you're going to hurt yourself you have to at least do it somewhere it doesn't show."

Her voice was strange and flat. I didn't really think about what she was saying. I was too worried I'd actually angered her. I couldn't afford to lose her affection, even for a moment.

"Okay," I said, trying to meet her eyes again, but she was just looking at my broken bites.

Downstairs, as the caterers started to prepare food in the kitchen and the waiters arranged tables outside, Lonnie floated candles inside paper boats on the pool. William watched her through the glass doors, eyes wide. I picked him up and put him on my lap at the kitchen table for his bottle. He was distracted by the activity around him and drank slowly, his head following the waiters in their white shirts and black bow ties. I kept shoving the nipple back into his mouth, willing him to drink, to be tired, to get it over with. Upstairs I rushed through a lullaby and put him in his crib, expecting to leave him there crying. He whimpered a little, but lay down and put his fingers in his mouth. I was caught off-guard with his goodness, and I paused at the bedroom door, watching him watch me leave from between the crib slats.

I smiled at him, though I was backlit in the doorway and he probably didn't see it.

At twilight the guests began to arrive in candy-colored sports cars. Though a party was the only thing a house of that size was good for, they didn't even bother to come through the front door, they followed a path of candles to the backyard, where a full bar and several tables of food were ready and waiting.

I wandered over to the bar and waited in a crush of people to order a drink. Behind me I heard Robert say in a low voice to James, "Did she have to invite everyone she's ever met? What the hell is wrong with her?"

The yard was already crowded, with still more couples spilling in along the candlelit path every minute. Behind me all I heard were people chiming, "Where's Lonnie?" to one another.

"Here she is!" a familiar voice rang out, and I felt myself encircled by a thin papery arm. I turned to see Gigi, martini in hand, her face nightmarishly close to my own.

Robert whirled around at the exclamation, his mouth agape in confusion. I didn't wait to see what would come out of it.

"Excuse me," I said immediately, knowing I had to find Lonnie, had to ask her why, oh why, she'd thought it would be okay to invite the woman who didn't even know which of us was her.

35

It took a long time to wander through all those rooms. The house was completely empty. It was too early for the guests to dribble over from the yard, seeking private spaces. Eventually I found a locked bathroom door, upstairs, one of the unused guest baths. I knocked. "Lonnie?"

She didn't exactly answer, but I did hear a woman's faint moan from somewhere inside, and then a choked sob. "Lonnie?" I said. "It's just Elle, are you in there?"

I tried the doorknob, thinking about the time she'd walked in on me on her birthday, but it jiggled uselessly in my palm—locked.

"Lonnie? Do you want me to get James?"

I heard another muffled sob. "Or . . . Carlow?"

There was no answer, and I was getting worried. I ran down the hall to my room and grabbed the first thing I could think of—my pocketknife. Back at the bathroom I slid it against the doorjamb, right next to the knob, until I could feel the lock catch, then pushed the door open.

The room was dimly lit, faint evening light trickling in from a fogged glass window above the empty bathtub, where Lonnie sat. Everything around her was pristine but a little musty from lack of use. She was crying. She was a beautiful crier. Her face didn't swell or redden, tears just spilled out of her green eyes, trickling down her cheeks, like a painting of the crying Virgin. The tub was huge. I climbed in next to her, careful not to slip on the porcelain in my heels. My dress bloomed across her lap. Our hips touched each other, touched porcelain; we were scooped against each other.

She told me she was having trouble being alone in a room. She had cut bangs in her hair, the stray tendrils in the sink. She kept touching them, brushing them one way and then the other, feeling the tips, just above her eyebrows. She looked different with bangs, younger somehow, a little more disheveled but in a way that appealed to me. It didn't matter what she did; she was a beautiful woman.

She said she's been dealing with a crushing nostalgia, running over these same places again and again, unable to accept the fact that the past is over. She said she felt like curling up in bed in the morning, in the dark, closing the blinds, longing for a dreamless sleep. A dark space of nothing. Because the something is sad, no matter what it is. It's sad because it ends. Beauty is pain because it is not eternal.

She said, "This happens sometimes. Thank you for being here. I was fine. But my hand won't stop hurting. Ever since I got drugged. I can't sleep at night. And I guess there's something about this place. When you're separated from it you expect it to stay the same, but then you come back and it isn't."

I didn't know what she was talking about to be honest, not really. The big old archaic house, the beach, the town, everything seemed to me like it had been this way forever. I had managed to not return to my own home for three years at that point, since I'd moved to the city. I didn't really know what it meant to go back. It was easier not to, financially of course, but also just easier to keep moving forward, to forget the loons, the pines, the boys, my father. People weren't meant to exist in so many spaces. We were supposed to immigrate to a new country and never return, to write home only occasionally, hoping the letter somehow survived the distance, and then lose touch, as everyone had always done until very recently. We were supposed to be allowed the capacity to start over, to be swallowed up in a new place, to grow up, to change.

"I cut bangs," she said, her eyes watering, spilling over. "Because I used to wear my hair like this in high school. Something ridiculous is happening to me."

I tried to remember the photo in my notebook, Lonnie next to the falling white sheet. Did she have bangs there? How had I not noticed?

I leaned my head over onto her shoulder, my ear pressed up on her bare skin. I thought about her on the beach, feeling her shoulder with her cheek. She was warm, feverish; she was giving off so much heat. I had the urge to lick the tears from her face.

"I like the bangs," I told her quietly, a stupid thing to say. I had bangs myself, of course I liked them. Though my skin hadn't darkened much, my hair had lightened in the sun over the past two weeks. My body right next to hers, so similar in size, our hair in the same style now, I imagined we were two halves of a ripe fruit—one half in light and one in shadow.

It was starting to rain. I could hear the drops on the window above us and shrieks coming from downstairs.

"My paper boats," Lonnie said, still crying.

I put my hand on her waist, rested it there for a moment, and then started gently rubbing her stomach, moving my palm back and forth. My heart pounded from the close contact. I wasn't really trying to make her feel better; I didn't know how to do that. She nuzzled her face into my neck, the way I was used to her son doing. Her vulnerability seemed a blessing. I could've kissed her then, just because she was crying.

"We need to get you a drink," I said instead. "I think you could really use a drink."

She nodded. "Okay, but just stay here for a minute. I can't face everybody like this."

"Okay, of course."

"Tell me how to stop crying," she said.

"We have to do something else," I said, turning over the knife in my hand. "Look, do you want to be blood sisters?"

Lonnie smiled, sniffed. "Where?" she said.

I calculated her body, calculated my own. I couldn't let her bleed on her white dress. I moved to the other end of the tub, so we faced each other, and then, sliding off the heel, brought the sole of my foot to my lap. I cut it along the ball, underneath my toes, pressing down until a line of red emerged.

"Do you want me to do yours?" I asked.

As Lonnie wasn't wearing shoes, she just held up the bottom of her foot, leaning back in the tub, her arms pressed against the porcelain on either side of her body to brace herself for the pain.

I studied the small perfect object in front of me, her pink heel cupped in my palm. She wiggled her toes, her face twitching, her nose wrinkling, reminding me of the rabbit I killed as a child. Steadying my hand against the side of her foot as if the knife were a pen I pushed the blade into the flesh once, then twice, forming a small red X. She didn't make a sound. Blood pooled quickly around it, her soles were so smooth and thin; I must've cut her pretty deep.

I pulled my leg up, lined up our matching wounds, and pressed my foot against hers.

Outside, the rain was violent by the time we made our way downstairs—beating against the windows, making a mutiny of the pool's surface. Paper boats were capsized, run ashore on the patio. Guests were damp, hair flattened. It had started suddenly, waves of it, and they'd had to run inside. Waiters were passing out white hand towels, women were fanning their faces, patting the skin, trying not to smudge their makeup. Everyone laughed. "It wasn't in the forecast!" "Where did it come from?"

"Gigi's here," I told Lonnie, remembering the reason I'd gone to find her in the first place. "Why did you invite her?"

She laughed maniacally. "I thought it would be funny. We'll just switch back, she'll think she's crazy."

James was in the kitchen. I was still holding Lonnie by her waist, though she'd stopped crying. "I found her," I said. James smiled at us, lecherous. "She needs a drink, a strong one."

"I have something better," James said, winking at me as if we had a plan and pulling a plastic bag from his pocket.

I didn't know what it was. Inside the bag were what looked like three tiny wads of toilet paper.

"This is what I need," Lonnie said.

"You want one too?" James asked. "You haven't had much to drink yet, have you?"

I shook my head. "What is it?"

"It's Molly I stole from Carlow," James said. "You ever done MDMA before?"

"No," I said.

"Don't worry," Lonnie said.

I didn't particularly want to be high, but looking at those three bundles on the counter I couldn't refuse. They were meant for Lonnie, James, and Carlow, but one was being offered to me instead. To refuse would be to accept exclusion. To accept would be to overthrow Carlow in some small way.

We tossed them back.

The lights in the kitchen flickered. Thunder clapped outside. I sputtered at the chemical taste, choked a little trying to swallow the paper.

Lonnie leaned her mouth to my ear. "Don't leave me alone," she said.

I pulled her closer, her hip into my hip. "No, no, no. Of course not."

The drug hit after only a few minutes—a sweeping sensation over my body like water. "It's starting," Lonnie said, as soon as I felt it, which reassured and excited me. We were having parallel experiences. Like our bodies were intertwined. I'd read somewhere that MDMA was originally developed for therapeutic benefits, to lower defenses and increase feelings of empathy.

In this way it felt like a housewife drug—the perfect drug for Lonnie. Lonnie, who should probably not exist within the context of a housewife, but continued to do so anyway. Lonnie, who hated everyone at this party, but didn't want to be alone in a room. An escape in order to stay.

"I want to go swimming," she said.

36

Lonnie, made of water, hair plastered to her face and spread out around her as she floated on her back, lips and fingertips turning blue, nails painted black, in the pool, in the rain. I walked around the edge, complicit in whatever was happening to her by her request. Both of our light dresses were see-through now, hers with pool water, mine with rain. I walked around the deck and bent to throw the soggy boats back into the water; they unfolded, sprawling out and turning into flowers around her. I felt invincible in her heels, not worried about slipping, not worried about any of the people inside the house or what they thought about us.

We were in something together, though I didn't know what it was. Thunder clapped overhead. Someplace, far back in my brain, I knew this wasn't a good idea, for her to be in the pool, during a thunderstorm, but I didn't feel any danger. I felt like singing.

Sun machine is coming down and we're gonna have a party
Sun machine is coming down and we're gonna have a party

My dad had given me that record, I remembered, eyes welling up; he'd handed it to me when I was fourteen, saying, "Here's something weird you might like."

Eventually, I climbed into the pool too, my heels catching and falling off on the ladder, floating away, the water swallowing me up for a moment before I remembered to kick and I reemerged, next to Lonnie's cold slippery body. The water was all lit up with colors.

Lonnie laughed, a sob of a laugh, spitting water from her mouth. She turned her face up, treading water. "Then rain, rain, rain," she said.

I grabbed onto her too hard, expecting buoyancy, and we sank down, light shining through the water and then suddenly not. Everything on the other side of my eyelids went dark. I could feel Lonnie's dress, Lonnie's hair underwater, floating through my fingertips, between my thighs. We emerged into a dark world, a streak of lightning, a thunderclap, screams. Something was wrong, somewhere else, but I didn't feel concern, didn't feel fear.

I pushed Lonnie underwater again, without knowing what I was doing, wanting to encase her in something as if to save her. It was Carlow who grabbed her arm, pulling her to the surface, yelling over the roar of the storm, "You fucking idiots, you have to get out of the pool!"

Inside, the guests had cozied up in little clumps throughout the sitting rooms and the library. Most of the food was ruined, but the alcohol was all right. Waiters were weaving through them, lighting candles and handing out flashlights. The house was dark, the power out.

I was trying to put sensations into words in my head, and having some trouble. Lonnie was shivering next to me, grinning and shaking, goose pimpled, jaw clenched. I noticed these things about her body as if it were my own, as if I could feel her temperature, her heart rate. A wave of heat came over me when I saw her jaw relax. Such pleasure in that tiny motion of her face; watching her mouth open slightly, her lips go slack, I could've cried. She wrapped herself in a towel, wrapped me in a towel. We were so similar. Something wonderful about being two people at once. What did we have to fear?

And then, the answer, the little bald-headed man in a wingback chair, leaning close to Gigi and eyeing the two of us.

"Be careful," I whispered to Lonnie. "Dad."

"What?"

"Dad."

"Shit," she whispered back, understanding my fear exactly, feeling it too. He was coming toward us then, his face still smiling politely at the guests, but I knew underneath he was outraged, having just learned I'd pretended to be his daughter in the Adirondacks. I knew he just didn't like me, knew he was thinking about the holes in my underwear. And I knew he'd succeed eventually in getting me fired, despite what Lonnie wanted.

We needed someone to protect us. Where was James? We left to find him, left to escape her dad.

It was Carlow we found in the hallway outside the kitchen, not James. All these people. All these extra people getting in the way. I had to get rid of him, had to get him alone for a moment. I pushed him down the hall and into the half bath under the stairs. He had to stoop against the sloped ceiling, putting his face very close to mine. I couldn't see him in the pitch-black, but I could feel his breath.

Lonnie started knocking on the other side of the door as soon as I shut it. "Don't leave me alone," she said, into the gap between the door and the frame.

"I'm right here," I said, pressing my face to where I'd heard her voice, and holding the knob so she couldn't turn it.

"That book," I said to Carlow. "You remember?"

"Did James give you something?"

He always sounded so amused. There was nothing funny in that little bathroom. I pulled the pocketknife out of the clutch Lonnie had loaned me, my left hand still holding the door shut.

When I didn't respond to his question he said, "What book?"

"*Laughter in the Dark*?" I said. "The one you left at Lonnie's house and came back to get the night I was working."

He laughed. "What are you on?"

"I think you should leave," I said, moving my foot

against the doorframe to keep Lonnie out and opening up the blade of the pocketknife.

"Did James give you something?" I knew he wouldn't take me seriously. I wanted to slash his mouth open from the corners downward, to peel that smirk off his face. I couldn't see it, but I knew it was there. I had a vague blur of a plan coming together—luring Lonnie into a bedroom with her husband. I had something sordid to do and he was too light, too good.

"You're going to ruin everything with your loyalty," I told him. "You're so faithful to her. We can't have that. We can't have that."

A scratch, only a scratch. Not on his face but his stomach, the part closest to my hand. I couldn't see it but I felt the rip of the blade. I knew dark red would start to seep onto his white button up, that he'd need to leave to avoid questions. Did I realize then that it would be the final nail in my own coffin? Was it worth it?

"What the fuck, Elle, that fucking hurt!"

"You're part of our blood pact now," I said, my voice unnaturally light, bouncing off the walls of that little room under the stairs. "How lovely."

"It's really bleeding! It's all wet!" He sounded scared. "You fucking crazy bitch!"

He pushed me aside, rough enough for my body to crash into the sink, breaking the porcelain soap dispenser. When he opened the door he pushed Lonnie too, who let out a short howl. "Both of you! Crazy bitches!"

I heard him run into the wall in the hallway. He wasn't walking straight. "Shit," I heard him whisper. "Shit. Shit."

I grasped around in the dark until Lonnie's shaking arms met my own. "You said you wouldn't leave me alone."

"I'm sorry, I'm sorry, I'm sorry," I droned into her wet hair. "It won't ever happen again."

In the kitchen, the waiters were picking up dirty glasses in the dark, washing them, drying them, putting them away. An assembly line of waiters, working, magically, without breaking anything. The glasses caught the light of Lonnie's votive candles, glowed, left trails—lines of light from one set of hands to another. I caught sight of Robert again and pulled Lonnie into the next room. Lonnie's hair was snakelike, still dripping. Water trickled down her face like tears, down her arms, down her chest, like her whole body was crying.

Every time I saw something I thought of something else. Was this what I was supposed to be feeling? Lonnie slipped a white taper candle from the dining room table into my hand. The wax warm and soft like lips.

We moved, stepping lightly, in sync, down a hallway to the library. Lonnie clutched my arm and wax dripped onto the back of my hand. The skin bubbled, rippled. I was a girl in a horror movie, the too many rooms, the wet dress turned transparent, the fragile flame in my hand, an angry patriarch right behind us.

The books were breathing, the pages rippled in the

dark. Stray guests giggled around us. They felt more like props than real people. It was getting worse, weirder, darker. I didn't feel ecstatic. I was not overcome with empathy, unless I considered the dissolving lines between myself and Lonnie a form of it. My heart raced in a way that made me feel dizzy. We moved along the windows, touching the cool glass. I put my face against a pane, expecting relief, but the glass pressed back into me, and I sputtered, trying to catch my breath before it swallowed me up.

Suddenly, I was overcome with the urge to find Sienna. I had an image of her in my mind as a teenager, with her friends at Coney Island, her greasy hair hanging flat over her ears and streaked with bleach—smiling but desperately unhappy, wanting out of the whole thing and perfectly willing to talk to strangers. That's all that had to happen, really, to end up with someone like LeRoi. You just had to want out and not know where to go. What was going to happen to the poor little thing?

"We have to go to the beach." I grabbed Lonnie's shoulders—my shoulders?

"That's where we're going." She laughed. Of course she already knew what I needed. She pulled on a bookcase, which swung out, revealing a dark hole in the wall, a secret passage. "They were paranoid about burglars," she said, pushing me forward, into the dark, the breathing salt-smelling dark, hanging on to my waist, moving me like a doll, like a puppet, my flesh like mud, like clay, not fully formed. I could watch my body as I could watch Lonnie's. "An escape route," she whispered.

The passageway led up and then steeply down. The candle blew out, so I felt along the sides of the passageway, to make sure they weren't narrowing. I tried to pay attention to what it felt like to be in her body. I understood that I was being given a rare gift, but I could only manage to think of movement—all the different motions that lead to a step—the knee bending, straightening, the foot pointing and then flexing, the hips swinging. I could feel the sting of the little X on the bottom of my foot.

When the next door opened we were outside, on the edge of the woods, near the boathouse. I watched myself run up and down on the wet sand just past the trees, my feet creating sparks, the brutal waves crashing beside me, still glowing green. I didn't understand why I couldn't find Sienna. I started yelling for her. If I was on the beach, she should be too. That was where we met.

But she wasn't there. I couldn't find her. I knew I'd never see her again, would never be able to save her from any of this. My clay legs gave out eventually. I watched myself lie down in the earth, clay to clay, earthworms surfacing as they had in Oregon during a rain. Stones surfacing around me too, pushing up through the ground, as well as other things, the bones of birds and rabbits and mice, arrowheads, the anglerfish. The big slimy body of the anglerfish at the feet of that clay person in the ground.

I picked up a stone from the ground, wiped it off,

expecting it to be jagged, but it was smooth like a river rock. I knelt beside the girl in the ground, opened her clay mouth, and slipped it inside.

37

When James found us on the beach I fell back into my own body. The rock in my mouth brought me back to myself. I discovered that my body was not made of clay, but rather covered in it, a thin layer all over. The three of us walked back to the house, our feet crunching over stray twigs and pine cones. James told us it was nearly one a.m., that most of the guests were gone, that Lonnie's father had fallen asleep. There was no longer anything to fear. Upstairs, he drew a bath in the big tub next to their bedroom. Inside the water I bloomed out of the clay, the skin underneath warm and soft and clean.

James bathed me, the water sparkling like it was full of glitter in the candlelight of the bathroom. I felt warm and safe as he scooped up water with his palms and released it over my shoulders so it trickled down my back, down my front, over my breasts, in gentle trails. I felt the pressure of his hands against my back, along my ribs—soft and reassuring.

When I closed my eyes, I saw indistinct designs on the backside of my eyelids, light and shadow, movement. The light had neon colors, but they changed too quickly for me to identify them. I remembered, as a child, rubbing my eyes one afternoon until I saw spots, closing my eyes and pressing down, watching the vague, neon-lined spots my fingers created. It had seemed then, as it seemed now, like some kind of paranormal occurrence. The experience I was having now felt more like a return than a divergence. Maybe, I thought, all divergences, all distractions, are just returns. In light of this, I had misinterpreted my experience with James in a basic way. My longing for him, for Carlow, for Lonnie even, felt new, stronger, more necessary—but maybe I was only searching for something unrecoverable from the past—the ache of youth itself, which is dispensed to everything and nothing. Hadn't I read that somewhere? We experience everything by the time we're nineteen or twenty—the rest of our lives are just long processes of remembering.

I suspected, opening my eyes again to the sparkling water, that the MDMA had been laced with something else hallucinogenic, or that I'd been given far too large a dose for my small body. I briefly wondered if I should worry about this, but instead I moved my hands around in the water, feeling the rippled texture of it. The more I could concentrate on observing sensory details, the less inclined I felt to panic about the way the drug was affecting me. A lack of awareness would signify danger, I decided, and settled back into my contentment.

I felt oddly close to my dad, being bathed by this other father, thinking that I might have accidentally taken LSD. He'd often told me about the time he'd tried it, as a long-haired teen in the sixties—how he'd stupidly decided to drive, and how the road had gone vertical in front of the windshield. I dreamed about that a lot, driving and the road unexpectedly surging upward—and, instead of crashing, the car going with it. I'd never realized his connection to my dreams before. I'd always thought it had more to do with growing up near a mountain, remembering the terror I'd felt as a child sitting high in my dad's truck, driving up and up along narrow curved roads with sharp overhangs, the guardrail looking far down outside my window, short and worthless.

That's when I realized I had no idea where Lonnie had gone. Lonnie gone was not good, Lonnie was having trouble being alone in a room. I shot up in the bath, overwhelmed with worry. James put a hand on my cheek; his hand was big, enveloping my face. "What is it? Are you coming down already?"

"Where's Lonnie?"

James's hand cupped my breast. I didn't know how long he'd been fondling me. "It's okay," he said.

"Where's Lonnie?" I repeated. I felt like crying. William had a children's book where an elephant, distraught over whether to share his ice cream with a friend, suddenly panics about where his friend is anyway—never mind the sharing. I felt like the sad, scared elephant. My eyes started to well, thinking of Lonnie alone somewhere, crying, and thinking of the sad elephant. I wanted to stop making these associations, but I couldn't.

“It hit you really hard, huh?” James said, tilting his head, understanding.

“I have to find Lonnie,” I said, thrashing in the water.

“She’s here,” James said, smiling at me, moving his hands up and down my arms.

And she was, below me, on the cold tile floor of the bathroom. Her hair and dress had dried. She was staring up somewhere past me, at the ceiling. I couldn’t read the expression on her face. It was blank, terrible in its blankness, like the dead eyes of the woman who’d had LeRoi’s baby and then disappeared. I didn’t want to associate Lonnie with her. I didn’t want to associate Lonnie with anyone. Lonnie was different, singular, alone. Poor Lonnie, who had everything but was all alone.

I wanted to climb out of the bath, be closer to her. James wrapped me in a thick towel, rubbing it up and down my body. He picked me up and carried me into the next room. I fought against him, wriggling. I didn’t want to leave Lonnie, but when he put me down on the bed I found I hadn’t, she was already there, next to me.

Though we all knew what was going to happen, it was obvious very quickly she wasn’t having a good time. I was not far gone enough to ignore it. I took her hand and put it between my legs. Looking at her face, her precious frowning face, I expected her to pull it away. I expected her to say, “What are you doing?” But she didn’t. She didn’t look at me. She didn’t look at her hand even. She just stared ahead as if I weren't in the room. I rubbed her hand against me. Her hand like a soft clay mold. The melting. The utter limpness of the thing.

How could I jolt her awake? How could I pull her into this moment? I stood on the bed, my legs shaky on the moving surface of the mattress. I pulled off my towel, conscious of the fact that I didn't look sexy as I did so. I was incapable of a striptease, now, because of the drugs, but also probably always. Performance had nothing to do with the sex I had. I took what I wanted from my lovers without finesse, without worrying about them. The fact that they had wanted me back, each of them, with equal force, with equal disregard for erotic buildup, had been lucky.

I tried to make up for my gracelessness with speed, so as not to draw attention to it. I hurled the towel to the floor and collapsed again on the bed. James was behind me, touching my back and shucking his own pants off. I ignored him. I went for the hem of Lonnie's dress, tugging it up. The skirt was short and she didn't need to move for me to lift it. I manipulated her arms to take it off her head, like I was undressing a sleepy baby. Her breasts appeared, braless, starkly white compared to her browned chest and stomach. I thought about Carlow touching them, under her robe that first night I saw them together. I cupped one in my palm. "Do you like this?" I asked her.

She didn't answer. I put her nipple into my mouth, flicked my tongue against the tip. It was dangerous, her lack of response. I could do anything I wanted to her.

I wanted to eat her. I wanted to take some small part of her and put it inside of my body, in my stomach. I thought of Christ's body, Communion wafers. I thought of a giant slug of hair I saw in a museum once, one of those museums of medical history full of human oddities—skeletons of two-headed children, Siamese twins sharing organs, skulls ballooned out from inflamed brains, all the strange things that can happen to a body—the hair had been removed from a woman's stomach after she died. It was the size and shape of a large eggplant and ruddy brown in color. Hair was nearly indigestible, like chewing gum; it just sat around inside people when they ate it. This appealed to me. I nuzzled into Lonnie's neck, mouth open, trying to catch some of her hair between my teeth and bite it off. I sucked it in, my mouth open by her neck, the strands catching in my incisors. It smelled like coconut oil, but tasted bitter.

I grabbed a hand and put her fingers into my mouth, listening to James grunting on the corner of the mattress. I was glad that what I appeared to be doing was pleasing to him—his pleasure a happy, innocent by-product of my own intense desire for consumption. I sucked on her fingers, as if to appease him, but I was actually seeking, with the wet tip of my tongue, a stray fingernail to bite—a snag of cuticle I could rip off and keep inside my own body. Her nails were uncharacteristically dirty, little crescents of darkness under the tips, all that sand she had run through her hands, you couldn't ever get all that sand out. But they were still smooth and long, I found as I flicked my tongue against the tips, her cuticles flat. I bit down on her index finger and she didn't even flinch.

I'd come so far, made it so close to her. I couldn't stop. I still felt she might reciprocate if I could just push a little more. I pressed my whole body against her and she fell back on the bed. Our legs were interlaced, so I pushed my thigh down, pushed myself on top of her thigh. She was waxed completely smooth now. I'd never waxed, never been waxed. I hadn't felt that skin so smooth since I was a child. I touched her and then couldn't stop touching her, the smoothness addicting, encouraging perpetual motion atop it.

I put my fingers inside her and found polished rocks—crystals—amethyst and rose quartz. They fell out into my palm. I recognized them from the jagged innards of geodes I'd kept on my windowsill as a child. I held them in my hand, rubbed them against myself. The source of her power.

Behind me James angled my hips up, away from Lonnie. I drew them back down, but he insisted, shoving himself quickly inside me, deep deep, all of a sudden so deep it was painful. Above Lonnie, my body casting a dark shadow over her, James gripped me by my waist and moved me back and forth, back and forth. I thought of the swings at the playground. The way you could move and move and move without going anywhere.

I couldn't see James. Lonnie was looking off somewhere behind me, but it didn't appear to be at him. She was conscious, blinking up at the ceiling, but what was wrong with her? If it had been Carlow's cock inside me would she be getting off on it? I was between them, experiencing something, but it didn't seem to have anything to do with the sex they had. That time she had told me, "We still make love all the time." The way she laid her legs across him, kissed him, smiled at him. This somehow wasn't the sex they had, even though this was the sex we were having. Why was she ruining everything? This was supposed to be an enlightening experience for me. I was supposed to be let into something intimate here, but she was keeping me at such a distance. I wanted to yell at her, "Stop moping!" I might have said it. I know I hit her lightly across the cheek and then harder, the way James had hit me. It didn't change anything. She just lay there blinking. *We can only understand "Lonnie" in relation to "Elle."* In resignation, I just took her limp hand and rubbed it against my clit until I came, shuddering, bucking against James. It didn't take long.

38

Lonnie slept the sleep of the dead next to me that night and I didn't sleep at all. I had the sensation of trying to hold sand, but terrible, grotesque, nightmarish. Everything was slipping through me, slipping away.

I could still touch her, it occurred to me in the night as she slept.

My hand on her chest. The way her body collapsed a little with each exhale—chest caving in like she was imploding in tiny degrees. It fell and rose but did not seem to rise as much as it fell. I touched her in different spots—a shoulder, her stomach, neck, cheek. I slid my hand under the sheet and slipped my fingertip across the soft bump of her nipple. I ran my fingertips across the waves of her hair, spread out around her on the pillow. I was gripped by panic. All those cells already dead.

It seemed to me the bed I was on with Lonnie and James was huge, a monstrous piece of furniture. Just softness, softness, so much softness it made me sick. I put the sheet inside my mouth, saturated the cotton threads with saliva, but it was softer still, slick with wetness. There was nothing around here to grasp—nothing hard.

And somewhere outside the bed there was still rain. The rain, the rain, the unholdable rain.

39

The next morning my limbs and eyelids were so heavy. I tried to swim back to reality when I heard Lonnie and James rise and felt a hot strip of sunlight across my legs, but I was tangled in blankets and couldn't compete with their weight. I'd never felt so strange before. When I drank I woke at dawn, fully conscious with pounding headaches, no matter how much I longed for sleep. That morning, I felt as if I were being twisted in the blankets like a dishcloth. I was wrung out. Void of emotion, memories, even my most basic sensations, like smell and taste, had disappeared. Sounds came and went but I grasped only partial meanings. Lonnie and James would board the boat. Little blips of phrases pulled at me. "Do you have everything?" "I feel like shit." I could sense Lonnie's body moving next to the bed, slow and stiff. They did not shake me awake to join them, they just left me. I did not yet wonder if they meant to let me sleep as a kindness or if they were discarding me, if they were done. I didn't wonder anything. I only lay there, sweating, naked, the world around me static and dry.

How they were able to leave at all eluded me. Eventually, I crawled to a bathroom somewhere distant in the house, like an animal wanting to die in private. I lay on the cool tile, my legs drawn up to my chest. The room was so small; it must have been servants' quarters. And for hours, as the sun burned through a tiny window onto my skin, sweating, death was all I could think of. At some point—I have no memory of the time—a maid, one of those mysterious house fairies that appeared only when everyone was out, found me. I don't remember either of us saying anything. She knocked, and when I didn't answer, opened the door gently, until it pressed into the back of my naked thigh. I felt a rush of cool air, a relief. She disappeared for a moment and then returned with ginger ale, the kind that burns hot on the way down, assuming I was hungover and stomach-sick.

She left me alone without comment, probably thinking I was a member of the household and not a fellow paid employee, but I wished she would stay despite the tears and my inability to move. The ginger ale was the best liquid I'd ever swallowed. I wished I could thank her.

By evening, I'd managed a shower and a scrambled egg with some crackers. I tried to remember how I'd felt after James's and my first encounter, when he'd come on my stomach. I tried to summon the unaffected person I'd been the next morning but something had changed. I was still coming to. Still underwater. The various pieces of the previous night were arranging themselves, some of them still missing. I could smell Lonnie on my body, her cologne, her cunt, her sweat, as if our bodies had really merged into one, but instead of satisfaction there was a deep embarrassment in the pit of my stomach. I could see her blank face from the night before, I could picture myself slapping her. I couldn't remember quite how it all had ended.

I put on an old pair of shorts and a T-shirt. I guess I knew they'd be coming back, that I'd have to face them all again. I had no idea what any of us would say. I thought if Carlow was with them it would be a protection, that we'd just never speak of it again, the way James had never mentioned our first kiss. Robert would've gone back to the city, I remembered with relief, he was staying only through the weekend.

When I heard voices in the foyer I ventured out to find them, my heart pounding. I didn't want to be alone anymore.

I remember there being a fire in the fireplace, but there wasn't—there wouldn't have been in September, I'm clearly conflating memories from upstate, but I can hear it crackling behind me, feel the flush of it on my back. The room was hot. Maybe there was a record crackling, the needle all the way at the middle, circling around and around playing only little pops and static.

Lonnie was curled up in the corner of the pink sofa, her feet stuck between two cushions. She looked tiny and years younger, more like a child of ten or eleven. Her arms were folded around her legs and she kept putting her cheek down on her knee, so I could see only the top of her head, the white line that parted her hair.

"We expected you to be gone, honestly," James said.

His tan had darkened that afternoon on the boat and his teeth looked shockingly white in contrast. I thought about teeth, how they were the only visible part of our skeleton. The thought distracted me. It took me a moment to realize what he was fiddling with as he spoke: my notebook. He'd been through my things. He was flipping through the pages right in front of me. He paused at the photo of Lonnie, but didn't show it to her. Maybe she'd already seen it or maybe he meant to protect her.

"This is a lot, Ella," he said, dropping my nickname just like that.

"I guess you're going through our stuff? Making lists for some reason?"

"It's for a project," I muttered, "for a book."

"Lonnie told me you were really interested in this serial killer, I guess you were going on and on about it at the artists' retreat. But this—" He thumbed the notebook pages. He didn't have to tell me the first half was just stupid little maps charting my route past the LeRoi house to theirs. "This is more than interested. You write down every time you walk by the house? Why the hell would you even do that?"

"Research," I said, looking toward Lonnie, hoping for sympathy, but her head was still down.

"This doesn't look like much of a book."

I wished I could come up with an artist's statement for some kind of experimental project like the ones I'd heard about at the retreat, but all I could think of was the man in the swimming pool with all the cards floating away from him. I couldn't pay attention to what James was telling me.

"You must understand you can't work with us anymore."

I couldn't wrap my head around it. I was in shock, my body shaking. I tried to imagine my life before Lonnie, but it felt blurry and vague—just wanting and hunger and loneliness. I didn't have any other friends now. I didn't have anyone.

"Listen, we wanted it to work out, but it's just not going to, you must understand why."

That *you must understand*. He wanted me to be complicit in my own demise, but I couldn't be complicit. It wasn't going to work. Thinking back over the summer, I could see Lonnie deeply unhappy, putting on a front. They both drove her crazy, she'd said so to me. *If only last night hadn't happened, I could've found a way to replace her.*

Lonnie, on the pink sofa, all folded up. Was she heartbroken too? "Lonnie," I said.

She lifted her head to look at me, but her eyes were the same dead pair from the night before. I knew it was over when she looked at me like that, but I didn't want to accept it.

Vertigo feels not unlike witchcraft, altered reality, a departure from gravity. If my own body could mess with one law of physics didn't it call everything else into question?

"Lonnie, this isn't what you want."

I kept focusing on the room to steady myself, as if going over all the details could preserve me in that space.

I wish I could remember it all, but I know how dangerous that is.

"It's been the worst summer of my life," I said, when Lonnie didn't answer. Not true of course, or maybe completely true. *There has to be some kind of explanation for that in physics.*

I'd quit a million jobs but I'd never been fired. There was no precedent for how I was supposed to act. I started crying. "Lonnie," I muttered miserably, the words catching in my throat, the room spinning. "Lonnie."

I was desperate to sit down.

"You know," James said. "Maybe I shouldn't bring this up, but you were the one who found Lonnie when she was roofied. She said she didn't feel strange until she got home."

"You can't possibly think I did that," I screeched. I had no control over the volume of my voice.

"I didn't think so at the time but there's all this"—he tossed the notebook on the ground—"and it got me thinking. You didn't call the cops until I got home."

"You got home right after I found her!"

"I had to tell you to do it."

The pattern on the rug, the pink and green and navy swirls, the little corner cabinet with all the antique figurines and vases that probably would've meant something historical or financial to someone else from a different background. I stared at everything, trying to take it in, worried it would be the last time I'd see any of it. Why do we do that to ourselves? Why do we implant all those stupid details on our brains? We always think we want to remember the things we so desperately need to forget.

"You brought this on yourself," James said. "Robert says you pretended to be Lonnie in the Adirondacks?"

"Lonnie wanted me to!" I shouldn't have said it. Turning on her wouldn't accomplish anything.

"I thought you were my friend!" she spat back, lifting her face from her knees. She wasn't crying. She was supposed to be the one crying. If she cried, I wouldn't have to. I tried to think of some words I could stab back at her, something to provoke tears, but I came up blank. I shook my head; there was nothing I could say, no way to argue.

"More importantly," James continued, "Carlow says you threatened him with a knife?"

"Pocketknife," I said, desperately, remembering what I'd done in the little bathroom for the first time. "I was high."

"He says you stabbed him."

He was referencing everything except the final act, the really important one. The way we'd both betrayed her body, pushed her into something she shouldn't have been a part of. He was just as much at fault.

If he gave them parties, sex, drugs, he could do whatever he wanted.

"Last night was your idea," I said, a little sting of a sentence.

Lonnie rose then, unfolding her body, throwing her shoulders back, transforming back into her adult self. From the table behind the sofa she grabbed a vase and flung it into the hallway, the blue-and-white porcelain shattering across the marble floor. "Fuck both of you," she said as she walked out.

James laughed a little, and then, kicking my notebook over toward me, said quietly, "I think you'd better leave now."

40

As I packed my suitcase, I tried to think of all the other larger failures I could be living with. People accidentally kill children. They drop babies on cement, on slippery rocks. They run innocent people over with cars. They have to live with themselves after that. They have to eat dinner, pay rent, build a little life around themselves. I thought about my own ancestors, the ones who chose to pack up and move their family across the country by covered wagon. Would they not have felt they'd failed as they watched their babies die of dysentery?

They must have had some other understanding of life. *So,* I asked myself, *have you seen the elephant yet?*

I could still feel James's cum dripping out of me. I'd never had anyone finish inside me before, without a condom. I wondered vaguely if I'd get pregnant. The semen itself disturbed me more than the idea of a baby. I didn't ever consider how it must come back out. Such a strange sensation—the body cleaning itself. I read once that a woman can carry around DNA from the men who've ejaculated inside her for the rest of her life. They cut open a bunch of dead women's brains and found male DNA, which at first they thought was from pregnancy, but later they realized it was in too many women, not just ones with sons. The sperm, they reasoned, are basically moving DNA, and they don't just burrow into available eggs but any cells they can find. I didn't want to house his genetic code. What did it do inside you? Why was he making me carry it?

It was a long walk to the train station, longer than I'd anticipated, especially while still hungover and wearily lugging my duffel bag. By the time I arrived the train—the only one for hours—had come and gone without me. This felt absurd. I hadn't really expected it to happen, though I knew I was running late. It was too absurd to leave and then have to go back. So I didn't. I picked a big house with no car in the driveway and sneaked around to the backyard. It was easy; all the houses had hedges instead of fences.

How long had it taken me to get from the house to the train station? Take in how long an hour is. How much space fits inside a length of time. The pavement, in fresh repair, still all wet and shiny from the previous night's rain. All the square green lawns, perfectly preened. The cool wet wind. The fat man standing outside his house smoking, watching me curiously. The escaped family dog, trotting toward me, then sensing my mood, running away.

I felt like I should've been going over something in my mind the way I did as a child when I argued with my mom, but I found myself unable to really think about Lonnie at all. I sat down in a lounge chair next to a covered pool. I dialed my dad's phone number, not expecting him to answer, but his voice came through clear on the other end after two rings.

"Ella," he said. "How are you, Smalls?"

He sounded fine. He sounded normal, and for some reason that made my throat start to close up.

"Dad." I choked. "You're okay?"

"It's going to take more than that to finish me off," he said. "They say I gotta quit smoking, but I'll survive."

I was crying now, tears falling down my face, but I tried not to let my voice give me away. "I told Wendy I didn't have the money to come home, but that was stupid. I want to come home."

"You don't have to come back for me, Smalls. I'd love to see you, but why don't you get a ticket the next time you have some time off work. Don't waste your money on those last-minute tickets, the way they jack the price up is criminal. Don't let them take you for a ride. I'd feel guilty."

"I'm still going to come home soon," I said. "It's been too long. I owe you."

"You have to live your life. I remember what that's like. Maybe one of these days I'll get out there to visit you."

"That'd be great," I said, though when I pictured him in New York I could only see him disoriented, fumbling with a MetroCard or struggling to make it up a staircase.

I knew he'd walk around Crown Heights with the sad scared look of a parent who could no longer protect his child from the outside world.

I asked him how they were treating him in the hospital and he told me only one of his nurses had a sense of humor. "Anyone without a sense of humor should not be allowed to handle someone else's body," he said.

He told me one of his nurses was a Seventh-day Adventist who kept trying to convince him he had something to fear. "I told her religion is just a way to sedate the masses. 'The meek shall inherit.' In other words, don't fight back, stay down, stay poor, rewards are coming, you only have to *die* first. Just because I had a heart attack doesn't mean I can't recognize a crock of shit."

It was a speech I'd memorized, but I enjoyed hearing it again, like replaying a favorite cassette tape—Dad's Strongest Opinions.

"You getting out soon?"

"Tomorrow."

"Dad, was it a bad one?"

"Don't worry about me. They're calling it mild. It only hurt like hell."

Hanging up made the distance between us feel very great. It seemed to me that he existed in the past. It was strange, how I could call him from the future. I thought of him wearing his blue terry robe even though I was pretty sure he'd thrown it out long ago.

I pulled on a sweater and fell dead asleep on that lawn

chair for several hours. I woke shivering, covered in salty mist, and grateful to the house for being there, for not ejecting me, for not giving me away. I was just in time for the six a.m. train. And that was it.

As it happened, I never had a chance to book any plane tickets. My dad went out for a beer later that week and collapsed face-first on the bar. They told me it was a case of sudden cardiac arrest, that he probably didn't feel any pain.

41

I saw Carlow one more time. I was out drinking alone, between bars, shuffling down a street on the border between Chinatown and the Lower East Side, in the middle of a sort of run-skip, trying to stay warm. It was spring, but the weather had turned cold again as it sometimes did and my coat wasn't thick enough. I didn't notice him smoking on a street corner until he grabbed my arm with a sudden forcefulness that made me scream. A group of passing girls started yelling at him to leave me alone. In the confusion it took me a moment to register his face. When we all finally realized what was happening he said, "Can we talk? Can I buy you a drink?"

We walked into the closest bar, which was grimy and tiki-themed with bamboo posts lining the booths and a leopard-print pool table in the middle of the room. It was crowded and we had some trouble finding a place to sit. We ordered beers at the bar and then sort of stood next to each other, getting bumped on all sides, trying to drink quickly so as not to spill. The strangeness of two bodies coming together again, after a time. The actual physical reality of a person's height next to your own. It seemed like such a significant thing. Carlow looked different, though it could've just been the falseness of memory, only the usual distortions falling out of focus as the fact of his body stood before me. He seemed distracted; he kept looking around at everyone but me. When we finally managed to find two bar stools next to each other he said, "She's gone. Did you know that?"

He had to say it loud, to compete with the noise of the bar. I followed his gaze to the pool table, where a girl in leopard-print pants was lining up a shot. Or maybe she wasn't wearing leopard-print pants. That seems more like something my mind made up to emphasize how ridiculous that bar seemed right then.

"Lonnie?" I said. By then James had already been to my apartment. Already come looking for her or for comfort or whatever it was he wanted. Since that night, I'd often thought about how it was possible that James was lying, or exaggerating. In the end, I have no real idea of how long she was gone, or if she came back. Maybe she only meant to get away for a while, to prove a point.

"Yeah, James told me." I stared at him, unsure what else to say.

He stumbled, shaking his head. "There was, I don't know. It was just something that happened." I recognized that the change on his face was grief. She hadn't run off with him; there was one possibility crossed out.

"I guess she was just your employer for a short time," he said. "I don't know if any of this matters to you."

I nodded. "It does," I said.

"I guess you knew everything that was going on too."

The dates in her diary worked out so the affair had to have started before the baby. William looks so much like James, I don't bother questioning his paternity. It must have been strange, though, to watch someone else's baby grow inside a woman you're making love to. That point she mentioned, in the second trimester, when she could ravage any and all food within sight, was he there? I picture them naked, him feeding her mangos, smoked salmon, avocado—foods smooth and slippery, like the inside of mouths.

Did he wonder if it could be his?

I nodded again, slowly, trying to meet his gaze. I felt like if I could just make eye contact with him we could communicate some kind of understanding about Lonnie—about how she had meant something large to both of us. I felt like we could regroup something somehow if he would just look at me. But his face was still turned slightly away.

The not-knowing. All of life's unanswerable questions—the matter we cannot see, the mysterious randomness that allows birth and death—were bottled inside my inability to truly know Lonnie. If only I had given it a little more time. Maybe she would have unrolled her life like a rug in front of me, laid it down in front of my feet and said, "Here, look at this. This is everything."

I thought, bitterly, here's your story, Sienna. It's another bad one; in fact, I'm not convinced it's any better than my wrapping-paper story. I was expecting something from her, something large, but what I found was as banal as a pun—love. Just a dumb love story. It was love, whatever that means, and I messed it up. I'd really got it all wrong. I'd wanted too much from her, wanted to conquer her, to become her, to encase her in my life in order to write her out of her own.

"Did she really leave William?" I asked. "James said she left him."

"I don't know," he said, vaguely, like he hadn't thought about it and didn't really care. "James and I haven't exactly kept in touch."

He finished his beer in one last gulp, said, "Excuse me," and headed to the bathroom.

By the time he returned the moment had passed. I no longer cared where he was looking. "Do you want to get drunk—really drunk—with me?" he said.

His asking made me realize what I actually wanted was to go home—alone, to find that notebook with the lists of her things, the picture of her as a teenager stuck to one of the pages with the bit of used chewing gum—but it seemed callous to say no, so I let him order us more drinks, tumblers of whiskey and beer this time. He downed his whiskey while I sipped mine slowly. He ended up drinking both our beers, and then another shot. We moved to a corner booth and I could see, thanks to a string of white Christmas lights, that his eyes had turned red and watery, though we didn't talk about Lonnie again. He told me about his art and some debacle with his landlord while I sat there, crossing and uncrossing my legs against the cracked vinyl of the seat until I noticed my tights start to run on the backs of my thighs.

At one point he took out his phone to show me the photos he'd been working on. Photos of women, body parts chopped up, repeated. The white of a sheet, streaks of blood. Slowly, staring at a black-and-white one, I realized it was my body on that wooden beam, suspended, arms splayed—my face.

All I could think about was how dead I looked, my eyes closed, like a body on display, ready for dissection. I must have touched my face after I cut myself because there was blood on my jaw. In one shot I could see Carlow's foot—he was barefoot, though I don't remember him taking off his shoes—right between my legs on the beam. I kept expecting him to say, "Touch yourself," but he never did. I had thought about doing it anyway, but I wanted the direction, the command. I'd wanted him to look at me the way he'd looked at her, or rather the way I imagined he looked at her when they were alone. It felt like a faraway desire.

He left with me, throwing a crumpled stack of uncounted bills onto the table. There was a moment on the cold dark sidewalk when we faced each other and I thought we might have a nice goodbye at least, something I never got with Lonnie, but in the next moment his mouth was on mine, his tongue sour with the taste of alcohol, his lips sloppy and wet. One of his hands held my shoulder so tightly it hurt and the other was in my hair. I found my body rejecting him before I could even really understand what was happening. I shoved him off.

He whispered something desperate and sad about always liking me. He said *please,* but I wasn't listening. I'm not quite sure how I got away from him or whether my pitiable image of him watching me go is imaginary or not. In my mind I was already underground, racing beneath the foul expanse of the East River on a hard plastic seat, thinking about how we love alone.

42

My dad was not a rich man, but he worked steadily over the course of his life, first in auto restoration, then briefly as a truck driver, and finally in construction. The only time he'd been unemployed was during the first two years of my life, during the tail end of the recession of the eighties.

He'd been on his feet, using his hands every day, which meant his salary had never risen very far, but he hadn't spent what he did earn on anything unnecessary. His house, like my Crown Heights bedroom, had stayed empty. He never bought basic furniture beyond beds for the two of us, a sofa, and a small kitchen table. He didn't travel. He drove that busted pickup for nearly twenty years. We watched bad movies on that same box TV for my whole adolescence.

He did, however, pay off his little house in the woods and save for retirement. What I received was enough, if I lived like him in my empty little bedroom with cheap clothes, to support me for a while.

Nearly every day is the same. It's not unlike unemployment, though I afford myself enough food and the luxury of alcohol at night. I get up early. I grab a notebook and walk. It's funny; at one time I would've gone straight to

James and asked for my job back. Or I would've let him stay over that night he showed up drunk to tell me the news of Lonnie's departure, but I no longer trust him. I no longer trust myself. I don't want to become Lonnie anymore. The seasons have changed.

I stop at a rotating selection of cafés and order a black coffee. Sometimes I pull out my notebook and other times I just sit and watch, my hands cradling the cup, trying to stay warm. I'll recognize a certain feature or mannerism—that upturned nose, the way she shrugged her shoulders, and I'll have to look again, just to be sure.

I can feel the slight weight of William on my hip like a phantom limb. I've written everything I can remember from her journal. I've written everything I can remember about her. It still falls hopelessly short. You don't ever stop missing someone, not really—or that version of someone you once knew, that little part of their existence. The missing just changes, it moves around inside your body, affecting different spaces at different times. It strikes me how much like death this leaving is. I have a notebook full of lists—the only thing concrete from that summer—but what do they mean? They're just facts, like the dates and names of those ghosts in the Adirondacks. What do they really add up to in terms of knowledge, in terms of meaning?

Sam thinks I need to find a new job or finally go to school. She thinks I should take my health, my security, and use it for something. I think I'm just going to see how far this money takes me. "Why must we do things?" I tell her. She doesn't know that I've been writing this. She doesn't know that Lonnie ever existed. Sometimes it all seems illusory to me as well—some other life I'd accidentally slipped into in a dream.

I've been holding on to it all this time, slipping it from one pocket to the next. In Oregon I might have buried it in the dirt among the pines. In the city, I move my mattress aside, then take my pocketknife and carve a little hole in the wall; paint chips, probably lead, float to the floor. The choir down the street starts singing—high and clear. I think of the way that choir used to sing at odd times to cover the sound of women's screams. No one missed most of those women when they disappeared.

I slip Lonnie's tooth into the crack in the wall. The white enamel vanishes into the shadow and I push my mattress back into place.

I've started walking past the LeRoi residence again, every day. Sometimes there are men on the porch or in the windows who say hello. I never respond, but I try to get a good look at them, try to figure out which one is the oldest son, which one I talked to that night as I smoked. I maintain the belief that somewhere Lonnie's bones are still together; however, if she had been born someone else that's where she might have gone. That's where the city's lost girls went.

*

Lonnie's thin arm, scattered with fine brown hairs. The muscle of her thigh, the planchette-shaped knot of her kneecap. I furtively stare at women on the street. I often see the back of her head on the sidewalk—those thick wilted curls, sometimes drawn up to show off the elegant stretch of her neck, like a fawn's. Though I don't exactly want to find her, I run to catch up anyway, wait for her to turn so I can catch a glimpse of her face. I can't decide if I expect to find those lovely features, or, as in a horror movie, some demon mask—bloodied sagging skin, pus seeping from the eyes. It's always neither. The woman turns and it's just someone else's face—ordinary and nothing like Lonnie's, so much so I can't believe I'd thought it could be her. I walk away disoriented, confused.

I am in an art museum again, desultory pieces of her accosting me from all around. Sometimes, it really does seem to be her. A double of her. As if she'd been someone else the whole time.

I saw her once crossing Fifth Avenue. Her face flashed toward me; she looked beautiful in the sun.

She was heavier the next time I spotted her; her frame had filled out around the middle in an unflattering way. She was ducking around the corner of an aisle at the Strand.

The third time, I was absolutely sure it was her. We were standing next to each other on a crowded train, our hands nearly touching on the pole, and I could see her reflection in the window as we passed through the long tunnel between Fourteenth Street and Brooklyn Bridge.

She looked older, tired; her skin was bad. Our eyes caught in the window, both of our faces twitching with recognition—her lips forming a smile for a brief second, and then settling back into a firm line. Was that smile meant to mean forgiveness or was she merely fighting off a whole life of politeness? Was she trying to place my face? Had I changed too? I'll never know.

There are a million different ways life can spin out away from the present moment. Sometimes it seems that everything was always happening all at once, the way when I was high James and Carlow had been old men and young boys at the same time. Lonnie was there, standing in front of me, and also Lonnie was gone, gone, gone.

We didn't speak. I couldn't think of a single thing to say. At Fulton Street she left, her hand brushing my own. It was exactly the same as when I imagined myself returning to my hometown—running into one of those old girlfriends from all those slumber parties, pretending to only halfway recognize each other. I could see her walking down the platform for a moment, as the train gained speed, and then I couldn't see her anymore. I started to cry, abruptly, unexpectedly.

Part of the story she had me read upstate returned.

After she watched the girls board the bus from the window, Karen heated up the car, scraped the ice off the windows, and drove to the store. Hardly anyone was around. She pushed a cart down the wide aisles, past the waxed apples gleaming in the florescent lighting, to the milk. The dairy aisle was always so cold. Even in the summer it was uncomfortable. She skittered through on tiptoe, keeping her coat zipped up past her chin. When the cart was going fast enough she lifted her feet onto the bar below the handle, propelling it forward at a reckless rate as she had seen other women's children do when their mothers were distracted.

Gliding down the long aisle like that, weightless, the cart shaking with speed, was a marvelous sensation. She closed her eyes, only for a moment, and opened them just in time to catch someone else, a woman peeking down the milk aisle as if she couldn't remember what she needed, then turning and retreating back where she had come from. Karen's heart pounded frantically. She abandoned her cart, and quickly followed the woman. She caught sight of her again examining jam jars a few aisles down. She was about the same height as Karen, the same weight, the same flat brown hair. She was even wearing the same coat. Her boots were the same brand, but a different style, one that Karen herself had tried on at the store and then decided against.

Karen stood back a little, twirled a jam jar around on the shelf as if she were trying to read the label, glancing at the woman from the corner of her eye. When the woman moved to the register Karen followed, hanging back a little until she had finished checking out, then Karen pursued her out the sliding glass doors to the parking lot.

It was snowing again outside. Karen's boots crunched loudly in the snow behind the woman. She turned a little, looking back, and then kept walking. Karen knew that flash of face, she knew the high cheekbones and the shadow under that eye. When the woman reached her car, she turned again, all at once, catching Karen off-guard. "Can I help you?" she asked, annoyed.

Something happened. The woman's face changed when she viewed it directly. It wasn't her own face at all.

Karen stammered, alarmed. "I'm— I'm sorry." Then she meant to say something else, but couldn't think of what it would be.

On that train, speeding away from that strange other version of Lonnie, an old woman walked up and down the aisle, asking for money. I gave her a twenty, because even if it was a scam, she deserved it all, she deserved to swallow the wealth of this city like a black hole. She took the bill, snatching it away from me with dirty arthritic fingers, and said she'd dreamed about me the night before. She'd dreamed Jesus cut off my head so she could have something to eat.

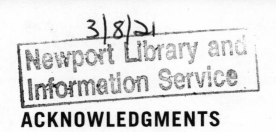

ACKNOWLEDGMENTS

I would like to thank my agent, Stephanie Delman, for believing in and fighting for this project, as well as Stefanie Diaz, and everyone at Sanford J. Greenburger. Thank you to my editor, Megan Lynch, for her sharp eye and immense intelligence. Also thanks to Angus Cargill, Libby Marshall, Sara Birmingham, and the whole team at Ecco.

So many fellow writers have had a huge impact on this book. Thank you so much to my workshop group: Karen Havelin, Iris Cohen, Hala Alyan, Yardenne Greenspan, Matthew DiPentima, and Lauren Schenkman. I love you all. Thanks to everyone who read or listened at Sundays at Erv's. Also, endless thanks to Matt Lally and Joe Ponce, as well as Saxon Baird, who was there every step of the way.

Thanks to Tad Beck and Grant Wahlquist for lending me the use of their house and studio. Thanks to Jeff Peer for the story about a girl.

Thanks to all my writing teachers, but most specifically Emily Barton, for helping me get through Columbia (and beyond), and Lidia Yuknavitch, my first writing teacher, the one who started it all.

Thank you to Michael Assous for so many small and large things. And finally, thanks to the world's best parents, Gary and Diane Stevens, without whom I'd be lost.